S0-AVK-331

The Jack of Justice

The Jack of Justice

Sam Hill

FIVE STAR
A part of Gale, a Cengage Company

**LIBRARY OF CONGRESS CIP DATA ON FILE.
CATALOGUING IN PUBLICATION FOR THIS BOOK
IS AVAILABLE FROM THE LIBRARY OF CONGRESS.**

LCCN: 2020008532
ISBN-13: 978-1-4328-7527-5 (hardcover alk. paper)

First Edition. First Printing: May 2021
Find us on Facebook—https://www.facebook.com/FiveStarCengage
Visit our website—http://www.gale.cengage.com/fivestar
Contact Five Star Publishing at FiveStar@cengage.com

Printed in Mexico
Print Number: 01 Print Year: 2021

The Jack of Justice

PROLOGUE

July 1878

All of Crooked Creek, Wyoming, had come out to bury Emilia Porter. The cross-grained old woman had spit more tobacco juice at more folks' shoes than any ten men combined, but that didn't matter. What did matter was that she was the mother of Charlie Porter, a thief who stole from the railroads as well as any man if not better, left no witnesses alive, and feared no person on earth but the mother he lived with in between raids.

Emilia had died two days back. There were proper calling hours at the house and as big a church funeral as a tiny church on the Wyoming prairie could muster. Now they were at the graveyard, where the Farrell brothers were leaning on their shovels, sweat still staining their shirts from digging all morning in the July heat.

Preacher Ephraim Patterson was giving one final prayer. His words trooped on into greater and greater excesses of theological zeal—so much so that there was more than one man shuffling and a few sidelong glances at noble thoughts far removed from reality. More than one mourner appreciated the preacher's creativity even if they deplored the lengths to which this summation had gone.

At long last, Charlie Porter interrupted.

"Time, Preacher."

His head moved up as he spoke. Four horsemen riding hard approached. His lips tightened. No respect, to be this late.

The men dismounted as the cloud of dust they kicked up filtered across the mourners, leaving a taste on their lips and a layer of white on suits and dresses that would need cleaning before being carefully stowed away for the next funeral.

One rider walked ahead of the rest. He ignored the minister and the coffin and stopped a few feet from Charlie Porter.

"Hello, Charlie."

"Dirk." The outlaw nodded at Dirk Rawlings as he recognized a man who once rode with him and had supposedly changed his ways. "Boys came late. Guess with the ranch and now, fine upstanding citizens you became, you almost forgot your old friends."

"Not a social call. Got a bounty on you for that Union Pacific job in '74. We aim to collect it. Figgered this was the time." He looked meaningfully at Porter's right hip. "Guess we figgered right."

Charlie Porter had broken a lifelong habit by coming unarmed to the funeral. Being taken and being delivered were different things. Best to roll with it.

"I'll come quiet. We got business to finish first."

"Not havin' no trouble. Not waitin'. Plannin' on havin' you come dead. Now move away from them other folks, and no one gets hurt. 'Cept you. Call it a double funeral, Charlie."

Charlie and Dirk and Dirk's men watched each other like cats. Charlie wore no gun, but they expected he had one somewhere.

How much could he accomplish with only a bluff, Charlie wondered.

"Bad manners, boys, killing a man at a funeral that ain't his," came the voice behind Dirk and his men. They stopped.

"Thought since you boys who are so brave and all to back-shoot women were lookin' for ol' Charlie there you might want to grab him while he was at his mother's burial," croaked the deep voice that crackled and wavered from behind a heavily shaggy salt-and-pepper beard.

A bent back testified to age, as did white hair spilling out from under an old black hat that had seen many better days. Leathery skin and dark circles under the eyes completed the picture of man all but spent. That is, if you ignored the hand by his right hip, fully alive as it hovered by the butt of his gun. His left, equally steady, held a shotgun.

"About your speed, Dirk. Pretend to be an honest man in public, do your dirty work in private. Sneaky. Remember Cheyenne Sally?"

"Can't say I do," replied Dirk.

"Cabin by Brown Deer Spring. Lived there. Died there. Couple days ago. Remember now? Fellas shot at her boy; desecrated her body."

"Don't remember every Injun I killed," Dirk replied loudly. Few would care about a man killing an Indian.

"Gonna remember her." The beared man shifted the shotgun. "Friend of mine. Don't like friends killed so you can lift her hair."

"Didn't need it when she was dead."

"Won't need yours either. Then again, not much market back East for prairie trash scalps, is there?"

The funeral crowd melted away out of range. Dirk and his men moved slightly apart.

"Ride on, old man," Dirk called.

"No."

"Put the popgun down, old man."

"When you are dead."

The man had done this before. He jammed the shotgun against his body. His left hand squeezed both triggers of the shotgun as the two of Dirk's men to his left went for their guns. They were lifted off the ground by the impact, then crashed as shotgun slugs tore into them. Dirk and his remaining partner then drew their own guns, but they had made the mistake of watching their comrades' death.

The gunman facing them had already dropped the shotgun and pulled his Colt. The younger men might have been a heartbeat faster, but their bullets were sailing wide of the stranger as his slammed them in the midsection.

The old man sighed deeply as he watched the men lying on the ground, dying. One man in the crowd had a reflex to help. One click of a Colt hammer cured that notion. The preacher knew only fools went to funerals unarmed.

"Charlie," the stranger called. Porter took a step forward. "Far enough. You make sure they bury these fellas? Not by good folks, but some place?"

"I will," replied Porter. "Why'd you do this? I owe you."

"Nope," said the old man, walking towards where the bodies lay. He coughed. A drop of red fell on his dust-encrusted boot. "Personal business."

"Tell me your name, so I know who to thank."

The old man reached into the pocket of the vest he wore. Extracted something. Tossed it on a body.

"Call me Jack." He turned away, shuffling off with the walk of a man who had done what he came to do and needed to move along. He stopped at the horses, went through the saddlebags. No one saw what he walked away with, curiosity being in limited supply when a man kills as well as this one did.

The preacher walked over by the body. A playing card lay face down where the man had thrown it. Blood tinged on its edge, he turned over the jack of spades as Crooked Creek looked on at the birth of a legend.

Chapter One

Deadwood, South Dakota, April 1879

Crayne had seen and sampled it all—the dynamic raw energy of the dreamers flooding into Deadwood, South Dakota, to strike it rich and the mire of filth and corruption into which so many fell.

Death followed life as bust followed boom in a dizzying race that defied logic but was testament to the inner workings of man when all was stripped away but the desire for instant wealth. It had been raw and often revolting, but never dull.

Now, he could leave it behind. The stories were all filed. The *Global Reporter,* the weekly news magazine that sent him there in the heat of the brutal Plains summer and kept him there through the harsh winter that was just now breaking, would have enough dispatches to keep readers satiated with gunfights, gambling, gold, and the grotesque for weeks to come. He hoped whoever drew the illustrations was good. He'd never seen a single copy, but that was just as well. Deadwood wasn't easy on correspondents.

As he walked from the room he took boarding with the Casper family, he found he was feeling regret. The summons to return had been welcome; enough was enough. And yet going back seemed almost as pointless as his life before this assignment. He had never gone back to the East when this chapter started; and now he felt he was going to a land as foreign as the one he left behind as a child.

"Mister Crayne!"

Harrison—the Caspers' youngest—was running down the street, long, black hair flapping because he had run out without the hat he almost always wore. This must be important. Crayne stopped.

"You got a telegram," the boy said worshipfully, never having known anyone who received one of the tissue papers with often cryptic messages missing letters to save space. "Mr. Francis came to look for you, but he could never catch you. I did. It must be important."

As Harrison handed over an only slightly crumpled piece of yellow paper, Crayne flipped the boy a silver dollar. Way too much, but the boy was a good one, and, since he was leaving, he would be gone before the boy told tales that would make his simplest journey a beggar-filled gauntlet. Deadwood children were as good in business as any sharp soul in the East. Generosity to one meant walking through an ocean of urchins even crossing the street.

DO NOT LEAVE STAY WAIT COMING WED DO NOT RETURN STAY THERE

It was signed "Sull." Crayne could not repress a smile as he pictured the man who sent it and the frazzled telegraph operator who would have had to compose the message ten times with a manic presence hovering behind, packing passion into the fragmented, barely coherent prose of the telegram. It was perhaps the longest message Sullivan had ever sent.

Matthew Michael Sullivan was barely over five feet tall, with more energy than a steam engine and more schemes than the Grant administration altogether. The bandy-legged man with the flowing, red curls and vast, red sideburns was perhaps Crayne's only friend in the world. He rarely came West . . . had been as far as St. Louis once that Crayne knew of and that was under protest when the magazine thought of putting offices out there. He wondered if there was a problem. No. Problems never were solved in person. Curt notes reading, "Your services are no longer required," were invented for that purpose. He knew that all too well.

It would be good to see someone who understood the odd world of a man who lived his life off to the side of human experience, jotting it down and acting as commentator, philosopher, and entertainer, writing the rough draft of history or the first strands of a myth as the case may be. Crayne would wait. He retraced his steps to spend another couple of nights with the family that had tolerated him these past weeks.

The 4:37 p.m. train from Chicago was not really a train. It was a stagecoach that came from Rapid City, the farthest point on the rails. Not only was the coach beset by ills that went from terrible weather to pits in a roadway that was barely more than mostly flattened, rock-hard dirt that could break an axle, it was the last part of a journey that could take hours, days, or longer depending upon the condition of the rails, the weather, and the temperament of the various Indians who could flummox an entire railroad by riding around on their shaggy ponies and making a fuss by firing guns that were usually defective. The coach was guaranteed never to arrive at 4:37.

The stationmaster commonly tried to adjust his "official" watch to make the coach's arrival as close to its theoretical time as possible. Crayne had caricatured him in a piece that had not yet been published, or at least not been seen. He was hoping he would be gone from Deadwood before copies of it filtered around. Magazines were like that. One day fifty old papers would show up, and everyone would know everything from a month ago. The East thought it mattered and would have been deeply disappointed to know how much it was regarded as a curiosity by men and women who had much better things to do with their lives and could happily be weeks behind the rest of the country.

Crayne's watch read 5 o'clock when the first traces of dust were visible. The stationmaster announced the on-time arrival of the 4:57 from Chicago. Crayne admired the stationmaster's devotion to his railroad's image.

"Does the hotel serve good food?" Sullivan asked as he hopped down from the coach, eyes taking in every sagging inch of Deadwood, where painting what was built happened rarely. "Bags will go there. I want good food. I'm starving. The stew they served at the last stop was water and shoe leather. Are there places to eat here or only drink? Has anyone been shot here today? Can I see a gold mine?"

"I'm fine, Matthew, thanks for asking," joked Crayne, a smile crossing a clean-shaven face few ever saw break into the relaxed grin now creasing it. "Yes, the hotel has good food. No, no one got shot today, but if you want to stand on the street long enough, we can arrange something. And I have to tell you, Matthew, that most folks shoot strangers who approach their claims. If that's what you have in mind, I can let you entertain yourself while I watch."

The shorter man blinked, looked around with bird-like glances at the town, the mud, the passengers, and the hole in the station's roof when a shotgun went off, a common happenstance when combined with the presence of a drunk. Distaste and disbelief mingled. "Cute. Hurry up. I don't have all day. Is it always this filthy?"

"It looks much cleaner at night," Crayne observed, taking the lead as they jostled past miners, cowboys, drunks, and gamblers. Crayne had not realized how different it was to have anyone he knew within five hundred miles. It was nice. So far. Sullivan was a quick study. He noted the various stores and saloons Crayne had mentioned in his dispatches. They stopped. Crayne pointed.

"Here?"

" 'Bout twenty feet down," Crayne said. "Mob chased him and they had them, then he realized he had that gun. Lynching doesn't work well when you let your victim keep his gun."

"I'll remember that. That was my favorite."

"We're here."

Sullivan looked at the hotel, lines appearing in his forehead above thick, raised brows. "Are you sure it won't fall down?"

"Not enough wind today," replied Crayne, not seeing the disgust on his friend's face as he surveyed the ramshackle structure in which he was expected to sleep or Sullivan's fruitless efforts to hide his revulsion at the caked mud covering the hotel floor.

Sullivan's bags were being taken to his room as the two men found a table. Sullivan ordered the best of everything, such as it was, and reached into his valise.

"French wine," he said, producing a bottle. "I came prepared. Out here they pickle frog sweat and call it whiskey. The vile stuff at the last stop was poison. How can anyone drink it?"

"Maybe it depends on the breed of frog."

Sullivan laughed loudly. Crayne had always been an oddity, shunning whiskey. He sipped the wine for politeness, but, in the end, Sullivan reached over and drained the glass in a swallow. Mostly, Crayne looked on contentedly as his friend ate and drank, having only a steak that was devoured in moments.

Sullivan could see some changes in Crayne, who had been a presence at the end of a telegraph line for the past few months, and a troubled memory before that after Crayne assassinated his career in one grand bit of writing after the Custer massacre in 1876. Crayne was still thin but looked weathered. No one would think he was a writer. He was eternally vigilant, with his eyes constantly moving from place to place and face to face. Crayne was average in height and build, with brown hair and features that were neither pleasing nor notable, except for the broken nose and deep, dark circles under the eyes. His face could be transformed by a rare smile, but, most of the time, Crayne looked like what he was, a man who sat off to the side of life, blending with the crowd as he took in everything and revealed nothing.

Sullivan filled in the silence with chatter about the others at the magazine Crayne knew, and many he knew only as faceless names who read his dispatches, drew illustrations, or otherwise connected the magazine's vaunted hundred thousand subscribers with the writings of its so-called Wild West correspondent.

It was not until a meal far too large to be consumed so fast by a small man was history that Sullivan eased back in his seat and contentedly smiled. "There," he said. "My ribs are no longer poking through my back."

"I was worried." Sullivan trended to being fat; it was a point of pride with him to insist he was not.

"Here is the plan," said Sullivan, who ignored Crayne and his legendary hair-trigger temper as could only an old friend and launched directly into business. "You're not coming back East."

If Crayne cared, the poker face didn't show. He had not realized until he heard the words how much he had not wanted to go.

"The Old Man wants you in Wyoming," Sullivan said.

"Why?" Crayne was not going to tip his hand.

If they thought he wanted to go back to the crowded streets of New York City, let them if it helped him strike a deal to avoid that sentence. After the work he did in Kansas and his return to writing in Dakota, he had become used to space, not crowds. Anyhow, New York held memories he would just as soon keep a thousand miles away. An extra few miles West would do nicely.

Sullivan slapped an envelope jammed with stray clippings, notes, and other papers on the table. "You know about Lincoln

County? Billy the Kid?"

"Hard not to. Young fella kills a few hundred men or more a day with a pistol at the range of a mile or two and can pull his gun faster than spit freezes in January. So they say. Wonder anyone is still living down there in New Mexico Territory. Fella who thought him up was a great writer."

Sullivan shot a glance at Crayne. The writer's self-mockery eluded Sullivan.

"Old Man thinks there's someone better to cover. Wants you there."

"Why?"

"Deadwood stories were great, Crayne. Maybe your best ever. With those and those pieces on the gold rush out here, Old Man has forgiven you for that Custer thing. He still calls you obscene names but now adds 'but he can write, and I want him writing for me.' "

Crayne's skeptical glance spoke volumes.

"Well, what did you expect? You practically wrote that you wished Sherman and Grant were at the Little Bighorn. Did you think you could actually do that in a magazine as big as ours? Old Man fought for them both and worships them. He still sends fawning letters to Sherman every time the general is in the news. He's about the only one in the world with Grant's picture still on the wall. Telegrams from both of them were on his desk the day your . . . comments . . . were printed." Sullivan was getting loud, and his arms were waving.

Crayne shrugged. He should care. He did, but distantly now. Almost three years ago. A lifetime ago. A different man wrote that—a man who cared. Custer. Glory. So many dead. The army kept most of the writers away. Crayne had thought he was lucky, until he reached the sun-baked, death-strewn Little Bighorn to see for himself what an Indian attack looked like. He shut his eyes for a long moment to help keep the past at bay. It didn't work well.

When he opened them, Sullivan had a contract in his face and was pretending he had no idea where his friend's mind had traveled.

"Sign. You need this. You should have been as famous as Twain, but maybe we can still make that happen. Write something to start the series before I leave whenever the next coach departs. Why do they call it a train? No, don't answer. Sign. With what I have for you, the first month should be easy," Sullivan said

"You had nothing to do with this, Matthew? The Old Man picked me because he likes my work? Am I really supposed to believe that, my friend?"

"I was taught God looks out for drunks and fools, but there are so many of the former I thought some assistance with the latter might be necessary," Sullivan riposted. "The Old Man has developed a very strong fixation on Wyoming Territory of late and the Indian problem. I do not know the full extent of it; you know he has business interests that go far beyond the extent of the magazine, and I think I am best to not know any of that. When he first started talking about this story he wants you to pursue, I brought up your name. I was certain he was going to say no—you had not been in Deadwood all that long—but he was intrigued. So, you have made a believer of him."

Sullivan was aware that Crayne was giving him a thorough inspection. Crayne made a rude noise. Crayne could see Sullivan relax.

"I wanted you to have this because I thought it would be good for you—something big, something bold. You were my friend, Crayne, when I had one friend, one shoe, and no home. This mad world of journalism has become my home and my life. I owe you for it all. And, you know, the more we sell, the higher my bonus goes."

Crayne laughed. For all the years they had worked together, Sullivan had never cared a thing for money or anything else but the wife who adored him and the magazine he edited. And what a magazine it was. Modeled in format after the highly successful news magazine *Harper's Weekly* in appearance, the *Global Reporter* claimed that its niche was telling "sophisticated and discriminating readers of the myriad events transpiring in the far reaches of America and around the globe." It offered a mix of "dispatches from intrepid correspondents who brave the wilds of the untamed West" with "inspiring literary masterpieces" from writers "whose works of literature grace the homes of the refined." The *Global Reporter* also offered "practical advice" for those "keeping a home, ordering the affairs of servants, or running a business." It did not note that its "latest telegraphic news" from "dark corners of the civilized and heathen reaches" was often culled from rumors sailors brought into the taverns from Manhattan's wharves.

In its editorials, the *Global Reporter* thundered with the crusty voice of founder, editor, and publisher, Jacob Southern. It praised U. S. Grant, castigated the notion of female suffrage, called for the extermination of the Indians, and supported spreading the light of civilization into the dark corners where savages dwelt.

Illustrators whose images graced the weekly publication's pages were "drawn from the ranks of skilled artists whose mission it is to convey the world and its wonders to our readers." Left unsaid were complaints from many clergymen that the sketches of missionaries braving the stewpots of the far-off heathen showed an unrealistic preponderance of attractive young women, many of whom appeared in relatively immodest conditions. The weekly journal of "the latest developments in the march of civilization" was presented "on the finest newsprint" and produced by "a press that is the wonder of modern machinery." The press's German origins had been trumpeted until the Franco-Prussian war revealed a reservoir of anti-German sentiment that prompted a revision. The *Global Reporter* augmented its columns with advertisements that, it told its readers "were reviewed with care by those who care for the welfare of our readers." It noted that "all claims of healing benefits" of its many patent medicines were "thoroughly verified," although it did not say by whom.

Sullivan had been running the place for eight years, since his incredible talents were discovered when Crayne found him in a Harlem street, half frozen, and dragged him into the office to be given a meal and a job. Sullivan went from copy boy to editor after a loud, long, and highly accurate rage one day over some very inarticulate prose submitted by a senior writer whose research usually extended as far as the nearest Manhattan watering hole. Southern recognized talent. Sullivan's career began.

Crayne signed. He barely looked at the money. It would be fair. Sullivan would have it no other way.

Business over, they talked of politics and war, of gold and gossamer dreams. Sullivan rose to go to his room.

"Fifty-eight hours on a train, Crayne, and that horrible coach contraption is far too long a journey. I want to sleep in a bed and not a train seat. And you have a few thousand words to write. We can look them over tomorrow when I am rested. I shall return the next day when I feel up to the journey."

"No one told you?"

"Told me what?"

"Coach leaves at noon," he said.

"What?"

"The way the schedule works, Matthew, is that the train leaves Rapid City again tomorrow if the eastbound is on time, which it never is, but no one knows how late it might be, so you have to be there. Next coach comes in a week. A week in

Deadwood might be just the thing, Matthew."

"Noon?" Sullivan sighed. "Then I shall see you in the morning."

They shook hands and sauntered out of the dining room. They passed the door, opened onto the Deadwood street for the sake of getting air in a building that smelled too often like unwashed men.

"Indulge me," said Sullivan. They moved to the doorway, then stood outside. People passed back and forth, some hurrying as fast as if they were in New York City, others ambling along as though hurry were a concept foreign to their world. The cloudy sky darkened in the west as the end of the day drew near.

"There you are, you miserable cur," said a voice from the pack. A figure stopped and moved closer.

"Go on up, Matthew," said Crayne, in a voice tinged with resignation and regret. "I have business."

Sullivan did not move a muscle. He had caught the challenge in the tone of the man in the street. The meal had revived him. His insatiable curiosity was stirred. Something was happening, and his friend was in the middle of it.

A roundish man in a bulky, cloth coat with a gun belt strapped around his middle was looking from the street into the doorway. A rough beard flowed from under a dark hat.

"What do you want, Jasper?" asked Crayne, who was reaching in his own coat for something bulky.

"Deceiver," called Jasper, throwing crumpled pieces of paper in Crayne's direction.

Crayne cringed. Nope, folks in Deadwood did not like seeing how someone else looked at them. They ran the reporter out of town who wrote about the women smoking pipes and chewing cigars. And that was only the women.

Amid the scraps at his feet, he could see the distinctive design of the *Global Reporter.* He hoped the week's issue that lay at his feet did not contain the piece on Jasper's brother's saloon, where adding water to the whiskey was a daily ritual he had chronicled with some verve and no little sarcasm, given that on days when the weather was bad the water came from the horse trough and not the filthy creek a mile from town.

"Sam will be done up by nightfall thanks to you," Jasper fulminated.

"Not me that watered his whiskey," Crayne observed placidly.

"Nobody had to know. Everybody does it."

"Said so in that, if you read it," said Crayne.

"Sayin' I can't read?"

Sullivan watched Crayne seem to lose all interest in the man. All animation left Crayne's face. His friend's usually crisp voice took on a slow, almost slurred diction.

"Jasper, he might lose sales for a day, but no one cares, and no one reads, so tell him to take a day off, and, in a couple of days, business will be better. Think the miners read that when they are thirsty? Nothing they don't already know. Go home and tell Sam it will be all right. I'll buy a round or two if it helps make amends."

"No, Crayne. You can't buy your way out of this. I told Sam I would set things right. Casper folks where you been boarding had not seen you. Should have known you'd be in a fancy place with a fancy meal and a fancy friend. Now you got to pay for what you done."

"And what does that entail, Jasper?" asked Crayne, who knew the answer and who, Sullivan thought, looked abysmally bored as though sitting through a bad play at a Manhattan theater. "What recompense could possibly be required for the non-existent affront to a saloon that in itself is an affront to so many things that water in the whiskey is but the tiniest tip of the vastest iceberg?"

"You and me in the street. Now," said Jasper.

"Should I affect surprise, Jasper? I suppose I should be pleased that I am affirmed as a man, for only men are called out." He turned his expressionless face to Sullivan. "I am sorry about the interruption."

Sullivan was flabbergasted. A gunfight? Crayne? The writer? The man who helped stray dogs and cats because he hated seeing animals suffer. Did they all assume out there that everyone had a gun? Why, Crayne would never . . . His eyes widened as Crayne, in fact, very deliberately and gradually pulled a pistol from the coat's inside pocket and held it up, by the barrel, for the man in the street to see.

"No holster, Jasper, but I have this pistol here. It's loaded. I can accommodate you. Wish you wouldn't though. Not worth it."

"It is to me."

"If you have been drinking your brother's whiskey without the water, Jasper, as you usually have, go sleep it off, and we can talk tomorrow."

"Now."

Crayne sighed as he shucked off the bulky coat he had been wearing. He shivered in the chill. Deadwood had two temperatures—oppressive and frigid—that worked their way through the calendar, each often sharing part of a day

"Matthew, take this. Don't want a hole in it. It has been a good coat, and I shan't wish it damaged." He jammed the gun in the waistband of his pants and walked away from the wall of the hotel. Sullivan followed, perplexed.

This was not the way a proper gunfight between contestants was conducted, surely? There was no drama, no spectacle. It was merely grubby and ordinary.

"Crayne, this is . . . absurd. Don't you need something . . . more? Things don't simply happen like this out here, do they?

Are there not rules, or some protocol to follow as I have read?"

Crayne laughed.

"Welcome to Deadwood, Matthew. Ought to be glad Jasper's got some kind of breeding. Other men would have shot toward the hotel without much of a thought for other folks. That would have ruined your dinner. Now stand back to avoid either a stray bullet or being shot by some fool who thinks they need to help Jasper because he's outnumbered. Some people can't aim worth a hoot."

He walked down wooden steps to the uncertain dirt and mud of the street. Even over the smells of the mud and mire, he caught a whiff of the pungent fumes of cheap whiskey emanating from Jasper.

"Hate doin' this, Jasper." Jasper stood as if he had grown roots while Crayne walked past him until he stopped ten feet down the street from Jasper and turned to face the man. Sullivan marveled. Neither tried any tricks. Each could have killed the other already, but this Jasper let Crayne take his position, and Crayne never tried to shoot Jasper when the man wasn't looking. Was this the code of the West?

"Shut your mouth, Crayne." Jasper had his hand out in front of him—ridiculously far in front, thought Sullivan, who had seen a thousand illustrations of how artists who had been in the West said it was really done. The man's fleshy hand, dark with hair and dirt, hovered over the holster. He could pull his gun clear faster than Crayne. That much was obvious. Sullivan wanted to shout at his friend.

A cart of barrels rolled past the two men as they stood. They watched it roll by, taking time out from preparing to kill one another. The driver barely turned his head. Talk on the street eased away as passersby realized there was a confrontation in the making, but so common was gunplay that many merely walked closer to the buildings or ducked as though sheltering themselves from hail as they continued on their way.

"Waitin' on you, Jasper," said Crayne at last. "If you changed your mind, tell me, and I'll put my coat back on. Chilly out here without one."

Sullivan was aghast. Crayne was asking the other man to start a gunfight. Sullivan was sure Crayne had never fired a gun.

The rounder man moved with a jerk, awkwardly clawing for the gun in its holster, fumbling to level and aim it. Crayne, Sullivan saw, was not going to fire first. The larger, rounder man fired a shot that seemed to pass Crayne by with no impact. He was thumbing the hammer of his gun back for a second shot when Crayne finished pulling the gun clear and, firing from his hip, fired twice at the bulky form of his opponent.

"Stand back, Matthew," Crayne yelled as he walked deliberately forward. Jasper was holding his fleshy right side. He had fallen to his knees. As Crayne came to stand over him, Jasper lifted the gun. It waved and wagged in all directions.

"Matthew! Move out of the way, man!" Sullivan was rooted to the spot as he saw the gun turn in his direction as the bulky gunman coughed and spit blood. The man kept looking at Sullivan.

Crayne's pistol boomed twice more. One shot hit Jasper's arm. The gun he was holding spun to the dirt. Then Jasper slammed back and then recoiled forward until he was lying on his side. This time, as Crayne stood over him with his hand on the trigger and a cocked gun pointing at the fallen man, he did not rise. Crayne eased the hammer back down.

"Is . . . Crayne, is he dead?"

"I hope so." He saw the shocked look on his friend's face. "This is not chivalry and fair fights, Matthew. People who want to kill someone want only to see them dead, and they will do anything they can to accomplish that end. See? I winged his coat there. Barely even touched him here, see? Hardly bleeding.

The coat and the fat were wounded, but I almost missed him. Remember that Matthew: good gunfighters should be skinny." He clapped Sullivan on the shoulder as he rose from his examination of Jasper's body, then saw the revulsion on the man's face.

"The dime novel gunfights are like battle scenes in the theater. Guns don't always shoot straight, and neither do the men using them. Some old pistols can kill the man who fires them as easily as the man he's aiming at. Here in Deadwood, my friend, it is ugly and quick, and very often deadly to everyone but the one who wanted to fight. Reality and the written word rarely meet when two men go out to meet each other."

A dray man was yelling for the mess blocking the street to be cleared.

"Help me. Take his feet," Crayne told Sullivan. "They will come around at night and collect him to toss him in the ground tomorrow," he added. "In the meantime, it's an unwritten rule that, if you kill someone, you should move them to the side of the street so that no one is inconvenienced in their passage."

"This is barbaric!"

"It's the West, Matthew. Someone manages to be killed about every day. Somehow. When a gunfight takes place between two miners who are good and drunk, they can yell at each other for half an hour, but then they usually miss everything they shoot at. It would be comic, but they are serious. Sometimes they miss and kill someone, but usually they shoot high and miss everything except anyone spectating from an upstairs window. Then they forget what they were mad about until the next time."

"You killed a man."

"Matthew, you forget that for two years I worked with the Pinkertons in Kansas and Missouri. I learned a lot about survival. Life out here ends in death very suddenly. I could either be ready to die or be prepared to live." Crayne took his coat from Sullivan's unresisting grasp. "No holes. Now, you can go to your room, and I shall go to my writing. Good evening."

Matthew Sullivan watched his friend saunter down the growing dimness of the Deadwood street, clutching the envelope with one hand and his coat with another. For the first time, Sullivan realized his friend had irrevocably changed. He wondered exactly who was being sent to Wyoming and what might happen.

Then the thought arrived: it was not his worry as long as the dispatches were good. He shivered, from the cold or the scene that had played out. Then he turned and went into his hotel, happily turning his back on the sights of Deadwood.

The bed had been as soft as promised, wonder of wonders, but sleep had not come easily to Matthew Sullivan. The dead, frozen or stricken as they slept, were common in New York City. He told himself that did not shock him as much as the sight of a man he knew as violent only with his words walking calmly out into the street, shooting a man, and showing no emotion. Did the West so change a man? Or was all this within the man all along and hidden under the trappings of civilization? He knew correspondents tended to embellish the truth for readers hundreds of miles away, and there were times when he wondered who was accurate among his writers and who was not, but what he had seen in a few hours rang so true with what his friend had written that he was once again amazed that Crayne could take the rawness and violence he seemed to barely notice and make it come alive on the page.

But above all he wondered who Crayne had become, and how that would affect what was going to happen in Wyoming.

The coffee at the hotel had been strong, and Sullivan was coming awake as he paced by the hotel waiting to board the terrible coach that would take him to the less-jostling but even more stultifying atmosphere of the train. He looked up and down the street. No Crayne. Could he produce this fast? There was still time. He looked at his watch again. 11:38. Twenty minutes until the alleged time he would leave. And there, walking down the street, was Crayne. Sullivan watched him walk; there was wariness in the step more than jauntiness.

Sullivan thought of the man who had once been the best in the business and would only become more famous with time. Crayne took care of that. After the Custer massacre, Crayne had published a livid tirade against generals who sent troopers to be slaughtered—drifting close enough to defending the Sioux that, even without the pressure from above, there was a groundswell of anger against a voice that had always stirred the water. This time he drowned in his own tempest. That man from 1876 was as gone as the wind, Sullivan realized. He'd seen changes in language and changes in tone and passed them off as changes in style. These were not superficial elements; these were glimpses into a deeper metamorphosis.

The grin, however, was the same as Crayne held out an ink-stained hand. "Matthew, I trust no rowdies shot up the town to keep you awake or entertained, as the case might be?"

"Perhaps a little more noise might have been useful," Sullivan replied.

"Here are six pieces, Matthew, about four thousand words each. That should take care of you until I am settled and can send a dispatch. Of course, I know you will not cut them apart to suit some editor's fancy and stretch these six stories into ten."

Sullivan blushed. The better the writer, the more tempting it was to add to the piece until what was planned as a story for one week carried over into two or three. It was good for sales.

"We have a Western Union account, Crayne, so if you need to use it, do so. Communication with the New York City office is your most important task. It is vital that I know as soon as you have found this man. You cannot roam in silence around Wyoming," he said intently, his voice rising.

In response to the odd look Crayne was giving him, he added, "It's what the Old Man wants—what he expects and demands."

Crayne shrugged.

"The Old Man wants you to give your copy to Elezial Newsom of the *Territorial Reporter* in Cheyenne. Go there first and meet him to settle how you send your dispatches to him. Stay in touch with him constantly. He is the one who told Southern about this. Old friends, I guess."

"I'll send what I can . . . more places in Wyoming than Cheyenne, though. Not sure if this man is reliable."

"If I say he is, he is."

"Didn't sleep well, Matthew?"

"Crayne, this is very important. It is your best chance at full redemption, and since you are my friend, if this fails, it is on me. I don't know what it will be like out there, but send whatever you can as soon as you can. We are a magazine and not a newspaper, but if there is a story that we can break, it would be a coup. Oh. There are an extra ten thousand copies being sold now from St. Louis west, so that you know. Mostly in Denver and some to the forts."

"I shall expect my neighbors to have read it, then, even if they are antelopes and bears," Crayne replied. "Here, take the clippings. I have everything I need. Paper lasts not at all out here, so if I miss a detail you wanted, it is best you have them."

"If this story lasts the season, I shall see you in the fall," offered Sullivan. "If not, I shall see you sooner."

With an expression that showed Sullivan his friend was clearly humoring him, Crayne replied with a similar sentiment. Tomorrow was a concept that never mattered until it arrived. If it was not in his mind, it was not in his dreams. Having empty dreams was, he knew, the secret to living one day at a time.

The coach driver blew his whistle as the horses whinnied their complaints at the sound. Crayne licked his lips and swallowed.

"If they ask, Matthew . . . if she appears in the offices as she did from time to time and asks . . . don't tell her what I am or what I do. Her father did her a favor, I am sure, for I cannot see her here in this place, instead of the wife of a prosperous if portly builder."

"You . . . you know?"

"It was a chance copy of the Buffalo newspaper, Matthew, with a picture of a honeymooning couple at Niagara Falls," Crayne said. "What is gone is dead."

"Is it?" Sullivan searched Crayne's face for a flicker of emotion.

"It must be. Now enjoy your ride and hurry back to your teeming metropolis, Matthew. It will take me about two weeks to arrive in Wyoming, where the last incident took place, so you should hear from me in three."

He had talked with a few people from Wyoming. It seemed farther than it was. In truth, he could make it in a week, but the opportunity to ride the High Plains alone and free was one he could not turn down. For weeks he had looked to the West, wanting to explore. He would not miss this chance to do so.

He impulsively reached out and embraced his friend. "Godspeed, Matthew."

Sullivan boarded and waved, as did his friend. He had not gone a mile amid the dust kicked up by the coach's wheels before impatiently pulling Crayne's papers and beginning to read. He found the opening dispatch. It was datelined simply, "The Wyoming Shadowlands." It read, "They call him the Jack of Justice, and in his game, death is a card that is running wild across the prairie and plains." He stopped, closed his eyes, and sighed. Whatever else, Crayne still had it.

He looked at his watch and calculated his travel time, assuming the train would be at the station when he arrived in Rapid City. If he telegraphed this to New York from Chicago, they could make this week's edition with some of it. The Jack of Justice! It would sell a hundred thousand copies. He smiled happily and gazed out the window. He had succeeded already.

Crayne watched his friend and the coach fade away until there was dust, and then nothing. Sullivan, who understood that money was more than scribblings on checks, had brought a substantial advance with him. Hard money. Crayne knew where it would go first.

The horse was mostly white with brown on his legs and belly that looked like splattered mud. Crayne had happened upon him a week ago while writing one of his last dispatches. Being on the edge of poverty had taught him much about riding horses that were at the bottom of the barrel. This one was not even in the same barrel with the rest. Dakota had been kind to Crayne, and he took it as a sign, naming the beast for the new start they both had there.

His owner had won him in a card game and was far more interested in cash than an animal. Crayne wondered how many hundred more days he and the horse would be together than the man and the twenty dollar gold pieces Crayne gave him would share company, but that was not his concern. A used saddle, a new Winchester, a new Colt, boxes of ammunition, some flour, coffee, and other food to carry, and the tools for cooking completed the purchases. By sundown, he was ready to leave Deadwood.

The future was often a mystery, but there were two directions in life. His friend went back to the past. He didn't know if he would go there if he could, but he knew that whatever lay ahead for him and Dakota, it was better than what lay behind.

Chapter Two

The Shadowlands engulfed Crayne. He was fairly certain that the other day he had crossed the imaginary border that divided the land for the sake of those who said they ruled it and was now in Wyoming. If so, no one who lived in this rugged country knew or cared. Indians had competing claims to the land—or would have if they were not all forced off of it by the onslaught of civilization and the columns of cavalry that patrolled the plains. The mountains might hold wealth, but they were rugged and still distant from the creep of ranchers and railroads. The Cheyenne word he had learned fit them best—where shadows hunt shadows. Such talk kept people away, and, where settlers did not venture, those on the run did. He had heard much of the rugged nature of the hills while he was in Deadwood, and they lived up to the advance publicity.

Winter had lingered longer here than in Deadwood. Today, the sun was shining, still blinding off the snow that stubbornly clung to the tops of the mountains that, by the map, had to be at least forty miles distant. The rains of the past few days had stopped. Creeks, barely down from the snowmelt, were now rushing in a way that would contrast to the almost listless trickles of the hot season in the summer. Bare sticks were budding with thick, green dots; the forest would brighten soon with the new growth. The rocks looked cleaned and scoured like a soldier on inspection.

The stillness created by the sound of the wind rushing past

his ears was an illusion. The land was alive with sounds—from the bears combing the brush for anything they hadn't already found to the winter-thin packs of wolves waiting for an elk that was old and had spent its last winter alive. Hawks and eagles soared stiff winged above him, then plummeted to rise with their prey.

He had enjoyed his travels from Deadwood on horseback, alone with the world. He had changed plans and made his obligatory visit first. Cheyenne had been too busy, with too many people trying to be too important. Elezial Newsom, the *Global Reporter*'s head man in Wyoming and supposedly a friend of Southern, was one of them. The man had been borderline rude to Crayne, starting with comments about the Custer piece. He wanted to know every move Crayne was planning. A young man who seemed to hang on Newsom's every word was there as well. He looked no different from the Five Points toughs Crayne recalled from Manhattan. Even if Crayne had a plan, which he did not, Newsom was not going to hear of it. The man was so overbearing Crayne was happy to leave Cheyenne as soon as he could. Newsom had wanted Crayne to have "protection." Crayne worked alone. He slipped away early to avoid a squabble.

If the unlovely man was a friend of Southern's, there was no point in offending him. He would find a way to get the job done without him. There were telegraph lines at Laramie City and Fort Laramie. Maybe other places. For now, he was on his own.

He had come to enjoy the hills and the solitude. So far from the teeming cities where he had spent much of his life. What would they say on the docks at the idea of waving brown-green grass that grew as high as a horse? Or a land where a day could be spent without hearing a human voice. Yet he felt as though he had come home. Often on the way, as with today, when he looked out across the land, he recalled his teacher reading from

Genesis: "And it was good." It was.

He had spent too much time wandering, but the land was an endless thrill as the greens and browns mingled with the grays of the rocks and endless blue of the sky. In a day or two, he would need to turn back toward civilization. Duty called. There were scribbles to file and news to share from among the scraps that had brought life and textures to the words on the paper Matthew had shown him almost three weeks before. He had stopped at the stray ranches, one-room trading posts, and spare crossroads collections of buildings that were hailed as towns. So many people had so much to say based—he was certain—upon scraps of information as insubstantial as the cloud of a man's breath at dawn. It was, however, a good story. It might not be a true story, but whether it was Robin Hood or the Jack of Justice, men who gathered myths about themselves lost nothing in the telling. He would tell the story. Elezial Newsom and Southern and Matthew were waiting. He had to deliver.

Crayne's stomach reminded him of the deplorable condition of his food supply. His store of meat was about gone, but there was still enough for a few days if he ate lightly or for one if he ate as much as he wanted. He had lots of flour. It wasn't really bread, but it had mostly kept his stomach quiet. Mostly. He didn't look too closely at the carrots and potatoes when he threw them in the pan, but they hadn't made him sick. Yet.

He'd last made contact with New York City the day he left Cheyenne, when he wired Matthew and learned that the Jack of Justice was the cover of last week's magazine and that twenty thousand extra copies were being sent to Denver. The New York City newspapers that were experimenting with putting the new craze of photography to use in selling newspapers were already advertising it through some agreement Southern made to print the first of the series. Crayne was glad he had the forethought to use a pseudonym—Joshua Kershaw—so that he could gather his material anonymously. He had learned a hard lesson in Deadwood.

It was as good a start as he would have wished. There had also been letters from Matthew he had not wanted to read in front of Newsom and had stuffed in his saddlebags. He should read them. Soon. But the land . . . it had been years since he had been well and truly alone more than any man is in the press of others, and there was a part of him that wanted to keep riding deeper and deeper into the hills, no matter what lay beyond. Tomorrow he could return to his supposed reason for being there. The next day, certainly.

He was brought back to reality by the sound of a human voice. He cocked his head. The wind. It had to be. The nearest ranch he recalled seeing was two valleys away to the south, and that was only the range where the horses grazed most of the year, he was told. Indians would not be making noise like that if they were hunting. Although these lands were used by the outcasts of the reservations as well as white society, he could not imagine anyone who had fled to the Shadowlands seeking to advertise their presence. It must have been an illusion—thinking about civilization made his mind conjure it.

"Come on, Dakota," he said. The voice sounded odd. Men riding alone talked to animals because they went crazy otherwise. Who did horses talk to, he wondered.

He heard it again. A child? Someone in panic. He turned Dakota in a circle trying to ascertain the source of the sound, knowing how the wind distorted sound. That way. To the west. Then a gunshot. He started to investigate. Then he stopped. Why? He was past caring. Who did what to whom no longer mattered. Did it? He had a story to do, and, the best he could figure, the man who would live whatever life he had left as the Jack of Justice—if what the stories Crayne heard were true—was somewhere up here. He was certain he knew some of the reasons but not enough of them. He needed to focus on his mission—find the man, tell the story, and let the drama play itself out without him. Distractions never paid. They led men to do things that resulted in their deaths.

The panic-laden voice sounded again, slicing through good intentions to remain removed. The voice meant trouble. Dakota started grazing placidly. There was no reason to interrupt the horse for a whim. Crayne dismounted and walked down the hill toward the pine grove at the edge of the miles-deep forest. Perhaps some emigrant party had tried to get the jump on the season and a child had become separated. The gunshot might be a signal. That would mean searchers, though, and he saw none on any ridge, where even the least movement would be skylined. No other voices, no answering shots.

He was now low enough that the trees caught most of the wind. The scream came clearly to his ears. A woman. A girl? He grimaced and moved on. Somebody had run off and become lost. He'd help whoever it was find whoever had strayed, and that would be that.

The next gunshot echoed in the valley. Bird noises were an angry, frightened chorus. The underbrush crackled as rabbits and other animals fled. Only fools went toward sounds like that. He moved faster.

The next scream was off to his right, barely one hundred yards away beyond the screen of the trees. This one was angry. He could not decipher the word. The pistol was now in his hand as he ran faster, instinct from too many years guiding him. He took a wide turn around the last few trees.

He could see tracks in the soft ground. He could hear and feel the sounds of a horse. As the meadow became visible, he saw a man on horseback slowly riding back and forth across the edge of the forest, looking for someone hidden by the trees. The man was oblivious to Crayne's presence. Crayne moved closer.

His hand held the pistol cocked and ready.

One hundred feet. Fifty. Close enough.

"Problem, friend?"

The rider turned and cursed. The arm that held his pistol started to rise.

"Friend, don't!" Crayne yelled, throat choking on words after hardly speaking to anyone but the horse in days, growing even tired of that come lately. "Just asking! Talk this out!"

The rider spurred his horse toward Crayne, who, taken aback, moved to his right toward the trees and started to run. There was no way he could make it. He stopped again and yelled at the rider to stop. The rider fired. A miss. He galloped on toward Crayne.

"You're making a mistake!" Crayne yelled. "Stop!"

The rider fired again. Crayne felt the bullet sail past his face. He'd done what he could. He stood still until the rider was about fifteen feet away. He'd find out now how lucky he was, or maybe how good. Or bad.

Two guns exploded together. Crayne rolled in the dirt. Surprise mingled with pain on the face of the rider as he jerked back in the saddle. The horse reared. Crayne rose and yelled again for the man to stop. He didn't. The rider fired, but the shot was so wild Crayne didn't even hear it whistle past.

Crayne thumbed back the hammer and squeezed the trigger as he extended his arm toward the man. Again and again. The rider slumped as another bullet from Crayne's gun slammed next to the first. The horse moved a few steps, thought about running, then stopped.

Crayne waited. His heart began to slow down. Breathing came easier.

"Hey, horse." It eyed Crayne suspiciously as Crayne walked closer, talking soft. The first time Crayne put out a hand, it shied away but accepted the hand the next time. Crayne grabbed the reins. The saddle was splattered with the blood of the rider who, with two bullets in his chest, was either already dead or so close to it that this world was beyond his awareness. Two hits. Six shots. Lucky for Crayne, the rider was a worse shot than he was. Crayne pulled the man's legs from the stirrups, one by one, and allowed him to slump to the ground. He knelt over the man to check for breath; there was none.

Crayne wondered why.

Crayne moved toward the trees. "Whoever is in there, the man after you is dead. You can come out."

No one emerged.

"I don't know what this is about, but I'm not going to hurt anyone." Crayne holstered his gun. Peaceful intentions might seem more believable if he was not waving a gun around, even though it was empty.

"He's dead? You with him?"

The voice could have been a child, a girl, or a woman. The speaker was behind a tree. Crayne waited. No sense spooking whoever it was.

"Very dead. Come and see. I am not with him. I don't usually kill people I ride with. Here, I'll set my gun on the ground."

He did so and stepped away from it, not so far he could not dive back but far enough to look peaceful. Trusting was good. Trusting carefully was better; he could reach the gun well before she could. Still the watcher did not emerge.

"You are hiding behind the pine with the real crooked branch by your right leg, and you have something tan on that shows behind that branch, and something dark like a jacket, so if I wanted to shoot you I could have by now," Crayne called, wondering if his exhibition of shooting skill would result in a jeer. It didn't. "If you have someplace that you need to ride to, take this horse this man no longer needs."

Crayne saw the hidden watcher move as he spoke. He waited.

Eventually she moved out from behind the tree. She was holding a large branch in her hands, carrying it like a club. She walked as warily as a wolf as she stayed near the protection of the trees. He could see her take in every detail before her. She walked with the vigilant wariness of a wild animal primed to attack first. She also limped severely.

"Why did you kill him?"

"He tried to kill me," Crayne replied. "I warned him to stop, but he didn't seem to be of a mind to. I have never taken kindly to that sort of thing. I told you I never saw him before. Why was he chasing you? What happened to your foot?"

She did not bother with an answer. "Where did you come from?"

"Passing by."

"You followed me."

"Miss, I have no idea where you are going. I'm not sure if I know where I am going. I had no idea you were here until I heard you screaming." She continued to watch him. "Miss, if you have someplace to go, you have a lot of daylight left. Might want to use it. Promise not to follow."

"I don't have any place to go." She was pretty adamant about that. Too much so. Crayne wondered about the dissonance between someone who acted very sure of herself but sounded like something else. Traps were sprung every day for well-meaning fools who did not understand the full depth of the West. He should walk away. He did not.

Crayne, impatient with human contact as always except when it was business, waited for more words for barely a minute. She didn't speak. Enough. She was safe. He was not needed. The limp could have been from anything. Not his problem.

"Miss, this is what I'm going to do. I'm going to walk back the way I came. Ranches are south that way." He pointed as he recalled the terrain he had ridden through these past days. "The nearest pass over the hills to the east is about a mile south, but that will lead you nowhere but the Black Hills trail. West is a lot more prairie until you reach some ranches about three, four days ride if you head off southwest, so I have been told. I'd head south if I was you, but you do what you please. You take care on your journey wherever you go."

No response came. He wondered if she had been wounded, but he could see no blood on her. What he could see was a young, angular face marked with a long-ago scar, matted black hair falling down around her face, and a travel-stained, dark buckskin jacket and leggings with some pattern on them. Indian? Maybe part. He could never tell. Cheeks? Nose? Those were not Indian. Her face was too narrow for a full-blooded Indian. Maybe. That was something someone told him in Dakota, and it fit with the ones he'd seen.

He boldly inspected her. Hard to tell if she was dark skinned or dark from the weather. But there was Indian there, he was sure, even though he was a novice at trying to decipher the heritage of the many people he met who defied categorization. That would explain a fear of a white man with a gun.

"Miss, I'm going to go now unless you need help."

He resolutely stepped toward the gun.

"Don't go."

Unreasoning irritation gripped him. "Miss, I don't know what you want, or where you want to go. You have a horse to ride, and that man's gun for protection. If there is something else wrong, would you please explain it to me?"

"I'm lost." She was lying. Slight change in the voice, the posture. No one who seemed to possess such ingrained wariness would be lost in a few trees. Now he wondered who set traps for whom and what had taken place before he stumbled on the scene.

"Well, I'm new on this range myself," Crayne replied. He

could not leave her; neither should he trust her. "Heading mostly that way." He waved toward the northeast. He weighed what came next. Not much choice, really. She was a woman, and there were rules, even out here. "You can ride with me if you want."

She did.

"What do you want in return?"

Fair question.

"You're a woman; you must be a better cook than I am," he replied. "Come on. Name's Crayne."

"You may call me Dawn," she said.

He was more than sure that was not her name . . . maybe part of the Indian name she must have had at some point. If she was Indian. This was Wyoming. Identities floated around on the wind until folks found one they liked, then floated away when it was time for a change.

"What happened to your foot?"

"I fell. It twisted." The truth was, she had fallen when the fool horse that pulled the wagon she stole with the provisions she took had shied at a snake and upset everything. She had planned to buy food from Jack's friend, but he had become too afraid to deal with her now that she was known to be riding with him. She had grown uneasy with the looks she was getting in town from some cowboys, so she broke in to the store at night and took what she needed, leaving some coins in return. At first, she thought she had escaped. Then came the accident. Then she found sign that she was being pursued. And now? She was still not sure of this one—either dumber than most or more clever. She'd find out which before she gave him even a glimpse of the truth.

Crayne knew from years of practical living that the dead needed nothing. He bent over the rider, taking the gun, gun belt, shells, the few silver dollars in the man's pockets, and the coat he was wearing. It was stout and sturdy, with only a couple of holes in it. She might need it. He then took the reins of the man's horse.

"Mount up," he told her. "We ought to move in case he has friends."

She was wary. Mounting would hurt a lot. Only a fool jumped on a strange horse with a bad leg that might give way. She hesitated, not wanting to show the depth of her injury.

"I am not sure I can ride."

Crayne, taking her words to mean she did not know how to ride, snorted. They were born knowing how to ride out here.

He was impatient.

"Nothing to it; you can get the hang of it in no time."

Before she could stop him, he grabbed her thin waist and lifted her bodily, plunking her down on the saddle while talking to the horse. She grabbed at him, then the horse.

"We're only going to walk," he told her. "No time to waste. I'll look at your foot in a bit."

They soon reached Dakota. The white horse was pleased to see him but seemed to be reserving judgment on the rest of the party. Dakota was not friendly. That was fine with Crayne. He wasn't either.

The clouds were uncertain. Crayne could not predict weather as he had learned in the past week. There was a place he had passed with trees and shelter and a small creek. They ambled that way. It was a good spot. Thick trees on three sides. The fourth was an open meadow making surprise difficult. They would stay there for the night. He reached up for her, ignoring the distaste in her face when he touched her. She let him awkwardly help her down. He started a fire, made a rough camp.

"Let me see that foot," he commanded.

For a minute he thought she might refuse. Then she sat on a limb he had dragged to serve as a seat by the fire. His fingers probed her ankle as he gazed off beyond the tree line, as though he had done this countless times before. He had.

"Nothing broken. Sprain. If I take your moccasin off, it never goes back on, and it's a bit cold for walking that way, so I will wrap this piece of old shirt around it." He had long ago learned that scraps had uses sooner or later. "Ride the next few days and walk as little as you can, and it will improve."

"How come you know this?"

He thought of a world far away. "I grew up with a doctor. Back in London. Most of his job when he tried to help people who weren't stabbed or drunk or bleeding was bandaging people who did something stupid."

"Well thank you!" She mentally pictured her hand with a rock in it putting him in his place.

"Didn't mean anything about you, Dawn," he said without concern. "Just thinking back. Wait here."

From the condition of her ankle, she had walked hard for a couple of days on a bad leg. That fit with running away. No weapons, although he imagined if she was as Western as she looked, there was a knife somewhere. A woman on her own out here invariably had a knife somewhere.

He had strips of his old shirt for bandages ready. The white shone brightly in the evening's gathering darkness. It would look odd, but it would help her walk better and hold the ankle in place until it healed.

He could not help but notice she had a hard-muscled leg. In the dimness and the firelight, he still wondered how Indian she was. As a mongrel, and American as anyone else, he wasn't quite sure why it mattered, even, except that his encounters with the Cheyenne and Sioux—at least live ones or those not fighting for their lives—had so far been fleeting and few. Reality could not match the tales that were told, but he was curious to find out. His curiosity would kill him. He hoped, though, that today was not that day.

"All done," he said with a smile. "Need something hauled or moved, tell me, and I'll do it. Rest does more to heal than anything else."

The sky was now clearing. Some stray stars were visible in the band of dark gray that was the eastern sky. He thought about taking to the trail in the dimming day. In the wild country between settlements and the far wider gaps between towns, few traveled at night. Daytime was different. The comings and goings of small armed bands were as much a part of the innate savagery of life as the sudden deaths that came to take men who were healthy one day and dead of some disease the next. He was not worried about risk. The past few years had ensured that whatever danger there would be in a collision between him and any of the wild men who roamed the wilds of Wyoming Territory, it would be evenly shared. Yet he did not travel alone. How the unaccustomed burden would distract him in a fight was a factor to consider. She might be tougher than he was. She probably was. Then again, finding out she was not would be troublesome, as would learning she might not be on his side in any encounter. They would wait for first light.

She watched him, uncertain. He was neither of the East nor the West. No. East, mostly, but something outside the run of traders and merchants. The clothes were wrong for a cowboy. So was the attitude. He was neat, not in the fussy way of some, but like a man used to order and cleanliness. Civilized, they called it. He thought more than he talked. That made it easier. Deception was a way of life in the Shadowlands, but the less she had to pretend to be someone she was not, the better.

A cowboy would have already called her some Indian epithet. He was talking to her as though she were his equal, as though she was not more Sioux than anything else, although the bits of white and Cheyenne made her distinctive enough that her clan had thought of her as almost an outsider. She had been unwanted in any world to begin with, and, as the War Between the States ended and first Red Cloud and then Sitting Bull fought the whites, whichever camp she was in, she looked like she belonged on the other side. Until lately, it had been her and her alone most of the time, unless someone took pity, which she hated, or affected not to know she was tagging along.

She could not deny the stranger's arrival had been timely. She had been making good time with the wagon until that snake spooked the horse. His antics sent her tumbling from the unfamiliar perch of the wagon seat. Everything was in the wagon—not only their food, but her guns. She thought at first she could catch him, but he was running like the wind—first time she had seen that in two days. The wagon hit a tree and smashed; she had seen that. Her rifle was ruined as well. The horse kept going with what was left, leaving behind a cloud of flour and the wreckage of her plans. Having no other choice, she started to walk, no matter how much her foot hurt her.

She had been careful to stay in the trees. Very careful. For two days' walk. Then she had come to a wide meadow. Walking around would be prudent, but it would prolong her trip and add to her misery. She had been most of the way across it when she was spotted, and the chase was on. She was not the fleet-footed Indian of lore, and one bad leg made it worse. The best she could have hoped for was that the rider who trapped her was alone and might either make a careless mistake or leave. She hated screaming like a woman, but when the only weapon left was her voice, she used it. She had warned him she was not alone. She had called out in Sioux and Cheyenne for help, knowing that there was no one there but hoping he could be stalled until dark. She was certain that only his fear that she could somehow work Indian magic and kill him had kept him at bay. The worst had about happened when—as she knew—the spirits finally heard her and took away her danger.

She busied herself with the chore of making food. Whoever this Crayne was, he was cleaner than many. His clothes were a mix of new and old, the dashing and the durable. He was not an average cowboy, but she did not know if that was good or bad. She mistrusted his eyes. They were too probing, too observant. Although all of the worlds she grew up in looked down upon those not purely of one race or another, she had long become used to her own skin. She hated being observed as though she were a novelty.

He seemed as content not to talk as she was. She had a knife hidden that would protect her if he became a threat, but she doubted she would need it.

Dawn cooked what she could with what he had. They ate in silence. A clue, Crayne thought. Out here, meals were a time to eat, not talk. She moved with swift efficiency. She was no tenderfoot, but the rest was a mystery.

He told her to sit while he cleaned up. She bristled inside, but now that she was no longer running for her life every minute, she wanted to rest her leg. He gave her a blanket, propped his saddle under her foot.

"It'll heal better. Trust me." He moved away to the far side of the trees, obviously giving her space to make it clear she was safe.

Stars looked impassively down as he waited in the shadows of deepest night. His life had changed, but even as he tried to understand how, it had gone past him like a fast train, and now he was pulled in its wake. Long ago he had learned about God. The Indians worshipped the land and wind and sky. Perhaps it was all the same. Perhaps whoever and whatever looked down knew what was to come. He, for certain, did not.

Matthew would tell him to leave the woman and file his

dispatches. But Matthew was ensconced in his New York City offices. Crayne would follow where this trail led.

Morning dawned cold. Almost everything was frozen. The sun had not cleared the mountains to the east. She smelled the fire he had started.

"Almost last of the coffee," he told her as she approached the fire, having slept under the trees. Her leg felt wooden. She woke up to a blanket over her that had not been there when last she was awake. She was irritated that he was happily awake while she was trying to throw off the last vestiges of sleep. She should be more aware than he was. He offered a steaming cup and a smile. "Been savin' it. Might as well use it today. Need it. Ready?"

She wasn't, but after three swallows and a grimace as the boiling liquid hit, vowed she was.

"You know how to shoot?"

"A gun?"

"Yup."

"Rifle . . . not a pistol."

"Good enough. If I tell you to duck, gallop, anything at all, you do it. Do you understand?"

"I think I can—"

"We both know how that little dance with that gentleman back there would have turned out. I don't know you, and you don't know me, but I need to know that, if there is another dance, I can count on you to do what I say. Argue about it, if you have to, when you're alive to do that. Let's go."

She gulped, packed, and mounted. The leg hurt less. Perhaps the stranger knew what he was doing. Maybe in another day she could feel safe on her own. For today, in spite of herself, help was welcome. No. Necessary. She fumed inwardly at that knowledge.

The fire was still sending a thin, lazy column of smoke into the air. It would linger a while, slowing anyone investigating the fire. He half-helped, half-pushed her in the saddle. He guessed maybe his hand was in the wrong place on her leg from the exclamation and snarly glance she threw him. He hadn't been paying attention.

For the first mile or two he held the reins; then, as he watched her move in the saddle with ease, he figured she had been lying at first about not knowing how to ride, and he gave them to her. As he did so, he was asking himself if he wanted her to gallop away, or whether he wanted his hand free.

A swift-moving storm appeared, but the part that caught them was not fierce and was fortunately brief. The forest sheltered them. Wetness added to her misery, for he did not stop nor seem to feel discomfort from the rain; in fact, it seemed to her that he even enjoyed it, although, when he saw her misery, he added a heavy coat to hers and spread it over her already-soaked hair. It was a gallant gesture, perhaps, but of little use. She did not bother telling him.

He made a fire after they stopped, told her to sit near it to dry herself, and offered her a mix of bread and dried meat. "You need to eat. I would like to be beyond the next hills tomorrow. I have business I've let slide, I guess, so I need to finish it. Once you move along on your way, I have one last place to visit before riding down to Cheyenne or Laramie for a while." He gave her a disarming smile but kept his real purpose vague. "I am used to traveling. My work takes me to many places around the territories."

Her suspicions flared when he never said what he did. Men who went into those towns worked for the army or the railroad or even the Territory; they were surveyors, or they were men paid to hunt men who did not want to be found. Especially one. If he had been trying to fool her, he had just made a mistake. She would be very, very careful.

She vowed to stay awake as long as he did. Twice her head snapped up when she started to doze. Then, sleep no longer could be conquered by will.

Crayne put the last blanket over her. He kept the fire going—more than he would if he was alone—but she would need the warmth.

She was stiff, sore, and angry in the morning. He had saved one final handful of coffee with sugar. It was not much. It didn't take her long to drink it down. He'd have to find something to kill if they wanted more. He was not a good hunter, but he was what they had. Time to go.

They didn't get far.

Ears trained by the wilderness to hear sounds before they became threats heard the drumming of hooves. Her head snapped around as she sat her horse. "Crayne." He stopped Dakota. She pointed. He turned in the saddle.

Not one rider. Three. No, four. Crayne and Dawn had ambled through a meadow; their path would be clear through the high grass. There was a stand of trees fifty feet away. Maybe they could make that. She tried to make it clear to him the urgency of it all. He was clueless.

"What are you doing?" she asked as he turned to face the riders.

"You said we have company," he said. "I will try being polite first to see if that makes them ride on. Head off for those trees. Don't move or say anything or do anything until I tell you. If it ends bad, you might be able to slip away through the trees. Not sure how deep those woods go."

He gave her his rifle, hoping he remembered to reclaim it in case this was nothing. She didn't look like this was the first time she had ever handled one. Maybe so, being a woman who had to survive. Maybe something else. Time would tell.

The horsemen were closer now. Coming around a curve in the rough trail around rocks and marshy spots that nature made for men and animals to follow. Three. Not riding like pursuit. But curious—pointing at the tracks. Until they saw him.

He had two revolvers, one in his hand. He could give three men a fight and maybe even win it, even if he was still green in many ways. He didn't think getting lucky was likely, but he'd learned long ago that odds were what a man makes them.

"Howdy, boys!" he called.

"Howdy," one called back. Crayne reluctantly put the gun back in its gunbelt. The three rode loosely forward. If they were a threat, they were confident. None of them moved toward a gun. They stopped about fifteen feet away. Crayne waited for them to decide what this was going to be. The lead one looked where the woman was waiting.

"You passing through?"

"Something like that."

"Kinda curious, friend. Don't know you. Don't see many folks up here. Circle Seven range here. Don't mind sharin' but we like to know who with."

"Circle Seven," mused Crayne, who knew how they all talked if not what they said. "Never heard of it. New?"

"Last fall. Brother Joshua and his wife settled here."

"Thought the only ranch this side of the hills was down southwest a ways, old man whose name I can never remember." At least, that's what the man a few days back had told him.

"He died. Brett Orcutt. He was a mean old cuss who plain dropped dead one day. Sorry if he was a friend."

"He wasn't. Name's Crayne. Business up in the hills. Railroad still run down that way?" He pointed south. He had no idea if there was a line within twenty miles.

"It does," the rider replied. "Train don't stop anywhere between Crown Valley and Neck River, though. Not anymore.

Injuns, I heard. Then some other kind of foolishness with some town or other not wantin' more stops. Rails are more a nuisance than it's worth, you ask me. Scares the horses."

"Progress," replied Crayne. "Crown Valley's about straight south of here, right?"

"Pretty much," said the rider. "You're about fifteen miles away. Neck River's closer off to the west, but I wouldn't advise it, with a woman and all. Wild country."

"Obliged," said Crayne, not surprised they had seen her. Women were rare on the range, and cowboys knew when one was within a hundred miles. Especially a young, pretty one. "Problem if we head down that way? Our horses might eat a bit of your grass, and I might kill a deer or rabbit to eat along the way, but other 'n that we won't be a bother."

The man waved a hand. "No bother. Cabin a few miles south. Line shack is all it is. Help yourself to what's there. Josh, my brother, knows cowboys have to eat, and he stocks it pretty good for us. Just finished putting things up, so there's a lot."

"Thank you," Crayne said, marveling again at the hospitality so common on the range, hospitality that often ended quickly. His goal had been northeast, but it was simpler to head south for a few miles, eat enough to last a few more days, and settle Dawn on her way. Perhaps he should file what dispatches he had and then come back another day to explore.

"You run into someone, tell 'em Earl Colquitt said you could ride on through. Well, we better ride."

The men left. Taking no chances, Crayne kept one hand near his gun as he waved the woman out of the trees with his other hand.

The sun was high in the sky when the shack came into view. No smoke. No horses. They waited a while and watched. She was chafing to be off the horse; but patience was often all that kept strays alive. Nice words covered many intentions; for all he knew the men from the meadow were already waiting.

"Why are we sitting here in the sun when there is a place inside?" she asked. "They said we could use their shack."

"They did." He didn't move.

She was reminded of her childhood—men mounted on horseback knowing trouble was out there and waiting to pick up traces of it on the wind. This Crayne was not a frontiersman, but he knew something was wrong. Or thought he did.

He looked each way often as they closed the final one hundred yards to the shack. It was built to resist weather, tucked into the side of a slight hill that shielded the shack from the strongest of the north and west winds. A small creek flowed fifty feet from the west side of the south-facing shack. There was a long open meadow that led to the front. A shutter was closed securely over the only window. Nothing looked disturbed recently.

"Get down and come in," he told her.

She did so, stumbling as she dismounted. He caught her. "I'm fine," she snapped as he grabbed her waist.

"Easy," he told her. "I'm on your side, remember? Now go in, and tell me if there's food there. If not, I'll go hunt something."

It took a moment for her to adjust to the dimness, even with the door open. A few barrels of what was marked as flour were there, all the things she would need to cook. Potatoes and carrots. Onions. No meat.

"Make bread with what you can," he told her. "Let me see what I can find for meat."

"No!"

He waited for more. "Stay near, please. I know this is shelter. I also know that if you are not here and someone comes, I am trapped and alone. There is only one way in."

"We have a spare gun," he told her, wondering again how

helpless she was or how often she had told men she was. Since he was a pretty poor hunter, and slightly embarrassed he had not noted that what was safe was also a potential trap, he gave in. "I will teach you to shoot so you can protect yourself. For now, I'll stay here."

He moved past her and busied himself starting a fire in the fireplace, not seeing the glare of fire she gave his back. As if she needed lessons.

When it was burning, he brought in wood, then went back out. She sliced vegetables and made dough. They would have food for tonight and bread for a day or two. Everything was cooking nicely. It would be the most food they had eaten.

She went to tell him and found him slumped in the sun against the rough wood of the shack. Asleep. First, she was angry that he slept while she worked. Then she realized he stayed wakeful in the nights and let him rest. She also knew that while he slept, there was a chance that questions the man would never answer might be revealed in his belongings. It wasn't right, but in a world where survival meant unmasking deception before it turned on her, there were no rules except survival.

Chapter Three

The smell of tobacco woke him. He was no longer drifting between sleep and half-aware wakefulness. He'd come out of enough Pinkerton naps to cross that line from sleep to alertness quickly. There could be no one using tobacco except someone watching. Dawn had not smelled of it. Someone wondering who was in the shack? He shifted slightly. The three riders? Best bet. He knew from experience the best way to lower someone's guard was to act friendly in person and surprise them when they were eating. It had worked for him before. And if the riders didn't send him here, who did?

The hat over his eyes didn't block his vision as much as it might appear to do. He could see around the brim. There was someone there, still in the brush. From the corner of his left eye, he could see that Dakota was watching someone or something. That was two. If it was the three riders, the third would be in the back.

Crayne was wondering how much longer he should pretend to be asleep. They solved that problem. The two he could see moved.

Crayne did not have the knack of drawing a gun swiftly from a holster. That was why he napped with it on his lap.

"Far enough," he said, tossing the hat away.

The two men—both who had been in the group he had encountered that morning—didn't hesitate. They pointed their rifles in his direction and each moved away farther from the other as they fired.

Crayne's first shot brought a moan; no time for satisfaction. A rifle bullet landed next to his ear in the wood. He rolled on the ground; the next shot barely missed as well. Gunfire sounded from behind the shack. Crayne rolled again. He was almost to the trees. He jammed his boot hard into the soft ground and stopped. Then he dropped flat. The next shot anticipated his continued movement. Firing while lying on his belly, the next four from Crayne's gun framed where the shot came from. There was a noise of a voice choking and branches moving. He pulled new shells from the gun belt. Reloaded. Sprang up.

The woman was there, gun pointed at Crayne as though she had done this a thousand times before.

"Put it down," she said.

"What?" he said. "I—"

"Put it down. You shot them; I know; I'm glad you did; guess you weren't their partner; but you still better put that gun down now. I don't want to shoot you, but I will. That was too close. I'm not taking any chances."

Dawn had shed any attempt to appear helpless. Crayne had lost enough hands to know when the cards were against him. He dropped the pistol. "Are they—"

"Dead," she replied. "Good riddance. By rights you should join them, because I can't help but think you had something to do with it, but he said not to kill anyone I don't have to. So I don't kill you. Yet."

"Sioux or Cheyenne?" Crayne always marveled at the way his mind picked on irrelevancies.

"Both," she replied without the least movement in the barrel of the gun aimed at his chest. "Father was Sioux and Cheyenne with a white a generation back who was part Cheyenne, although you could barely tell. Mother was part Sioux a ways back and mostly Irish and Welsh from some trader. They say it's an interesting combination, whatever that means. Out here it means nobody wants you. Lived twelve years with the Sioux. They could overlook most of me. Then I became the enemy when the soldiers started attacking all the time. Then I moved away. Tried life with my Cheyenne half brother. Wasn't any better. Lived on my own until . . . well, it don't matter to you. Made a promise to kill any white man calls me squaw. Kept it. Drop the gun belt."

"Why?" The belt was in the dirt.

"Hands way up, now. I don't like shooting people who are not shooting back, but I can do it if I have to."

He complied.

"This is what happens. You go in that shack and load up some sacks of carrots and potatoes on my horse. You can eat the bread I was making. One false move and I will kill you. I know how. When you are done, I am going to ride away. You will stay here. I will take your beautiful horse—"

The gun shifted as he inadvertently tensed.

"—for a ride with me and leave him about four or five miles in that direction." She pointed northwest. "Not going to steal him. Seen the way he looks at you as though you matter. If you have a brain, you will find some other direction to ride in and leave this part of Wyoming alone. You've already done enough."

"I don't know . . . I really don't understand what this is all about. I don't mean you any harm. I don't know who you are and what your business is. You don't know a thing about me. Let me explain."

The sound of disgust was plain. The rifle wiggled a bit. He stopped talking.

"Crayne, the famous writer, aren't you? Think we are all blind out here? Ignorant? Can't read?"

"But . . . but . . ." Sullivan had assured him they would use the fake name.

"*Global Reporter* Western correspondent." she said. "Deadwood, right? Last month they wrote you were seeking"—her voice changed as she mocked the magazine—"the man behind the mask of the Jack of Justice.

"There were copies all over Laramie City," she said. "Your rag even had a sketch of you. Nice sketch. Not real flattering, and you had a mustache and funny clothes like they wear in the East, but nice. Wouldn't know it was you to look now. You in disguise, scribbler?"

Crayne was furious. They could run a five-year-old sketch; legally it was theirs. But they had a deal . . . Southern . . . He started to pace.

"Do *not* move," she said. "Thought you looked familiar when I met you. Could not place it. Figured it when I went through your saddlebags while you were sleepin'. Saw all them notes. We read some of your scribblings on Deadwood. I suppose they were good. Mostly I like the paper to start fires."

"Why? What is any of this to you? I did you no harm and meant you no harm. Who of yours have I hurt?"

"You are a Judas goat, Crayne. A poor dumb Judas goat. Going to find 'the Jack of Justice' as if you are the only man in all of Wyoming and Dakota and Montana looking for him. The man you killed was following me as a way to track down Jack. These three are not much different. Bad enough the past year, but the past month every man wants to be famous because you made it important for them to hunt him. Jack is worth a thousand of you, Crayne. I don't know how many others there are, but I think I am safer alone. Maybe you were sent to find him to kill him; maybe you are so stupid you don't know why they sent you; maybe you even told me the truth. Don't matter now. Thank you for helping my foot. It does feel better, but I can't risk being caught."

For a moment, Crayne's conversation with Newsom flashed into his mind. Protection? Or was there another purpose to giving Crayne an armed escort? Crayne tried but could not quite reject the idea. "I still don't understand."

"Mountain men and maybe a few Sioux and a couple of Cheyenne can make it on their own out here, Crayne, but it's hard. The man you are hunting for the sake of your magazine, your scribblings, is a real man who is one of the few men in Wyoming who will intervene when a Sioux is injured. Or a Cheyenne. He is the only one with the nerve to stand up to what you Easterners are doing. He has a price on his head—not the kind that the law posts, but the kind that people offer who want him killed any way the deed can be done so they can prey on us. Anybody who rides these trails knows he has help. He can't exactly go into town. I'm the one that rides into towns to pick up his supplies, cooks his dinner, and helps him hide. Patches him when he is shot. Helps him when the sickness gets him bad. It's not something you know, being a big fancy correspondent and all, but it's something the people that live here in the Shadowlands know. They're hunting me so they can find him, and if you are leading them to me, you are leading them to him. I'm protecting Jack. I'm protecting my people." She laughed bitterly. "I'm protecting my hair. No one will hurt us if I can stop it."

"Us? You're part white. I can see that. You . . . you said that."

"You people from the East; you are so stupid," she shouted at him. "My grandchildren can be blond as the sun, and to a lot of the folks out here, they will look like they have Indian in them, and someone will look at them as warriors. 'Nits make lice,' Crayne. Bet you don't know where that came from."

"John Chivington. Colorado Militia. Killed bunch of folks on a drunk one day during the Civil War. Sand Creek. 1864. Black Kettle was the chief. Man flew a U.S. flag, and the Colorado boys killed his people anyhow."

"Amazing." Her sarcasm and scorn were thick. "You actually have read something other than dime novels about scalping. That's how they think; that's how they act. I know who you are looking for. I will protect him. I will protect him until the day I die, if it takes that, and so will others. You think this is all about your magazine. This is about his life! He will stop them from killing and taking trophies for the fun of it, Crayne."

"You his wife? Tell me his name. Your name. Your real name. Let me talk to him. Tell his story."

"No; it is none of your business. No names. No hints. I've met others like you. Writers." The disgust was heavy. "Tell them it snowed an inch and you read a page of nonsense that never was. No writing nothing about a man whose boots you don't even deserve to lick, not with my help anyhow. Maybe you believe what you are saying, but I don't."

"You don't understand."

"Your readers can live without it. We are not characters in a story, Crayne. We are real, live people who can die if someone finds us. He is not dying to amuse some fat cow in a vest in Boston. Go write about something sensational somewhere else. Write about Billy the Kid in New Mexico."

Crayne groaned.

"Tell them Jack died or went to find Sitting Bull in Canada. Leave him alone. Figure it out, Crayne, that there are consequences to the things you write. Putting Jack in danger is one of them I ain't going to allow. I have every scrap of notes I could find. Taking them. Gonna burn them first chance. Unless you are smarter than you look and have a better memory, you won't have anything to write about, unless you make it all up, which I suppose you might well do. Give it up and go home."

"Or?"

"Or the next time this will not end so well for you. Can't say

I want to shoot you, but you know I will." Silence fell. Crayne had no options.

"Are you going to tell me your real name?"

She shook her head. "If you can follow, others can. Names are clues. Dawn is good enough."

"Who educated you?" he asked.

"Missionary school," she replied. "He meant well. I can read better than most white girls." She emphasized white. "I liked books. The rough men came one day and hung him for being kind to Indians."

"Sorry."

"Don't be. I killed two of them easy. The other one shot me in the face, but I killed him, too." He watched her relive the scene in her mind.

"Go! Give this up. Death is not for the amusement of your readers. You want to do something with your life? Quit writing about a man that is trying to do something right and risking his life to do it, and go do something yourself for a change instead of leeching off the lives of people who are better than you ever will be."

She leaped up on the horse's back, wincing slightly at the pain in her ankle but showing none of the timidity she had shown earlier. The gun never wobbled. She rode off at a leisurely pace, leading Dakota. Crayne sat with the dead and watched her go. Northwest.

It was not raining—yet. He might as well start walking. He looked around at the dead again. Maybe now would be a good idea. That was, once he had eaten what he could eat and packed away the rest of whatever she had made. Didn't matter if she hated him or not. A meal was a meal.

The smoke from the factories across New York City that made leathers and laces was blowing toward the office windows, making the Old Man's private office an even thicker haze than usual, because he refused to bow to the stench and close the windows.

Jacob Southern had been a commercial printer in Buffalo before a political connection vaulted him to a position on the staff of the headquarters of the Army of the Potomac. When the War Between the States ended, he was determined to make his mark on the publishing world. He brought his domineering energy to New York City to launch a weekly news magazine that would outsell everything else in the market. With a shock of white hair, and two massive white eyebrows, the burly, glaring, growling force that was Southern intimidated new and old writers alike.

"Well?" Southern growled as he greeted Sullivan with the cigar in his mouth wagging angrily.

"Nothing," Sullivan replied.

Southern's massive jaw clenched in what to Sullivan looked like a bare-knuckle boxer's fist. It had now been three weeks since they had heard from Crayne. Southern had made it very clear to Sullivan that, although Crayne was a gifted writer, Southern believed that man was a miserable, contentious, disloyal wreck of a human being who was tolerated only as long as he produced and only as long as Sullivan—the most gifted of all editors—insisted upon him. He recalled Crayne's writings after the Little Bighorn. The man all but reeked sympathy with the Indians. Contrary and cantankerous. What his daughter had ever seen in the man was something Southern had never been able to understand. At least he had been able to break that off while Crayne was off on an assignment, one from which he never returned, thanks to his own willful actions.

Still, so far, they had made a killing off of Crayne's Jack of Justice series, properly handled and revised to suit the taste of the readers, who expected their Wild West to have certain stock characters Crayne had omitted. There were three weeks left to go, though, and one of those weeks was—even by Southern's standards—stretching the material very, very thin to the point where the readers might not be satisfied.

Sullivan saw telegrams on Southern's desk. He knew word had come from Cheyenne, including one this morning, but not from Crayne. Sullivan was nervous. He had worked out a system of couriers to bring Crayne's writings East as fast as possible, if there was too much to telegraph. All Crayne had to do was obey instructions. Sullivan had told him to stay in touch. What could be keeping him?

"That Denver man," Southern said after belching out as much smoke as a steam engine on a steep grade. "The one we had to send West because of that . . . incident . . . the woman . . . Marshall. Find him. Send him."

"Send him where?"

"Wyoming," said Southern. "Cheyenne. Meet Newsom. We need someone there who will do what we say and tell us everything he knows. I want the job done. I don't trust Crayne. Never have. Let you talk me into it. I want someone who jumps when I say so and doesn't argue and will stay in communication with this office as he is told to. This is too important."

"Marshall can't equal Crayne, sir," Sullivan replied, trying to appease the Old Man's anger with the deference that the former War Between the States officer believed was his due. Marshall would never track down the Jack of Justice, Sullivan thought. Only someone as driven as Crayne could do it. Sullivan had been counting on that.

"Marshall is disreputable, dishonest, and personally a disgusting foul wretch," said Southern. "He has a good eye for the landscape and people; he will do exactly what we tell him. He will write what the readers want to read. You and I both know, Sullivan, that this story only ends one way. Sooner or later the army decides that it has to become involved, they hunt the man down, and they kill him. That Lucas fellow could probably write it from here, but he lies too much as it is, so do not encourage him."

The cigar wagged again like a stubby, glowing version of a cat's tail.

"Marshall it is," Southern concluded. "Tell him to go to Cheyenne and await instructions. Pay the usual rate; say more may be forthcoming. If we do not hear from your friend, he shall have the story. He may have the story anyhow if, as it seems, Crayne succumbed to his past ways of behavior. If he has taken this to be some crusade out there, I won't even bother to recall him again; I will cut him off. Wire him if you want. Leave."

Sullivan left. Southern had said "as it seems." He had heard something about Crayne he did not share. From whom? Newsom? Sullivan hoped not. He would have to find out, but discreetly. Southern had many contacts in many places.

For all he knew, Southern had heard gossip from Fort Laramie. Southern revered the army and its leaders and might have a friend who was an officer there. Officers there would hardly look favorably upon a man who castigated their Custer, even if privately and dispassionately many men believed the campaign of 1876 to have been so enmeshed in politics, rivalries, and ambitions, it was a wonder whether it ever could have succeeded. But that was a story that would never be told.

Crayne was digging his own grave if he failed to do what Southern wanted and what Sullivan made so clear. All Crayne needed to do was find the man—which should be easy for a former Pinkerton man—send in his dispatches, and not chase that which didn't produce anything. How much simpler could it be? If Southern was right and Crayne was up to something more than the story, then there might be nothing Sullivan could do to save him. It might be time to worry more about saving himself.

Walking through the endless miles of miles and miles of Wyoming Territory gave a man time to think, when not distracted by the contrasts of a land that could be flat for a few miles, hilly the next, and then rugged and rocky to the point where it defied any possible use. But the rugged plains and hills took Crayne's mind from his troubles, whether watching hawks hover and then dive, elk lumber across clearings, or antelope dash away from predators real or imagined.

There was much to think of. Much he did not wish to think of. Crayne had never thought much about the actors and actresses in the little dramas he wrote, arranging and rearranging the facts in such ways that would suit those who enjoyed the thrill of the chase from the comfort of a padded chair or a window seat. Life was the raw material of stories that were acted out by writers and readers, within limits established by the conventions of society.

The girl's impassioned denunciation of his work could not help but make him reconsider his life. Others were far worse than he; they would not scruple at setting a scene to cause a reaction, bribing a man to start a fight, or even—as Donaldson did—burning down a man's barn to write about the tardy nature of his neighbors' response to help a man they all hated. Some created people out of whole cloth; although he could never but be amused at Harbaugh's endless parade of feisty grandmothers who held off drunken ruffians. Readers either never caught on or were equally amused, as if they wanted the world they read about to be made up of stock characters who moved in predictable, orderly ways to act out the appropriate fates the polite readers of polite society wished to bestow upon them.

Today found him thinking more about what happened to

those he wrote about—how changes came to their lives because he chronicled their shortcomings, or even their attributes. How lives were altered to fill pages in a newspaper or magazine. Or, in the case of Jasper back in Deadwood, snuffed out before their time. It was never personal. On his end. He had not really thought about the other end. Until today.

As he walked, he thought about Maggie Noshoes in Whitechapel when he was a boy and her conception of God—that He walked the earth and one day would find you and make you look in His eyes so that you would understand right and wrong and what your life was worth. He'd had a taste of it from Dawn, or whatever her real name was.

Maybe she was right. He should do something more with his life than write what he knew were often half-true fairy tales about what other people were doing with theirs. He recalled the Pinkerton days with some fondness, because he was not chained to an assignment. He was often in danger, but rarely bored. Still, it was the person who hired the agency who was always right. The runaway wife had to be returned to the lout, although often the difference between the one she chose and the one she left was marginal. Crayne had enjoyed the hunt for the truth, or the person, or whatever it was he was set to track down, but morally life as a detective was as shaky as writing.

In short, the only thing he could do well made life worse for the people with whom he interacted.

And yet . . . he did want to know the story. He did want to write the story. Maybe not the story that Southern wanted . . . no, not that story at all. That story was one puny bit of the bigger, wider, more important whole.

From the start, it was clear to him that this Jack of Justice had been on some type of crusade and was clearly a man who was in the grip of an illness, even though no one said he was sick. Someone talked about coughing blood. It was death that made men realize they needed to balance the slate. What triggered it? No man could hope to kill every man who hated Indians. That would be most of several territories. And these were not only Indians. These were people who were castoffs, easy prey. He wished he had the notes he would never see again. No, there was something hidden in all the words people had told him that was behind all this. Something was stirring passions beyond the usual surface ripples.

What the girl had told him whetted his curiosity. There was a massive story taking place on this Wyoming range where one man was, from her tale, trying to set right many wrongs. That was the story he should be telling. Would Sullivan buy it? Matthew might. Would Southern? Doubtful, since he knew that the source of any changes from the plan he and Sullivan had agreed upon could only be laid at one man's feet—the feet of a man whose objectivity on the subject of Indians never recovered from being the first journalist on the scene of Custer's Washita fight in 1868 and one of the few at the Little Bighorn before he was forcibly removed and his notes taken from him. After speaking to survivors of the commands that barely survived the Indian onslaught that slaughtered Custer's command, Crayne had put in flaming prose his verdict of who put their lives in danger and why. Anything he wrote now about Indians would be lumped with the past and never see print.

The *Global Reporter* had spent a significant amount of time clearly—from the girl's words—selling the series. Probably everything he had written was cut to shreds and re-pasted together to stretch it as long as possible. He knew they would do that; it was the way the business worked when the writer was a thousand or more miles from the editor. Depending upon how well they had stretched the material, he might have a couple of weeks left, but not more. Filing soon would buy time. He could file more pabulum. Should he? Oh, there was the question to which the answer changed over and over.

Laramie City was probably three days away. He would need the telegraph there. Cheyenne was probably not that much farther, but it had left a bad taste. Newsom. Especially Newsom, whom he now thought of in a different light since the girl called Crayne a Judas goat. He might be too suspicious now, but he had been too trusting before, he feared. Judas goat? That would imply someone knew more about this Jack of Justice than he understood anyone to know. She was hysterical. Or maybe she knew a lot more than he did.

He'd give it a try. But first, he needed to find his horse. There had to be other places where the wires ran. This was almost 1880.

"Dakota!" he called, hoping the horse had learned its name and would come magically prancing out. It had not. On he walked, feet slogging as his thoughts raced and grappled with a question he had never fully pondered.

Top Hat drew its name from the scrawny, rock-strewn hill that led up to the small town, or so the locals said. In fact, Top Hat was created through the magic of a surveyor's pen when the Naming Commission passed through in 1858. A raging forest fire that year had swept through, leaving the surveyor to recall the place succinctly as "Tophet."

Since such a name was clearly not in keeping with what the commission wanted for names, the name was changed to Top Hat, which went along coincidentally with the rocky prominence of a nearby bare summit that was named after the bald head of a trapper until the Naming Commission gracefully consigned him to oblivion. Top Hat boasted a rough, rocky slope that attracted few settlers. Miners had tried to find something of value, but the half-finished shafts were evidence that the place was—so far—found worthless. Gold fever drew men to swarm, dig, then flee to whatever other spot rumor picked as the next major gold strike.

Failing to be useful to men, the wild hills enjoyed days without human interference in the lives of the animals that clustered in treetops and crevices and in the caves winding through the mountain like labyrinths. Legends passed down from generations of Cheyenne and Sioux as well as those started by white trappers talking of strange noises, ghosts, and riders who were never seen again after vanishing from view.

The town existed because such roads as there were in this northeastern corner of Wyoming petered out all at the same time in the same place. Its collection of buildings was a town insomuch as the unpainted, rickety relics of a more optimistic day were leaning into each other more than away from each other, showing signs of the hasty construction that followed the expulsion of the Sioux from their ancestral lands in the years following the Battle of Little Bighorn. Top Hat also was an object lesson in the slow death of towns that blossomed quickly in hopes of becoming another Deadwood. Some clung to the hope that when the gold fever broke, there would be other riches to dig. Coal, maybe lead. The forests would provide lumber if anyone could figure out how to transport the wood back to civilization so it could become houses and railroad ties. Inertia kept some who came for gold and had neither the means nor the energy to move on eking out existence on small ranches. And so Top Hat clung to existence, if not life.

In this time and place when the best barometer of civic health was the number of saloons a community could boast, Top Hat's status was clear by the fact that it had one, and only one. In fact, it had one of everything—dry goods store, stable, and blacksmith.

On this grim-sky day with lowering clouds threatening rain, that one saloon had three customers and a barkeep, all lost in the pause that begins when everything has long ago been said.

"Shh!" hissed one of the customers, an older, grizzled man who moved with the pain of old wounds and the alacrity that comes with scars of hesitation. His skin was leathery; the rutted darkness beneath his eyes hung far into his cheeks, almost touching the edge of the salt-and-pepper bread that hung from his gaunt visage. He held up his hand. The silence that had been in effect before he spoke remained.

Then a smile creased his grimness. "There! She's back at last."

The slow, rhythmic clopping of a shod horse on rock-strewn dirt was audible. The older man and a younger man each eased their guns from well-worn, low-slung holsters. They knew that no efforts to elude pursuers were foolproof. Readiness was synonymous with survival. The barkeep continued polishing the glass he had started cleaning what seemed like an hour ago.

"Shoot through that window, you buy a new one," he grumbled.

"No window there, maybe you can fit all them miners easier, Lew," chimed back the older man. "Pretty crowded here now."

"Town'll have its day again when they find whatever them mountains got hid," Lew replied. "Break the glass, Jack, and I break your head." He grinned at the other man, who replied with a smile of long friendship.

"Gonna have to stand in line if you want to do that, Lew," Jack replied.

"It's her," said the younger man as if announcing the official verdict, uneasily watching the older men banter in a world that excluded him and made him feel callow, ending the conversation.

The older man's face transformed as he walked through the doors and opened his arms for the girl.

"Thought you'd gone civilized."

"Problems," she said after a brief, intense hug during which she was certain his ribs felt sharper than they had a few weeks ago when she left.

"We do attract them," he replied. He had already noted what was supposed to be a wagonload of food was a few sacks on horseback. There would be an explanation, but he did not care. They would make do. She was back. Supplies would appear in time, from somewhere.

"Tommy, lend a hand."

In a moment, the sacks of food were transferred to the saloon's pantry. Then the young woman told her tale, from their friend breaking his promise to help them obtain food to her meeting with Crayne and the men combing the Shadowlands looking for him, or her, or both.

The older man said nothing about this mishap with the horse and wagon. They happened. Surviving them and adapting to adversity was all that mattered. Friends fade in the heat. He was, however, uncertain why, after a year of embarking upon the crusade that would make up for the wasted years of his life, he was suddenly of interest.

"That scribbler!" she said. "They are writing about you like you are some kind of outlaw. People out looking to make a name. I had some of the papers in the wagon, but they ended up scattered. Found one I could bring you so you could see how dangerous it is. They are printing lies, Jack. We have to do something about it."

He was silent for a moment, wondering at connections he had supposed but could not prove. Did the writer fit in? It was too tangled. He would finish his work, regardless.

His niece did right, he told her. She did not look pleased. He hated seeing her angry with herself.

"A writer? And that one to boot? You let him live?" He started to chuckle. "Feelin' poorly are you?"

"Didn't seem right. Wanted to; didn't want to. Owed him. Think I should have?" she asked uncertainly.

"No, I do not," he said clearly. "Not to lecture, but you can't do right by doing wrong, girl. I've read that man's work. He once savaged ol' Custer. Folks wanted to hang him in about half the states and all the territories. That was a few years back. I was in Colorado then. He disappeared; I figured someone killed him over what he wrote about Custer. Guess not."

"I don't know if he was clever or stupid, Uncle. Not sure if he led them or they all were lucky or everyone who was curious worked together, because that newspaper or whatever they call those fancy things with all the pictures set them all on your trail. Maybe we need another place to hide. Maybe you need to be careful. They're looking all over for you. Those scribblers set the hounds on you, Uncle Jack, as though that's what they wanted."

"Don't think they'll find me," he said, wondering if that had been the real purpose of the writer's trip. "Didn't finish my business last year before the snow and before that fella nicked me," he said, gesturing to the left side of his chest, where a bullet laid him low for several weeks at the end of the previous autumn. "We have our work to do, girl, and then maybe we give it up. I suppose we could go on forever, but nobody can make it all right. Make the price high enough, put enough fear into them, and they will stop. Find an easier way to make money—someone more vulnerable. It's the way of the East, child. The way of the East. Never used to be the way of life out here, but that was when you could talk sense to a man."

"Dawn, we can accomplish our work," spoke up the younger man with force and gusto—perhaps more than the occasion called for. "If you had come back sooner, we would have been gone. We only have a few more men we have to see, and then we can wrap all this up. We need to move, Jack, and we need to hurry."

The older man seemed to consider the speaker, as though from a distance. Then his mouth moved in a smile that never reached his eyes. "We will move soon, Tommy. Soon. And then we will see what we shall see. I will let you know when the time is right."

With that enigmatic remark he strode off to be alone with his thoughts. Dawn gave Tommy an angry look and went to stable the horse. Tommy looked around in indecision, worry plain on his face.

Chapter Four

The Laramie City telegraph operator was watching Crayne with disapproval as Crayne fumed again over Sullivan's parsimonious ways with telegrams. If the man said it the first time, plainly, he would not need to send more telegrams asking basic questions. He'd heard of an invention that would let people talk over wires. He could use one right here, right now to tell Sullivan exactly what he thought.

He had sent his telegrams yesterday explaining that the story was not what Southern thought and that there was a bigger story that was better. He may have oversold it a bit, but what was exaggeration when there was a chance to redeem his life?

The first reply had been there when he arrived early this morning after a night in the cheapest stable he and Dakota could find. The Western Union man had witnessed Crayne's rage when a single one-word telegram, "NO," had been received—rage that had Crayne screaming a name and waving both arms to the point where Bryce Smith was about ready to call for the sheriff.

More telegrams followed from the same unsigned sender. Why was he not in Cheyenne? Where were the stories? Crayne knew Southern sent these. He had fired off an intemperate question about the sender's sanity. Smith, he was sure from listening to the tapping of the Morse code, deleted some of the words.

Another came, signed by Sullivan from a different sender in

New York City. It warned Crayne about Southern's plan for Hiram Marshall. Crayne replied by insisting he was right. Every instinct he had was telling him so.

He had rehearsed the message to Matthew a thousand times. It was the right thing to do from any perspective. Matthew must have been able to see it.

Then silence. Crayne waited, pacing. The Western Union man was plainly scared, too fearful to leave his cherished place at the hands of a madman while he went for the law. The machine started clacking. It stopped. Crayne heard the pencil scratching. The old man put the paper face down on the table and slunk out of range.

Crayne turned over the telegram.

It had five words.

FIRED REPAY ADVANCE NOW SOUTHERN

Crayne had no idea how long he stood there in shock. The Western Union man, clearly frightened from reading the contents and knowing no man ever took such words gently, was stammering something. Crayne had no idea what he was saying until the man gingerly put another thin sheet of paper into his right hand. It was from Matthew.

"SORRY S THINKS LITT BIGHORN ALL OVER COME HOME REPLY," it read.

Crayne's eyes were unfocused as he stared dumbly at the pieces of paper. This was it. Being fired once happened. Sometimes more. Maxwell boasted every magazine fired him because he was too controversial. But Crayne knew that being replaced like this, and the Old Man's venom and willingness to blackball Crayne for good this time, would all but finish him. He'd burned bridges leaving the Pinkertons. His last chance at writing was gone. There was no place to go now. None.

"Sir?" The Western Union man. Hovering.

"What?" Crayne was angry. At everyone. The man was handy.

"New York is waiting for a reply."

"Yes." Crayne looked out the window. Maybe the Pinkertons would take him if he begged enough, but with the Old Man's connections, maybe not. Matthew knew everyone worth knowing in newspapers and magazines, but in a match between his well-meaning friends and his wrathful enemy, Matthew was a reed to stand upon in the face of a hurricane.

"Send a reply that says, 'Yes?' " asked the clerk.

Crayne's eyes strayed. He felt trapped. He wanted to tell Matthew he would make his own way. But he was no mountain man, no Wild West cowboy. He was a writer who could no longer write. There was nothing he could do. Nothing. He might as well surrender. He would never surrender. Yes, he would.

"Tell them . . ." He watched idly as two broad-shouldered cowboys forced a young Indian girl, running errands from the looks of the bulky package under her arm, off the duckboards where she was so busy with her delivery that she had not seen them, down into the mud of the street, where she and her package were soon covered with filth as the girl wailed and clutched the ruined package in misery. They pushed each other in glee as they doubled over laughing.

"Tell them to drop dead," Crayne said, stalking out of the office as the door slammed loudly behind him, cutting off the exclamations of a very confused Western Union man.

There was a story to be told. Sooner or later, he'd find someone to print it. First, there was business to tend to. Important business. Business maybe he was only now beginning to understand. He wished she could see this. Whoever she really was.

The two cowboys had entered the Black Bear. The trembling girl, somewhat reassured by the silver dollar Crayne gave her after a lot of soothing, waited by the doorway. He could not tell if she was Sioux or Cheyenne or whatever, but she was innocent of everything except existing. She wore a little dress like any white girl would wear and nothing that would give him a clue about who she belonged to. Her eyes were endless in their pain above cheeks where tears left their marks in the mud. That was all that mattered.

"Boys!" exclaimed Crayne buoyantly as the rush of leaving common sense behind engulfed him in the exuberant euphoria of the moment. Walking up to the cowboys and throwing an arm over the shoulders of each one, he babbled nonsense. "A while! A long time! Friends! The better bottle for my friends here."

In a place where men could come to deeply know one another and then see that close friend a year later or more, being friends with apparent strangers whose beards had undergone transformations was not uncommon. In a saloon, friendship mattered less, perhaps, than whiskey. The cowboys grinned. Crayne understood the looks they gave each other. The fool wanted to spend money on strangers, let him.

The barkeep poured them their poison—Crayne kept his arms around the two men.

"To friendship, boys," Crayne called, throwing his head back. The two cowboys raised the glasses to their lips.

Seconds later, shattering glass and cursing filled the air. The two cowboys were each holding hands to their faces to staunch the flow of blood. Crayne had reached down and pulled the guns from their belts after smashing their faces into the bar, crushing the glass in the process and splattering their faces with blood and cheap booze.

"My friends. On your way here you pushed a little girl into the mud and ruined her dress and probably the package she is carrying. I think she deserves compensation. Maybe a couple of silver dollars from each of you or whatever else you have in your pockets. Then you can crawl over to the doorway and apologize. Now!"

"She's just an Injun, mister," said one, recoiling when the gun hit him across the face.

"She's a little girl. You should pick on someone your own size," Crayne said.

"Planning to," came the voice behind him.

Not for the first time, Crayne wondered how, with his instincts for being in the wrong place at the wrong time and on the wrong side, he had lived as long as he had. He turned to see a cowboy stamped with the mark of the range—a lean, strong man who exuded authority and confidence.

"My men. Want to tell me why you're beatin' on 'em?"

Crayne could see other men rising from chairs where they had been sitting. What was going to happen next was as scripted as the lines of a play. Filled with more rage than sense, Crayne tossed the other cowboys' guns at the newcomer, who fumbled as the heavy objects came his way none too gently. One was caught; the other clattered across the warped mud-covered wood of the saloon floor.

Crayne touched the gun in the holster at his hip as he considered his options. "Hold this," Crayne said, taking the gun belt off and handing it to the bartender.

He was supposed to be afraid. He wasn't. He was too angry. He went to the saloon doors, saw the girl, and grabbed her roughly. "Sorry, little one." Fear coursed through her. "You know English?" She nodded.

"They start fighting, you run, understand?" She nodded.

He walked up to the man who had called him out and pointed at the girl. "This is why."

"Injun kid." The man shrugged. "Not theirs. So what?"

"They shoved the kid in the mud, fella. Little girl. Never hurt nobody. Package for somebody. Tryin' to make a penny or two.

A kid. You make war on kids? Who cares what she is? Just a kid, pushed around by two fat horses for fun. This common with your outfit?"

"You got a problem with something, friend, I can help you not have that problem ever again," said the man.

"Amelia! Amelia!" An older woman's concerned voice called from outside. The voice grew louder. "Amelia!"

"Here!" the child called, running toward the security of the woman's voice. Her bare feet slapped on the filthy wood floor of the saloon as she ran out the doors.

The doors kept swinging as an old woman entered with the child hanging on tightly. She was thin and tall, taller than Crayne. Her hair had gone to gray, and she wore it tucked into a tight little ball on the top of her head. She had a thin face, with intelligent eyes that took in everything with a glance around its interior. She was clearly used to being in charge of whatever she surveyed.

"Are we having a wedding or a funeral today, Mr. Johansen?" she asked the barkeep.

"Neither, Miz Taylor. Bit of a dispute."

The older woman looked down at the little girl holding her legs and gently disengaged her before squatting down in her deep rose-colored dress so they could be eye to eye. "Amelia, are you in this dispute?"

The little girl nodded.

"Tell me."

She pointed at the bloodied cowboys at the bar. "Them push hard; Miz Peabiddy's dress . . . landed in mud and is gotten ruining," Her eyes looked up at the older white woman in misery and fear.

"Pea*body*," corrected the older woman. "Say it again, dear." As though a saloon on the brink of a brawl was not a few feet away. "And the word is 'ruined,' dear."

"Miz Peabody's dress got dirty, and this man said he'd give me money to clean it, and then they started to argue, and this man and his friends over there are planning to beat up that man," she said, pointing first at the man confronting Crayne and some men who had risen from the tables where they were swilling down whiskey and then at Crayne.

" 'Bout right," echoed Johansen.

"And you are?" she addressed Crayne.

"Crayne." She waited for more. He was not inclined to give it. With a raised eyebrow she turned to Crayne's antagonist.

"And you?"

"Circle I," said the man. "Jed Loew, foreman. Now see here, ma'm. This man assaulted my men . . ."

"And you usually push little girls in the mud?" the older woman asked. "Do you deny that they did it? Well, do you?" She advanced upon him, a figure of implacable wrath. The foreman shook his head like a schoolboy.

"Are you going to order those bullies who assaulted that sweet girl to push me in the mud?"

"No . . . no, ma'am."

"Well, then. Amelia, let us go." She looked at the swollen, bloody faces of the cowboys. "Mr. Crayne, I think there has already been sufficient payment. And Ollie?"

"Yes, Miz Taylor?" said the man behind the bar, still holding a shotgun.

"Please be sure they all leave here alive, whatever they might plan to do afterwards," she said. "Gentlemen, for the record, I own this establishment, and if one of you were to be unruly here, I should hate to have one of my employees—and please notice there are several standing in case they are needed—use their weapons. There is always damage to pay for when that happens." She began to leave. "Tempers flare in places like this, but I do hope this ends here. Ollie, if any of the gentlemen with

Mr. Loew need a drink before they go, it is on the house." She paused. "One. And thank you, Mr. Crayne. Amelia is a little Sioux girl who lost her parents. The soldiers found her, and, when I saw her, I took her in. Should you return this way after an extended trip away from Laramie, for I imagine it would be safest to leave expeditiously and avoid a swift return, ask for the home of Martha Taylor, and you shall be welcome, or you may come here, and Ollie will find me." She glared at the cowboys, who were open mouthed, and swept out. "Have a safe and swift journey, gentlemen."

Crayne knew that overstaying a welcome was bad enough, but lingering where he was not wanted would be like giving a wolf back a piece of meat it had dropped. Loew, still awkwardly holding the gun Crayne had thrown at him, seemed to be biding his time. Crayne silently nodded at the cowboys, anyone else watching, took his gun belt back from the bartender and strapped it on, then left before whatever spell the old woman had cast began to evaporate.

O'Meara's stable was as cheap as any in Laramie. Its owner didn't seem to care if Crayne stayed with the horse; Crayne had experienced all the joys of Laramie life he wanted to. Stables were good places. Cool, relaxing—the place where a worried soul could rest his mind and his body. He did not need sleep; he needed to understand. He could only go on so long without a direction. Assignments had always defined life; the closest he had come in years to the windy freedom of not caring what the next day held was while prowling the Shadowlands, but even then some of the delight was the awareness that he was playing hooky—that sooner or later he would need to do the job he had been sent to do, a job that he was still going to do whether Southern liked it or not.

The young woman had made it clear that the Jack of Justice was drawn to protect Indians. All the accounts made it clear that he was most active along the Dakota border toward the northern part of Wyoming Territory. Then that must be where it all began—in the rugged fastness of northeastern Wyoming. He doubted he could find exactly where he had met the woman, but if she had sent him northwest, then she had to have traveled in another direction, and since there were settlements every direction except one, she must have gone northeast. If the region was as remote as it had seemed, there were only so many places she could have gone. Pinkertons taught well.

He had a destination with no real idea what to do when he arrived, yet there was within him that sense of windy freedom that comes when shackles are cast aside. Little money, no job, no prospects, and not a friend closer than fifteen hundred miles. How could one argue with a plan like that?

He spoke to God and Dakota the words he told them nightly, hunkered down in the hay, and slept the sleep of those who—even if only to themselves—are just.

Hiram Marshall was gloating. Crayne had been something of a legend. Showed up one day with an attitude and an accent. Wrote circles around everyone else who had credentials. Fate had helped him. Marshall and the rest of the decent people who worked at the *Global Reporter* schemed to manipulate Southern into sending Crayne West where nothing important ever happened and illness ended many careers, not to mention lives. Drat the man. He had all but stumbled into the Indian wars and the Battle of the Washita. He came back a celebrity among writers. He romanced Southern's daughter until the Old Man put a stop to that, headed back West to regain his reputation or simply to make another bid at fame, and was one of the few who saw the Little Bighorn while the battlefield was still raw with death. Crayne had then filed the story that destroyed him—a fluke really that would have been stifled by an editor if not for the fact that, at that time, Crayne was considered such a great and important writer that no one was editing what the man wrote, and no one thought to ask if this was really what was wanted to fill the magazine's lead columns. Then he was gone as if he had never been.

Marshall had come West to Denver to make a name because New York City and the offices of the *Global Reporter* were becoming more and crowded with inferior writers. Twain made his name out West; he could, too. A year later, he had achieved nothing but frustration. He read Crayne's Deadwood pieces with rage. Crayne wrote as if the dirty, filthy common people mattered. Now, he would be one of them. There was the real justice, he gloated.

Southern's telegram was direct. Marshall owned the Jack of Justice story now. He knew what Southern wanted. He would give it to him. He had never been in the corner of Wyoming Crayne had been exploring, so he would ride there. Local color. The plot would be whatever he felt Southern wanted it to be.

He thought briefly of Crayne once more. Crayne had acted as though the education Marshall received at Princeton meant nothing. Crayne, he was certain, never went to a formal school. The man was a combination of urchin and savant. If he met Crayne again, he was ready. Southern, in an especially verbose telegram that would have the old skinflint beating his clerks in a rage to recoup what he spent, made it clear that Crayne could be arrested for theft for taking money from Southern. The charges might never result in a conviction, but they would finish ruining Crayne.

And that would be a good deed done, thought Marshall. He wondered if Twain's publishing house would have an interest in the book he could write based on the true story of this cold-blooded killer. Perhaps. He might need to work around Sullivan, who was Crayne's friend, but if Southern ordered every scrap on the man be given to Marshall when he went East in triumph after having exposed the killer, he would have it. Yes, he could be famous and rich. He wondered how much the ladies would appreciate a tall, distinguished man who was ever-so-famous. He would find out, for certain.

"You are troubled." The older man lifted himself up to the fence rail with some effort to sit beside her.

"I am worried," Dawn said, looking at the man the world knew as the Jack of Justice and she knew as Uncle. "It is getting too dangerous."

"I am going to die, child. Perhaps a season. Perhaps less. More is not very likely. I do not expect to see the next snow. I have been given the choice to either die doing what I want to do or the way my body insists it will do if I live long enough. I am a selfish old man. I will do this my way."

He did not share his worries with her. There were signs, but, until they came to fruition, it was cruelty to make her think ill of anyone. Imaginings were easy when there were hours for them to probe the mind. All would soon be revealed. Death was, after all, only a moment that must be spent in crossing over . . . only a moment.

"Is it worth it?"

She had the sense of him gathering words as a man sorts rocks when looking to build a wall, picking some and discarding others.

"The first one, yes. Some others, yes. Some? Perhaps not. The weak who do wrong sometimes pay for the sins of the strong more than their own. I am sure you saw many of the Sioux and the Cheyenne and the others in your travels. What do the People say?"

"You should hear. They think there are spirits walking. They believe anything, everything, and yet, at the same time, nothing.

A Cheyenne woman I met is sure you are a sign. Many white men fear so." She did not hear the scorn with which she said "white." She had long since realized that even if to the Sioux and Cheyenne she was less than a full member of either nation, to many whites she was barely human. "There are those who say one day there will be a return of all the People as if by magic."

"Hope lives within us, child. When that hope goes, something takes its place, even if we know it is not the hope we once held. The missionaries taught you about King Arthur, did they not?"

She laughed. Uncle loved old stories. She nodded.

"He lived hundreds and hundreds of years ago, if he ever even lived at all, and in that land, people still tell their children he will rise to soothe their ills. Perhaps one day the People shall say so of me."

"Do you like being called the Jack of Justice?"

"Your young man."

"Hardly, Uncle."

He laughed. "It is a worthy name. He understood this was justice and not killing. That is perceptive for a man as young as you say. Were it not for the danger, I would have enjoyed a talk with him. Most of the scribblers see the world in a very set way; I believe your young man was different. I have wished at times I could explain to the people of the East what I wish them to know, but I do not have the words, and I do not think those who write magazines and newspapers would print them if I had them. Perhaps he could have told my story. Perhaps not. That is a burden that shall fall to you as you tell the People."

"He is not my young man, Uncle."

"But every time I say it, you stammer and flush, child. At my age, I shall not deny myself this entertainment."

"He is gone. I do not think he will be back, and I do not think he was as evil as some, but there will be others. They hunt you, for their own purposes."

"And child, I too hunt, for my own purposes. The best hunter shall win."

He grunted as he slid down from the rail and hit the ground. He moved off in the night, the silent confidence and purpose stilling her fears—for the moment.

Matthew Sullivan was a disconsolate man walking home to his luxurious Manhattan home. Crayne was not another adventurer scribbling for pay. He sought some sense of justice in his work, amid all the blather common to one's lot. The end of his career provided, sadly, a moral to what happened to idealists when they faced reality.

Crayne had never quite been at home anywhere. Sullivan knew he'd been born in London, fled it young, and ended up in New York City in that way loose leaves flow down a drain, with an education that was vast in some areas and nonexistent in others. And an attitude. He had seen Crayne walk alone in parts of the city where police feared to tread. There were charges once from a man behaving toward a woman in a way Crayne thought was unjust.

Sullivan was one of the few who saw behind the fearless façade Crayne projected to the world. Crayne had never, Sullivan realized, gotten over being at the Washita when Custer and his soldiers raided the Indians there. Crayne had made his mark writing about it. He had once confided to Sullivan that, if the fame was welcome, the nightmares were not, and they lasted longer. Sullivan had been making a trip to the presidential nominating convention when the Little Bighorn fiasco took place. At the time, it was a tragedy. In time, he had come to see it as inevitable. He had given Crayne an opportunity. More he could not do, unless there was something he could do to rectify the situation, should it come to that.

He shrugged off the memory. Annie would be waiting. A home. A purpose. His life was stable and solid. He had invested well and wisely and was reaping the rewards of acting where there was opportunity. His friend was the flame of a candle, flickering its way in the wild winds of Wyoming. Perhaps soon to flicker out. It was a tragedy. But it did not touch him. It would not touch him.

Laramie City was a bad memory by the time the sun had reached its peak. Crayne had picked up bits of small talk from the stable owner before he left.

"Most Indians know that old days ain't ever coming back, any more than the buffalo. Some of our boys still think an Injun can sneak up on 'em and lift their hair and carry a buffalo or two while stealing fifty horses, and every Injun should be killed because of what happened to Custer. Nonsense. Right now, the way I see it, more people are doing wrong to the Injuns than they do wrong to us. This fella those easterners call Jack of Justice is scaring a lot of proper men because he fights back, but he has discipline. The ones I hear he's killed were not much good. Makes me wonder if this fella, this Jack of Justice, has a list of who committed certain sins, and he's working through that list like God's hand coming down. These folks are not scared of one man, fella. They are scared of judgment."

Fort Laramie was off to the east. Crayne gave it a wide berth. He had not been an admirer of George Armstrong Custer. Still wasn't. He'd made that clear, and made it clear that, when a man's home was invaded and he was lied to and preyed on—white, red, black, any color—a man was going to fight back knowing that the dignity of war might be the only thing he had left. Nope. No friends there. The frontier army shuffled officers here and there. He had no interest in seeing anyone from the past.

As he and Dakota continued their journey, he could feel the knot within him loosen. He was, for now, riding through a land that was rougher than it appeared but also filled with hidden delights from a bounding deer surprised in the tall grass of that meadow to a bear fishing in a stream who gave Crayne one glance that let a human know its place in the order of things. Once again, he thought of letting the journey roll along forever.

As he rode further north and further east, the topography kept changing—the trees as well. More pines. Then there would be a plain of grassland. It seemed that Wyoming could not make up its mind what kind of place it wanted to be.

One small valley appeared before him, a surprise carved into the rock. "Antelope Gulch Trading Post" was crudely carved into a sign that was freshly painted. He had never learned the frontier vernacular of what made a gulch different from a draw or a gulley or a swale. He wondered idly if anyone knew.

The post was small. One main building. Couple of outbuildings and a barn. No fence, no wall around the place. Somebody was cooking something. Crayne could barely cook to feed himself. Anything was a better alternative.

Jack Tanner's name was probably not Jack Tanner his whole life, but Crayne had long understood that, in the West, names were changed more often than boots. The man was probably trading rocks with his friends when he was three and getting the better of the deal. Crayne was not even going to try to compete. The man's wife was cooking, and seemed happy to make extra. Tanner was very happy to have a paying guest.

"Don't see much hard money up here," Tanner said, going on with the blunt summation of character Wyoming folks were quite often willing to provide unasked. "Don't suppose you want to tell me why a man with hard money is up here? You got East in you, but not lately, and you don't look like no surveyor. I'm stumped."

"Not worth the telling," replied Crayne, knowing that it was impossible out here not to be curious, and what would be impertinent in the East was the way a man talked in the West, but he also knew that everyone knew a man's business was his own private concern if he wanted it that way.

"No offence," said Tanner. "Man wonders."

"None taken," replied Crayne, who was amazed at the way his vocabulary changed from the world of the city to the world of the frontier. "Man does wonder indeed. Tell me. Cheyenne, Sioux, and whites up here. Figger they mix like sheep and cows. Where's the worst of it?"

Tanner and his wife looked at each other. Not a common question. Only fools wanted to see the worst.

"Follow the creek," he said. "Trail starts to fade out the closer you ride toward Top Hat, but, if you're looking for trouble, it'll find you. Trail down to the east there—big oak splintered by lightning years back. East there and a bit south, you'll find some people. Lot of Red Cloud's people, some of Sitting Bull's people drifted there. White folks live there, too. A few miners . . . small ranchers. Basque family that keeps sheep. Kind of odd but nice folks. Sing a lot in their lingo. Do great things with stew. Lot more of 'em down south but only that one family up here.

"There is also a man named Stivell. Not much of a friend. Walk soft there. Outlaw country, too, but nobody cares much, mister. Live around 'em, there's good and bad in the Sioux and the Presbyterians. Some of the Methodists."

"Don't disagree," Crayne replied. " 'Specially the Presbyterians. Don't know I've seen a Methodist lately, though."

Tanner smiled. "After Custer, it all changed. Lot of suspicion. Lot of fear. Folks who knew each other years, both sides, stopped being neighbors and started waitin' for the shoe to fall. Some folks think the Sioux are sittin' on gold. Some folks see land no other white man owns and want it. Sioux don't take bein' pushed well. Cheyenne have been pushed all over creation, and they don't take it lightly either. Indians are gettin' weaker every year but not so weak they can't ever stand up and fight back. Lot of whites want to see peace, but every time an Indian kills a white man—no matter what the cause—nobody wants to think about peace. You know 'bout Solomon?"

"Bible fella?"

"Yup. He might be the only one wise enough, son, to figger it all out, because to me it is a sin that, with all this land out here, everybody has to sit on the same piece of it. But that ain't all."

"Scalps," said Crayne.

Tanner's eyes went wide. "Know more than you look like you would," he said, biding time. "Talk going 'round that some whites hunt Indians for their hair. Might be true but a lot of scalps taken both ways around the time of the Little Bighorn. Men fight; they take trophies. Happens. Only hear about it one way now, but tales change a lot in the tellin'." He acted as though Crayne had touched on a subject he would prefer to avoid.

"Folks want to trade them here?"

Tanner nodded. "Not for me. I try to say 'Live and let live,' mister, but that's just plain wrong." He was silent. Crayne had a feeling there was more Tanner knew, but it was information he dared not share.

"Now I'm going to do something sensible and feed the horses." He stomped out.

"You are looking for that man," Canadee Tanner said evenly.

"What man?"

"Don't fool an old woman, Mr. Crayne. I know all the signs. You are not a killer, so I would guess you are another writer from the East, looking for a story. You are educated and clean. Your saddlebags had ink and pens and paper. You were fidgeting with your knife and cleaning the dirt from under your fingernails. There is ink all over you right hand, even though it has faded severely. The only ones with that disease passing through here are writers. You look at everything as though it matters, as if you are trying to decide how to explain it. I know your kind."

She had him. "Are there that many?"

"They pass through," she said. "Before Deadwood, we had more of them when they thought there might be gold here. If Deadwood was another hundred miles away, we would have even fewer of them, but we might not have any customers either. Thank God there is no gold here. It's not a simple story, Mr. Crayne. It is not simple at all. No one tells the story as it is, though."

"That is true, Mrs. Tanner," replied Crayne. "But life is simple in the East. Readers who flip pages in the shadows of smokestacks and in the wretched shadow of a filthy alley do not believe in Indians whose understanding of the land is greater than our own and who value life as precious. They do not understand that anyone would wage war to swagger and not slaughter. They see savagery and cannot imagine that beneath it is a view of this life in which time and space and all the world are seen in such a different way that the two peoples can share a room and have not one word in common. There is no conception among my genteel readers that these Indians have come to the place where they would rather turn and die with a bullet in the chest than wait for the one in the back."

"Mr. Crayne, you are a poet."

"And a writer who writes what no one believes is a writer no one reads and no one employs, Mrs. Tanner."

"Does that mean a good writer must sell his soul, Mr. Crayne?"

"That, my dear lady, is a question that we shall understand when we reach the end of the story." He rose. "I have pondered this since the Washita, Mrs. Tanner. In the mountain of wrongs, there remains a valley walked by a few who want to know the truth. There are days I believe there is no truth. There are days when there are vast piles of truth as big as the wrongs. I believe that the Jack of Justice walks this valley; I believe he has a mission, but I cannot discern it. I cannot explain it all, but I can tell you that finding him and learning this is more important to me than any story, any words I have ever written. I do not need to write it; I am not following his trail in search of an interview. I need to know it."

"Then I wish you Godspeed and the story Godspeed," she replied. "For those who sit and enjoy an evening by the fire more when they hear of our lives and deaths out here, those who read what you send them scrubbed of its realities and softened of things that are harsh, I must tell you, Mr. Crayne, I have contempt. If they are not bold enough to live it, then they should leave alone those of us who are."

"Another lady I met out here had the same perspective," he said, recalling the young woman whose name he never knew. "Perhaps you shall make a convert of me yet."

"Perhaps, Mr. Crayne, we already have. Good night." She rose and moved to the sleeping room behind the goods-strewn floor where he would sleep.

"If the cold bothers you, throw a skin over you," said Tanner as he made his final trip through. "Hot tomorrow, but it might snow early. Take what you need. Long's you don't bleed much on it, nobody'll know." He turned, winked, and was gone.

A faint trace of what looked like frost remained on the shadow-covered ground as Crayne moved across the trading post's yard to Dakota. The morning sun was sending steam from the roof as it melted the snow there; some places were already dry. It would be clear and perfect to make as much ground as he could.

He was barely out of the yard along the trail to the north when he saw four burly, heavily-clothed riders galloping toward the post. Men riding with a purpose. Too many years of being too curious were a hard habit to break. His head echoed again with Dawn's denunciation. *Judas Goat.* Had they followed him?

Their horses were saddled by the trading post by the time he cautiously rode back; the door was open, and loud voices were carrying. He checked the gun in his holster. Loaded. Loosened. He would be out-gunned, but he had learned that men who were not prepared for fights were the ones who lost them. He softly walked up the sagging steps to the doorway and walked in.

He slammed the door. Four hard faces turned; four right hands moved toward the guns at their hips.

"Something wrong?" Crayne asked innocently, appearing startled at the commotion. "Jack, think I dropped my pocket knife last night when I slept here. Seen the thing? It's about oh, yea long." He held his hands a few inches apart. "Little thing, but I've gotten attached to it . . . won it in a poker game down in Hays City. See it anywhere?" He moved as though looking, squinting into the dimness by the floor in the shadows.

"Excuse me," he said as he moved past one of the riders and went behind him. "Don't let me interrupt."

The four men had yet to say a word.

"I might have dropped it here." Crayne looked one in the face. "Can I . . . um . . . do you mind moving so I can look? Didn't happen to see it did you? Silver? Well, kind of that color. It has to be here somewhere." The man's eyes shifted to another man who appeared to be the leader as he stepped aside. Crayne continued his looking and talking.

"You best not be lying," said one of the men to Tanner.

"That fella's only one been through in a week," said Tanner.

"Find out you had 'em, you won't regret it long." His eyes lit on Crayne. Crayne felt the sensation of fear—that sense that said he needed to run or fight back. Then the eyes moved on, around the room, as though looking for a sign visible to only his senses. "Boys." The man led the way out. The others followed, mounted, and were gone.

"Put the gun down, Canadee," Tanner said when the hoofbeats that broke the silence were now muffled and distant. "Nobody left here to shoot but Crayne."

She emerged from behind a curtain that separated their room from the store, ready to lift the gun again quickly. She was clearly used to holding weapons.

"Want to tell me about that?" asked Crayne.

"Paul Danvers," said Tanner. "Gang of toughs. Ride for Old Colonel Anderson when they ride for anyone regular. Not men you cross."

"Looking for your friend, Mr. Crayne," Canadee said pointedly. "And I do not think they wish to entertain anyone but themselves." She withdrew behind the curtain.

"Story goes that the fella you call Jack of Justice rides with some Sioux or half-breeds," Tanner said. "Wondered if I'd seen 'em. 'Specially a girl who fetches things. Somebody saw her a while back. They thought she came this way. Body found in Bend Creek area. Guess they knew he was a man chasing her. Told them I had not seen her. Danvers knows I'd like to spit on his grave, and I have a soft spot for folks like the Sioux and the Cheyenne once I'm sure they won't be coming here with a thousand warriors to scalp me, and he wasn't quite sure about believin' me. Think he might have asked longer if you hadn't come back." A pause. "He don't ask nice. Obliged."

"They're riding after this fella?"

"Yup. Men like Danvers are good at finding secrets. Someone tipped them he was up this way. If they pick up his scent, they'll find him. Don't know why the colonel is interested, but there's probably a reward out. Why?"

"Might be lookin' myself. Follow their trail, or maybe you have a better idea?"

Tanner looked him over appraisingly. "Way I told you before, but if you want to take a more di-rect route to Top Hat, this is what you do. When you get to the creek making a bend like a *U*, lot of big rocks there, and it's all big timber, take the left fork. Top Hat's where you need to go. Maybe the hills beyond. Not sure they're there, but they will be. Might be down at Stivell's range, too. Heard things."

"Thanks for trusting me."

"Thank me if you make it out, friend," said Tanner. "And don't be surprised if you meet those fellas when you get there. They're riding hard. Not like them. Someone paying big money. Somebody wants that man dead."

"How far?"

"Start now, maybe tonight, tomorrow early . . . depends on how bad the rains left the trails."

"Then I better go."

"Take this, Mr. Crayne." Canadee Tanner had a pack of bread and meat made up. "We hope to meet you again."

Crayne had never tested Dakota. Today, however, he pushed the horse faster as they rode through the flatlands. The land changed soon, however, and they were picking their way through trees, following a track that—had Crayne not known it was there—might have simply appeared as a muddy smear from floods. He stopped once when the sun was high to eat what Mrs. Tanner had given him.

For the first time he wondered what he would do if he met the man he sought. Interview him for the magazine for which he no longer worked? If the man would even talk. How would he know him? Crayne had every description in his mind. Even though some were quite contradictory, he'd know him. Then again, he could be pretty sure Dawn would be there, too. Armed. The thought still made Crayne smile in spite of himself. Cross that bridge when we set it on fire, he told himself as he recalled old Emery's phrase when he was writing something and had no idea how it would end. He held the memory a moment, then let is dissipate and pushed on.

The trees were thick as he neared a creek. His senses told him he was once again not alone. He'd picked up a shadow early in the afternoon. He'd done enough of it himself to know the signs. The way the track wound, a man walking through the trees could easily keep up with a slow-moving horse on a trail where limbs hung low over the mud. Although the muddy way was smooth, showing that Danvers and his men had not passed this way, he had to wonder if Tanner had sent him to an ambush. Now, as it was growing dim, the trees could shelter any number of men if they were good at being quiet.

These were.

With the creek on his right, running fast and hard over rocks at a wide spot no man or horse could jump, he was hemmed in as they moved fast; one behind, one ahead, and one jumping from the gnarled roots of a tree whose trunk had hidden him.

The man, Indian from the fast look Crayne took at his hatless assailant with braids, went to grab Crayne around the shoulders. Crayne was more comfortable with tactics that did not involve shooting people. Street fighting taught that. The heavy Colt was swinging as the man leaped. It caught the would-be bandit in the face.

The man's yell of pain was loud in the stillness. He grasped at Crayne, but pain weakened his grip. Crayne shrugged him to the dirt, hands sliding off the greasy buckskin of the man's jacket as he slid down into Dakota's hooves with a cry.

Dakota was now running. Crayne barely missed being knocked out of the saddle by one low branch. The man he was galloping towards was fighting for control of his horse, which shied out of Dakota's way. A rifle shot barked behind him, but it went wide. The creek and road bent left, then right.

Pulling hard on the reins, he slowed Dakota about two miles down the road. He could continue with someone on his trail or deal with it now. He hated looking over his shoulder.

He dismounted, gun in hand, and led the horse off the path to a clearing. There were no sounds yet of anyone following, but in a place where no one else was on the road, no robber would let a victim escape.

Everyone thought he was a newcomer. Newcomers do stupid things, right? He'd do one and see what happened.

He worked to build a fire. Fast. Not much smoke, but enough. If they were walking, they would need a little time to catch up.

He led the horse through some bushes the horse did not like and tied him to a tree. Then he waited. The longer Crayne waited, the more Crayne wondered if hiding a white horse in the dark woods would work as badly as it increasingly seemed it might. He wondered what other mistakes he had made.

A voice. Either he was obvious or they were good, because it was coming from the woods behind him. He moved swiftly and as silently as he could back to Dakota and hauled the rope off of the saddle horn.

"This'll work, really," he whispered as the horse watched him finish tying a rope across a path to set what had to be the most obvious trap ever built. He moved back to be ready for what had to happen next, unless they were as bad in the woods as he was.

He could sense them. Could they do the same? Probably. Dakota whinnied. Good horse. Bodies moving through a thicket make noise no matter how carefully one walks. He waited to give them time to all be there.

Now!

"Hands up," called Crayne, waving the rifle at three Indians gathered by his horse after he ran to Dakota's spot. "Move away from the horse now. He does not care to be splattered with blood, but if pressed I will have to cause him that discomfort."

They complied. He ordered them to throw away their guns and knives. He was certain there were more, but at least a few weapons were out of their reach. Dakota did not react as though horses were near. Had they found their way through the woods without the path? He was in control for the moment, but out of his depth. He hoped they did not know that. He needed some way to be sure three did not overpower one. There it was, right under his nose or, rather, their feet.

"Bath time," he called. They looked at one another. No one moved. One shrugged as though indicating he did not understand. Rock fragments stung their legs as the rifle kicked up pebbles and dust from his warning shot. "Now!" He gestured with the gun toward the water. Again.

They wanted to resist. They wanted to rush him. He aimed at the man the others looked to. "Try, and the first two die where they stand." It was a line from a conversation he wrote about a killer backed into a corner. He hoped it worked.

It did. They started moving into the water. Taking their time.

"Faster," he said, gesturing with his chin toward the creek, which was knee deep.

He forced them to wade in until they were well out.

"Don't kill unless I have to," he told them. "Don't follow me. Next time, I won't hesitate."

Grunts were his only reply.

"You Sioux?" he asked. No answer. "That's rude." He shouldered the weapon.

"Cheyenne," said the leader of the group.

"Know this man they call Jack of Justice?"

They did. It showed.

"You see him, tell him Crayne's lookin' for him. I only want to talk. Tell him I could have killed you three but didn't."

"What do you want with him, Raccoon Eyes?" asked the group's leader.

Crayne had always disliked the dark circles that formed under his eyes when he went without sleep. If one old woman in London said they were a sign he would die of consumption within the week, a hundred had done so. For the first time, he was angry. He thought about shooting the Indian where he stood.

No.

"My business, Wet Britches," he called back, enjoying the snickering that came from the man's two compatriots. "You pass along the message, and you make sure you and any friends like you stay out of my way."

He lowered the gun. "Better go before you freeze or a bear eats you." But the impulse would not be stilled. He had to know. He had to understand. He had to ask.

"Why do you ride around to rob the few people who come this way?" he said to the three would-be robbers. "Why don't you live with Sitting Bull or Red Cloud? Why don't you live where you belong?"

Wet Britches spoke with an odd accent, but the words were clear.

"And you, Raccoon Eyes, belong with Custer."

There was nothing left to say. Crayne and Dakota moved out without a backward glance, pressing on as the shadows merged into a deep gray.

Chapter Five

Allen Stivell was one of those folks who just plain hated. Men. Women. Horses. Life. He was brutal in a good mood and deadly when not. His ranch barely eked out an existence, but he would never concede the battle. He started the season with six riders but was already down to the two he'd left to gather the main herd of cattle together. He started with ten cows, mostly picked off from Texas drives. He was up to fifty. Or had been last fall. Strays must have found their way to the north meadow, and so he was there alone to bring them back.

It was a hard life, but Stivell was a hard man. He never turned down the chance to make some extra money, even when it was work his hands wouldn't agree to do and that sent one of them off without two months' pay, cursing Stivell. Fool. Money was money. Didn't matter about the hands. The three new ones who signed up last week were hard cases, but they knew something about the hard ways of the frontier. He sent them off this morning with curses and instructions to find something to do before he fired them.

Stivell had a line shack with a small pen. He'd finished putting a cow inside when he saw he was not alone. Three riders had ridden up. The man who rode in front, with what appeared to be two young Indian half-breeds behind him, gave him no pause. Old man . . . sick looking. Stivell could break him in two. Woman was breathing fire; boy was scared and looking around. If they came to steal, they would be disappointed.

"Allen Stivell?"

"Who wants to know?"

"They call me Jack of Justice."

Stivell spat. "Eastern papers. Heard of that. Making things up. Be on your way, or I will kill you. You're trespassin' on private property."

"Callin' you to account. Rosalee Night Star. Wild Bear Thrushsong. Ezra Perkins. Tom Harris. Know the names?"

"Don't know. Don't care." Stivell had a gun at his hip, but he knew he was slow. The rifle was in the seat of the wagon a few feet from his right. He could hit anything with a rifle. "Got work to do, a ranch to run." He walked toward the wagon and the weapon.

"How fast?" said the man on the horse.

Stivell stopped a moment.

"Killed 'em. You did. Recall wanting to see who ran faster when they were runnin' for their lives, Sioux or white men?"

"No contest. Injuns always run away fastest."

"You killed 'em all. And you know why. Time to pay. Give you the chance to tell me who else is in this little game of yours. Dyin' fast beats dyin' slow. I can give you either. Slow sounds good right now."

The man had dismounted and was walking closer . . . white shirt and black vest—trademarks of the man Stivell thought was a myth. His throat was suddenly very dry. He ran for it.

His eyes saw the shiny Winchester in the seat for one second before two explosions filled his ears, he was spun around by the impact of bullets smashing into him, and he saw sky. He saw this Jack of Justice. Merciless. He saw a tiny bit of paper fall across him.

"Last chance to make things right with your Maker," the man said. "Make things right before the Great Spirit comes to drag you to a place where you will be given that which you deserve."

Stivell saw a silhouette looking down. Dark against light. Were those arms? Wings? Angels? Indians? No! He started to speak. Then he saw nothing.

"Ought to go," said Jack after Stivell had breathed his last. "Man might have a crew that was supposed to meet him. They'll find him sooner or later, I suspect."

He noted Tommy's pained expression, as though disapproving. Dawn never blinked. "Surprised he didn't prepare," mused Jack, looking hard at Tommy, who was sweating. "He had to know I'd be coming."

Dawn was listening but not to them. She held out a hand to still the talk. Riders! Hard and fast!

"What's that?" she asked.

"Nothing," said Tommy, who had been looking over his shoulder during Jack's showdown with Stivell. "Spooked a bear. Quit being so jumpy, Dawn. It is nothing. There is no one out there."

Jack felt the sadness grow. It had been a long trail. The young folks thought he slept more than he did; that he never knew what went on away from the clearings where they camped on the road. He had never embraced the mortality of fear; he preferred to battle the present than fret over the future. He looked at Tommy and Dawn. He wanted to tell her to ride hard and fast while she might save her life, but there was no time. There was never enough time.

He had suspected when Tommy rode out alone to scout, leaving Dawn behind. He'd known when Tommy fussed with his horse on the trail. There was no loose shoe. He thought he saw trail markers once, but he wanted to hope he was wrong. The boy had been asking when they were going to confront Stivell. Asking and asking until he received an answer. Then a scout. All alone. Now he knew why.

There was always one.

"Let's go, Uncle," Dawn said. "Somebody's coming!"

She was right, but it was far too late. Three horses galloped hard from behind a screen of trees. The riders, who had come to work with Stivell after being told their quarry would come to them in time, pulled up for one moment.

"Good trail, kid. Old man tried to lose us along the way, or we would have been here sooner. That him?"

Tommy pointed at Jack.

"That's him."

"Judas," spat Dawn, levering three shots in Tommy's direction and realizing as she did so that all the questions from the past weeks had pointed in this direction, but she had not wanted to see it. She thought he was leaving trail makers on the way from Top Hat but had told herself it was her imagination. The young man who had sworn to her they could have a life together was planning to betray them all the time. She worried when he scouted alone, he might be seeing another girl. If only that's what it had been.

She did not see him reel in the saddle and clutch the horn to stop himself from falling. Brought to bay by the hunters, she had no thought for anything except for how to kill the three men who had come to kill Jack.

Jack, who had not mounted, moved fast, for an old man. There was no escape. He was now in the storehouse doorway firing precious shells to save Dawn. She kicked the horse toward the shack and leaped, rolling until she reached the door as whining bullets splattered the dirt. He shut it behind her. Bullets thunked into the wood.

"Guns?" he asked.

She hefted the Winchester. "Handful or so of shells in each pocket," she said, digging out one handful of bullets from her coat. She opened her coat to show him the pistol jammed into the belt of the pants she wore. And the knife, a long, big-bladed one she used to hunt.

" 'Bout the same." Jack packed two guns on a belt where he stored spare shells. He never tried to draw two at one time but had learned the hard way that having a spare could save his life. "Can hold them a bit."

The heavy door was a barrier to bullets but also blocked them from knowing what their attackers were doing. Time ticked past. The shooting had long stopped, but for all they knew, the men were standing outside the shack ready to pour bullets inside.

"We stay here, we're trapped," he told her. "Move fast. If I fall, run faster."

He stood with his hand on the latch. "Fast, now," he said. He pushed it open.

The attackers were moving cautiously across the ranch yard, only ten yards from their refuge. Dawn and Jack each fired a few rounds and ducked back inside.

"Give it up," a voice called. "Might take time to gun you out, but we can burn you out. We only want you, old man. Woman lives if you give it up."

He smiled grimly. "Do you want to do the honors or shall I?"

"Drop dead," Dawn yelled.

Jack smiled broadly. "You have way too much of your ma in you, girl. You take one; leave me two. Girl your age can only be allowed so much fun. Meet you when."

She felt her eyes fill with tears, but there was no time. She nodded.

He pushed back the door. She fired until her Winchester was empty as they ran until they could hide behind a filled water trough. There were still three guns firing. They were running out of time and land. She reloaded, gasping.

"Have things your way," said a voice. "Let 'em have it. Keep firing until I tell you to stop."

The water in the trough began to splash as a fusillade of shots hit it. Dawn fired back with the rifle until its ammunition was gone.

Soon, the water was spilling through bullet holes, and the old wood was splintering. Their shelter was literally being shot to pieces. The guns roared on.

Eyes met.

"It is a good day to die, little one," he said amid the din. She should be afraid. All she thought of was taking them with her.

"It is a better day to kill."

Since the blood first bubbled up from his lungs, she knew this was how he wanted to cross the final river. She nodded. Whatever Sioux or Cheyenne spirit would be with her to cross with her, she would meet it soon.

She had the pistol in one hand, the knife in the other. He had just finished loading one revolver, and now held a gun in each hand. He raised his left hand, to hold her back. She waited for the signal. His fingers twitched. For a moment, she wondered if she should pray to the God of her mother or if she was already in the hand of the Spirit her father worshipped. She hoped they were the same.

A new wave of gunfire made them involuntarily duck in the act of launching their suicide attack. No lead roiled the waters. There was angry yelling. They could hear the pattern. One rifle firing steadily, others not. A pistol hammered. Angry words and screaming. Someone in pain.

Maybe Tommy wasn't dead, she thought. Maybe he had come to his senses. More gunfire. Then silence broken by indistinct, occasional moans.

Jack nodded. They rose from the trough with their guns pointed toward the last sounds their enemies had made.

One man with a rifle was turning to meet them as both their guns trained on him. He soon crumpled to the earth. A second man was already in the act of falling as they fired. His dying body jerked from the impact of the bullets.

"Tommy?" she called as she ran toward the only man standing. She reached him. It wasn't Tommy. It was . . .

He turned to her without words, reloading his pistol.

"Crayne?"

"The young man on the ground over there is probably still alive, but I don't think he will live," Crayne said. "If he was with your party, you might want to see him while there is still time. The three who were trying to kill you are either dead or will be soon. Thank you for getting the last of them."

He doffed his hat briefly and replaced it. "Pleased again to make your acquaintance, whatever your real name might be."

She ran past him. Crayne could only grin at the absurdity of it mingled with relief he had survived the scene he had stumbled upon. A wary man with his gun trained on Crayne approached. Witnesses could describe a man's features; only seeing the man in the flesh made him real.

Crayne holstered his gun and extended a hand as if this were Fifth Avenue by the park. He did not know an involuntary grin had sprouted.

"And you, sir, I would know best as the Jack of Justice," he said. "I had thought you might be somewhat broader and shorter; witnesses can be difficult. My name is Crayne, and I have been looking for you for quite some time. May I be permitted to know your real name? Is your disease far along? Can I help you?"

Jack surveyed the scene. He shook Crayne's hand politely, with no enthusiasm, as he focused on Dawn and Tommy.

"Perhaps in time, Crayne, I can give you some answers. I suppose we owe you." Jack looked around as though the trees might hold more riders. "I guess you writers will do anything for your interviews, but, if it is all the same to you, I would rather not have a conversation with dead bodies around. We made a lot of noise, and I think someone must have sent those men here. Someone will come looking, and I prefer not to be around."

"Then I shall ride with you, because I am certain that more company is likely on its way."

He mentioned Danvers.

Jack's eyes narrowed. "The colonel." He thought. "Stay here," he ordered Crayne. "What comes next is family business and it is private."

Tommy was passing the point where the pain dominated the little time he had left. What remained was a desperate need for atonement before whatever befell traitors was meted out on the other side.

Dawn's three shots had torn holes in his chest. The red bubbled by his mouth.

"Why?" Dawn asked. "Why, oh why?"

"Two hundred dollars," he said. "Ranch. Land. No life to keep running."

"He's my uncle!"

"Not my fight. Not mine." He was gasping. "No-accounts. All they were. Misfits. Crazy people. Not worth nothing."

"No!" she said. "They were people, Tommy. Think what was being done to them so that those fat Eastern people could have a trinket. Oh, Tommy."

The argument would never be finished. His hand opened. She reached for it. It closed. He shuddered a moment and coughed. Her uncle put an arm over her shoulders.

"Told you I should have traveled alone, girl," he said. "You would have had a life, then."

"No, Uncle," she said. "If he would betray you, he would

betray me. But I don't know why. Why? Why?" She was screaming.

"Some folks live their whole lives, never caring about the man next to them," said Crayne, who had ignored Jack's order to stay away. "Some folks can't stop caring. Guessing he followed along for you, miss. Some men can follow a dream until it dies; some others lose sight of it. Nothing more we can do now but bury him decently. Shovel around somewhere?" He looked at Jack. "You better go. I don't look dangerous enough to have killed all these people if anyone comes by to investigate. I'm only a writer, after all. You need to take her away. She's in no condition for anything with her man dead and all."

Dawn was silent. Her mind was showing her, each in its painful turn, memory after memory of Tommy. Even as she wept, she knew that the one she would never forget or forgive was him with his arm extended, pointing at Jack. She could not contain the grief that welled from her eyes at all she had lost.

"About five miles that way," Jack pointed, "there's a brook and a grove of spruce trees. We'll camp there."

"I'll find you."

"Not worried I'll leave you in the lurch?"

"Found you once. I'll find you again. She's in no shape for much, sir. You won't go far for her sake, not for mine. And you owe me."

The man smiled. "I do that."

Jack pointed his head toward the barn. "Tools ought to be over there. Make sure the card's there before you leave," he said as he fished a torn half of a filthy, worn playing card from his coat and handed it to Crayne. "Never know when some writer may want to tell the story that I want them all to know. Maybe you know some writer that can tell the story the way it ought to be told."

"Go," said Crayne. "You were lucky here once, twice is not

likely." He thought. "How'd they find you?"

"Not sure," replied Jack. "We travel back trails, so after we left Top Hat there was no way to find us. We're pretty safe there; there's a small cave that is like a fort. Folks there like us, too, and would fight anyone who tried to take us there. Tommy rode a lot alone over the winter, early spring while Dawn took care of me. Someone turned his head . . . poisoned his mind. He worked this out. He knew we'd be here sooner or later."

Crayne dug a wide, deep hole and rolled into it the three men who had chased Jack and the girl. He dug a separate hole for Tommy. It was work, but it seemed the right thing to do. The holes were in a small clearing screened by bushes. Critters might find them; men preoccupied with the spectacle of Stivell's corpse might not.

He had emptied all the pockets. Altogether, there was about a hundred dollars in coins. A couple of letters. He thought about privacy, then wondered if they might be useful for starting fires. He jammed them in the saddlebags. He saved the gun belts, guns, and the shells. He was learning.

There were about two hours of daylight left. He looked around the ranch yard. Musing at the concept that words were to him what liquor was to a drunk, he pulled some paper and a pencil from his saddlebag. There was time now. There might not be later. He put his back against a tree, looked around, and wrote.

Evening was dappling the ground with shadows as Crayne and Dakota arrived at the cluster of pines. Blue wisps he had smelled for half a mile filtered through the twisted branches. He wondered which one had him in the sights of a rifle.

He tipped his hat on the guess it was Dawn and rode toward the smoke.

She had the rifle in her hand when he reached the clearing. Something in the stew pot smelled good.

"Get down and eat," she said. "Uncle Jack is resting. We already ate. He said not to kill you."

Crayne could not help but laugh at the way in which she sounded like a child denied a treat.

"Shhh. You'll wake him. Now eat while it's still warm."

He did.

"Why did you come back?" she asked. "Is it really so important to you that you hound him? Do you make lots of money for an interview? Is all you care about having some important story for your precious magazine?"

He shook his head, mouth full. "They fired me."

"Then what are you doing here?" She was suspicious. Everyone was up to something; people from the East who looked at the West as a curiosity were the worst. The ones who meant well fumbled and failed. The ones who didn't took what they wanted without regard to the damage and waste around them they left behind. She wasn't sure yet which he was. Crayne did not seem to be ruthless or a fool.

He thought about telling her about his long conversation with himself after they had met before. He thought about telling her about the little girl in Laramie. It sounded like self-serving claptrap to make himself look better in her eyes. Maybe it was.

"Nothing better to do."

Usually, Easterners packed as many big words and tall ideas in their conversation as possible. Crayne's failure to do so took her by surprise. There would be time to learn if he was out for something more. She was certain that if he was, she could deal with it.

"Want to tell me what you know?" said Jack, walking stiffly over to the fire.

Crayne could see the pallor in the man's face, and the pain.

He waved away the beginning of Crayne's insistence that he should ask the questions with a weary hand.

"It is time, child," he said gently to Dawn. He sat across from Crayne, patting her on the shoulder as she began to object to him speaking to Crayne at all. "Old men have privileges. One of the top ones is having my curiosity answered. I am very certain that you have been stalking me from a distance like a hunter, and you know a lot more than any of them. Tell me about me. I want to know how good you are." Jack's eyes gleamed as he spoke.

"This started with a Cheyenne woman," Crayne said.

"Sally."

"Sally. Best I can tell, the man that killed her was trash who thought he was better'n her. I don't think the other thing started yet, because it was only one and you weren't sure. Guess here from me is that he had people who looked up to him. Guess you wanted to tell the world he was something more."

Jack's eyes glittered. "Like what?"

"A knave. Other meaning of the playing card you left. Don't know about them all, but I can guess they had one side folks knew and liked, and you wanted to tell them there was something they didn't know. Did it start with Sioux and Cheyenne or end up happening that way?"

"If you want the truth, a little of both. Out here, Crayne, there was kind of an uneasy way whites and Indians co-existed. Like too many cats in a room—lot of threats, not much action. Then something would happen. Fetterman Massacre way back in '66, Red Cloud's War. Black Hills. Each time it became harder to find that way back to that normal. Little Bighorn finished it. Some men thought it was their duty to kill any Indian, no matter how young or old. Fools out here, some of 'em, just like to kill. A sickness. They kill the weak because no one fights back. Knew Sally most of my life. Raised rabbits. Fed deer. Gentle woman. My last straw. Couple others. I was reading something, and it hit me that, if I could make them afraid, they might stop."

He gave Crayne a long, intent look. It made Crayne wonder if there was another level to the truth being told.

"People are afraid of what they don't understand. White man was calling out cowards who killed folks who were poor. They happened to be Indians. Come to find out, after I started, it made a difference. Dawn here started hearing about more people who had been killed. And more. It was bigger than I thought."

"Scalps."

"Watch your mouth," Dawn said, starting to rise.

"Very, very good," Jack said with a growing smile the longer he looked at the writer's intense form.

"Does that mean you will answer all my questions?" Crayne asked hurriedly.

"In time."

"There isn't all that much time. You have consumption, so you know you have nothing to lose."

" 'Bout right. Maybe until the end of the year if I am what they call lucky. Saw a traveling medicine show man back in Colorado about five years ago who said I might last another two or three. He was wrong, but it's gonna end sooner than later. If this ends badly, it does. Realized when I saw what happened to Sally that whatever held me back before had no meaning now. Even when I go, there's gonna be someone wondering where I went. Whether I'm around. And, if I am lucky, the men who need killing will be in the ground ahead of me."

"What about before all of this?"

"Never quite settled. Dawn's dad was a friend. He was a smith. Worked for him to help, but he died when a horse threw him. No hand to manage a ranch, run a stable. Did what I could; probably you can't imagine it, but, when you got bits of Indian and white in you, both of 'em think you belong in the other camp."

"Please do not lie to me. Are you trying to deny you were Powder River Jack, who, according to a Montana newspaper was 'half-Sioux, half-Irish, and all-around the worst enemy the U.S. Army paymasters and supply wagons ever had'?"

Jack looked at Dawn. There was admiration in his look at Crayne.

"You did not tell me, young lady, that your young man was this good." He turned back to Crayne. "You are diligent."

"I spent a few years with the Pinkertons."

Jack nodded. "Now I see. Most writer fellas out here hit the saloons, collect some tales, and find a soft place to write while they make up most of it. Who in the East is going to know? Guess you have a nose for sniffing out the past. Yup. Powder River Jack. Made a living off the army and the gullible for a lot of years. Was a time we had it down right—steal a few horses and then sell them to the army before the owner knew they were gone. Rob a paymaster here and there to steal enough money to live on and to share; never take too much. Young man's game. Territory started getting too crowded. Not that many hiding places. I suppose you could say I retired. Good poker player knows when to leave the table, friend. Sioux, Cheyenne, they were friends and scouts. Didn't matter what the government said or what the tribal elders said. We made our own rules."

"Why does Dawn call you uncle, then, if you are not kin?"

"Because I want to," she interjected.

"And she tends to do what she wants," he added. "Luck of the trail, Crayne. Nothing more. I met her about a year before all this started. Surviving alone out here is not easy, Crayne. We needed each other."

"Now what?"

"Thaddeus Anderson is a man no one crosses because he's rich," Jack explained. "They call him 'Colonel.' Civil War. Rode with Chivington. To hear him tell it, Chivington didn't do half the job that should have been done. He's been having every Indian or half-breed with any shack anywhere tossed off the land and then claiming it. Told folks he wants every single one either on a reservation or dead. Maybe had ten or twenty folks killed. If I can kill him, a lot of the bad goes away. There are a lot of folks who want to do wrong but won't if they see the biggest one is killed."

Jack looked at Crayne as though deciding.

"Trades in scalps, too. They all did. Folks in the East you come from pay big money for something like that. Disgusting. Indian man scalps his enemy to prove he's a warrior; pretty rough to see but it's a man trying to say he's a man. Man buys a scalp it says he likes me to do his dirty work for him, or at least that is what it says to me."

"They should be shot," Dawn growled.

"Some of the ones I tracked down sold to him. He sells to someone else. Don't know who. That's why I want to corner him before I kill him. Had him once last year, but he was too heavily guarded, and I could not close the deal. He knows I'm looking."

"And he's looking for you."

"He is. I have killed a lot of the men who work for him. Picture this like a pyramid thing, Crayne. Read about those. Out in the desert, like. One man at the top. Don't know him. Know Stivell was near the top. Men came to him to give him what they took. He would pay them. He took his merchandise to Anderson. Anderson's the next big one up, I think. Might be others beyond him, but I have not heard of them. One more to go before I get the colonel—man named Cheyenne Luke who helps make sure the colonel is protected. Part Cheyenne. Kills his own kind. He's in Laramie City."

"So you're bound for there."

Jack nodded. "The best I can hope for, Crayne, to give some meaning to the time I have left is to break this. Taking Anderson out of the chain means that it stops, at least for now. Times change. If it stops for a while, maybe it stops for good. I need to get this done, and then maybe we go find a place to lie low and let life take its course."

"End it? No more shootings?"

"Ever see a man at the end of consumption?"

Crayne had. It wasn't pretty. He nodded. He had more questions, and Jack talked a while until he had a coughing fit, and Dawn made them stop.

Now, for the first time, he understood. No one would ever print the story, because it did not fit in the form that good stories were required to have—the heroes and villains were not where they were supposed to be. He might never live to write it. But he would live it. This once, he would live life instead of writing about it. Even if, as it seemed very likely, it would kill him. He held out a hand as Jack turned to leave the fire.

"Maybe I'll ride along," he said. "Nothing else much to do right now." Jack's face did not move. Crayne wondered if the man was a step ahead of him. Probably.

" 'Spose."

He then turned to Dawn. "Unless you plan to point a gun at me again?" He was smiling the way men smiled at women. She was disconcerted. Her uncle had never been so open and trusting. Did he do this only because Crayne was good at guessing? What if he was another Judas? Why did he trust Crayne? Worse yet, why did she want to?

"I might do exactly that!" she exclaimed as her uncle laughed before a cough racked his chest and once again shattered the night's peace. "No more talk."

The next day was a slow and easy ride.

"We take back trails," Jack explained. "Not so they can't find me, but if nobody sees me on the trails, it seems like I mysteriously show up." He smiled. "Dawn's idea. She likes making this old man into a legend. You two share that in common."

He clucked and nudged his horse ahead, leaving the two of them ambling along together.

"Gonna ever tell me your real name?" Crayne asked after a while.

She made a sour face.

"That good, huh?"

"I told you, I am Sioux, I am Cheyenne, and I am white. Everyone had a name for me. My Cheyenne family named me Fire Buffalo Dawn, because of a dream of my father's. My Sioux family called me Red Coyote Dance. You do not need to know the reason why. To my white family I was Blanche. I use Dawn more than any of them when I speak with white people."

"Do you think of yourself as Cheyenne more than anything else? Is that why?"

"No, Crayne." She shook her head. He would never understand. "If I were to go see any of my Sioux or Cheyenne families, wherever they are, they would take me in and care for me, but I do not belong in their world. I have lived apart too much. If I see my white family, they would be kind, but it would be obvious that I can't belong there. If they tried to have me live with them, they would be insulted by their neighbors. Everyone lives in these boxes; I don't. Dawn is a name they can remember, and it makes my life simpler. What they call me is what they call me. Who I am is something very different."

"I know that feeling." The disparaging noise she made riled

him. He grabbed her arm.

"I'm sorry if nothing in the world matters as much as not being what the rest of them are, but who cares? Let me tell you this story. Rich English lord gets a servant pregnant. Terrible scandal. She's Irish. So what happens? She is dropped off by the London docks with a few coins in her pocket, and the lord goes on with life. She finds a man who will take in a pregnant woman. She dies. Little kid is passed around until he eventually finds a woman who will act something like a mother to him. She drinks. He lives on the docks. One day, there's a terrible accident. The man he knows as his father because he shelters the woman and the child gets killed in a factory accident. Lots of people hurt. A disgraced doctor who—small world—knew the lord is among those treating the injured. He sees the resemblance. I changed households again. He was a drunk. Terrible drunk. Brilliant doctor. Educated me; forced me to school and church. I helped him birth babies and stitch pub fight scars. One day, there was a union demonstration. He was for them. The police were not. One of them tried to hit the man who was as close to a real father as I ever had with a club. The copper ended up the one hurt. Hit his head on a paving stone and almost died. I had soldiers chasing me for a while. They almost caught me. For weeks the people of Whitechapel and the docks hid me until the search was off, then I was put on a ship with three pounds to my name, and I made it to New York City. I found work at a printer; then I started writing. When I was nineteen, I was given a huge opportunity to write for the *Global Reporter* in Kansas, to cover the Indian wars."

He paused. He was looking beyond her now.

"I was there about a week when Custer attacked the camp at the Washita. I was so excited. Big news. Big reputation. Everyone knew where the camp was. I snuck out. I was writing about what it looked like on the very morning Custer and his men attacked." His lips jerked as he paused. "Slaughter. Nothing I ever saw prepared me for it. I wrote it. The telegraph meant my dispatches reached New York about as fast as the ones for the daily newspapers, but I had a lot more to tell. The *Global Reporter* had a detailed article long before most other publications even knew about the attack. I stayed West a bit, then went back to New York. I discovered I was good at writing, Dawn. Then some things happened. The year of the Custer fight, I was sent out here again. I managed to sneak in with one of the first columns that went to the Bighorn after the massacre and before the burials. It was so pointless, so stupid. So many dead—Sioux and white. I wrote what I thought—that Custer and the army and the generals were all wrong. I was fired. Had a couple offers of lynching. An old soldier I knew who agreed with me put me in touch with the Pinkertons. I worked Kansas and Missouri a while, then I wrote those Deadwood pieces you mentioned. Then they sent me here, and you know what happened since. So I have no family, no friends, no job, and, if there is a place in the world I belong other than where I'm standing, I have no idea where it is."

He was silent as his eyes watched two crows try to distract a hawk.

"When you have nothing, Dawn, you have nothing to lose." He let go of her arm and drifted off behind her.

The door to the office of the Owner and Publisher, labeled as such, was never to be opened without the blessing of its occupant. On this morning it was thrown wide, slamming against a wainscoted wall amid the tremulous rattling of the glass.

"What are you . . ." snarled Southern, stopping in mid-word at the sight of William Tecumseh Sherman, the general in chief of the U.S. Army, standing in the doorway with the glowing red tip of a cigar pointed at Southern like the barrel of a cannon and a thundercloud expression on his baleful countenance.

"General . . . a wonderful surprise." Southern had served under the man and idolized him.

"That scribbler you have in Wyoming . . . Crayne," began Sherman. "Who sent him? Why? Well?"

"Oh, I fired him, General," said Southern, a picture of subservience. "Fired. Would not do as instructed. Please, take a chair."

"Not staying. Jack of Justice. All that. You printed it."

"Well, yes, General. The readers enjoy . . ."

Sherman gave a full and colorful assessment of the magazine's readers and his wishes for their eventual consignment to a place of eternal fire. "End it."

"End it?" echoed Southern.

"Your series. Stirring up troubles. Sioux. Cheyenne. Barely coming to heel; this gives them ideas. Gives whites ideas, too. Rumors out there of things that have to be stopped, if they're true. I want that series stopped. I want it all stopped before the damage becomes worse. Can you imagine what you would have caused if the Indians could read? What were you thinking? Stopped. Kill him off. Your writers make these things up, don't they? I worked with newspaper men in the war. I know how they are. You make up these things to sell your rag; you can end them whenever you want. You started it. End it. Is that clear?"

"Well, um, General, I, um . . ."

"Some weasel, Hiram something, works for you. Hanging around Fort Laramie. How many people do you have on this story, Southern?"

"Yes; he was pursuing the final parts of the series. He's the only one, sir, General, sir. The other one was fired, and I do not know what happened to him."

"Find him!" roared Sherman. "You set him loose out there to cause mischief and let him go? Southern!"

"I will find him, General. I'll . . . I'll do it," Southern stammered, wondering how on earth he could ever do this.

"Cavalry patrol is leaving to finish this. Your man will ride with them. He will write that the army brought an outlaw to justice. He will write that he is dead. Dead—hear? I will not hear or read about this again. Are we clear, Southern? There will be no threats to law and order on the frontier, and we will not encourage new Indian wars for the sake of selling your magazine. The Indian wars are over, and, if you start them up again, I shall give you a seat at the battle to end them. Do. You. Understand?"

Sherman was never anything but clear. Southern was trying to gain some advantage from the conversation.

"Exclusive?"

"What?" Sherman barked.

"None of your officers will say anything to anyone else?"

"If they do, they will find out what a firing squad is for," gritted Sherman from behind a cloud of foul, dense blue smoke. He pulled a watch from his pocket. "If this does not end, your man will find out what a good rope is for, and you will lose your license to peddle your paper on military posts. I'm late. Good day."

He spun on his heel and left, slamming the rattling door behind him, leaving Southern an exhausted wreck who was reminded once again of the vast powerful energy that was Sherman. He was also fiercely reminded of the menace in crossing a man who had spent most of the past fifteen years fighting the Indian wars and was clearly not going to allow the least spark to fan the flames.

Hiram Marshall was unclear whether the troopers riding with him were an escort or a guard. He had been told what to write, what to say, and what to do.

He had been experimenting with various ways to kill off the Jack of Justice at the hands of the cavalry, turning them over in his mind, ever since he received a telegram from Southern, and he had received a visit from the post commander.

This would be a coup. Crayne had built up the Jack of Justice. Marshall would take him down. Yet, for all that, this would ensure him speaking engagements in the East, as an expert on the pursuit of a deadly gunman, he fretted. Killing off the Jack of Justice with pen and ink was one thing; making sure the flesh-and-blood man did not take umbrage at this was another.

There had been an undercurrent of admiration for the man that Crayne had instigated. He would need to be sure that, after he filed the story, he himself went as far from Wyoming Territory as possible with the greatest possible speed. However, Southern had wired him that they would start a speaking tour once this was all over. Yes. He would not rush so fast that he missed out on fame. Good press to build up to the East would help. But in Denver. Where there was civilization. Not in Wyoming.

And there was Crayne. His rival never gave up willingly. Ever. Crayne had to know some of what was going on. He himself had heard rumors of what sparked the Jack of Justice to action, although all of it was delivered with a grin, a wink, and a nod. Crayne, the noble idealist, would be on the trail. Sooner or later, he would emerge. Marshall had warned Southern, and the bite of the response was clear even through a telegraph line. He had then sent his information to Sullivan and received a very warm response.

For now, Marshall was a cork bobbing along on a course others had set. This was too easy, and, when things were too good to be true, they usually were not very good for very long.

Chapter Six

The man's name was Luke. Jack had talked about him on the ride.

"Sells kids. Mostly Cheyenne or Sioux. Part Cheyenne himself. Sells them as slaves, workers. Way I hear it, if there's someone he can sell, he don't let the fact that the child has a mother or father stand in his way." Jack spat. It was tinged with red. "No race has all the good folks, Crayne. No race has all the bad. Luke is pure bad. If men are dealing scalps, Luke is in the middle of it. After this, we go take care of the colonel. Then we hide."

"You should stop now," piped up Dawn. "You've been spitting blood for two days."

"Time's running out," said Jack. "Means we need to go faster, girl." His eyes were burning with fever or fervor. Crayne knew the man was eating far less than a healthy man would.

"Maybe she's right," he said. "Maybe you need to rest a few days."

"No time," said Jack. "Gonna rest a long time soon enough."

"Maybe I can help," offered Crayne. "Don't need to do this alone."

"No," replied Jack. He stopped his horse. His eyes bored into Crayne's as dust filtered across their faces. "My game. Mine. Not anybody else's. Dawn, you make sure. Hear?"

"Yes, Uncle," she replied, eyes downcast. She was clearly unhappy but did not challenge him.

The Black Horse was filled. The big man in the corner was rocking back on the rear legs of his chair, laughing at something said to him by a greasy-haired man on his left. Rolls of fat spilled over his pants; he had put his gun belt over the back of the chair to ease the strain on his middle.

Jack sat his horse outside with a duster over his trademark outfit. Crayne and Dawn had gone in the saloon, armed with a description of Cheyenne Luke and a stern warning not to interact with him. Crayne grumbled, but Dawn told him he could either be quiet or dead.

When they emerged with their news, Jack gave a grim smile at learning his quarry was near.

"Never know," he said. "Have the horses ready, Dawn. Crayne, stand clear."

"It's not right," Crayne said. "Now that I started shootin' people, kind of like it. Need the practice."

Jack was not amused.

"Dawn, if he moves, shoot him." Jack looked at him. "Folks think that some man—a spirit, a cowboy, a ghost—rises up and strikes down the men who deserve it, it means something. Legend has more power to control folks than I ever could. Not killing the legend, Crayne, even if it kills this body. You kill him, it's murder. I do, it's justice. Stand aside."

Crayne did.

Jack entered to the universal disinterest of the customers. He shuffled across the room, an old man from his gait. Bent. He kept his head down. No one anyone cared to notice.

Dawn held the horses as they watched him through the saloon window. The time to untie them might be more than they had. Her rifle was in its scabbard, and she held reins in each hand. It was the best chance he would get. Crayne told her he was going inside.

"Crayne!" she said. "He said no. This isn't a story. This is real."

Crayne shrugged. "Maybe I want to see it to write about it." Her face spoke volumes of disgust.

Jack had crossed the room without anyone noticing. He was at the big man's table. Cheyenne Luke.

Jack kicked the table over. The smashing furniture stilled the room. The big man and the greasy-haired man rose from their chairs.

"Luke. Sell any Sioux children today? Anybody's hair?"

"Don't put my business all over the saloon," the big man said. "None of your affair. Run along, old man."

Jack shucked the duster. The white shirt and black vest, even as common as they were, were known. Luke swallowed hard but kept his face impassive.

"The man they tell stories about. Jack of Justice. I can have you killed, old man. Go away."

"You sell children, Luke. You sell your own people. I know what you send East every month. Ghost warriors will come and crawl into your soul, Luke. You will burn in punishment, Luke, for what you have done."

"You God?" called out Luke. "You here to preach?"

"I'm here to make things right."

Jack and Luke were ten feet apart. The greasy man was with Luke. "Shift," Jack said to the man. "Don't want anyone hurt I don't want to hurt."

"I'll take my chances," said the man, with a sly smile. "Maybe you want to take yours?"

It was quiet. The choking sound that emerged from Jack caused a start. He coughed; blood flew as his chest quaked, and his frame rocked from the force of the coughing fit that engulfed him.

Luke reached for the gun belt hooked over the back of his chair. The greasy man started to pull the one at his hip. Red spread across Jack's face, down his white shirt, and in a spray that covered the floor as another spasm rippled his chest. He was staggering as he desperately reached toward his hip.

Luke had the hammer cocked back when Crayne's first shot, going wide, slammed into the wall behind him. The half-breed looked at the man at the bar instead of the bloody apparition in front of him.

Mistake.

Jack had pulled his gun clear and was thumbing it back as Luke realized his danger. Their guns went off together. The greasy-haired man screamed shrilly as a bullet from Crayne's gun shattered his wrist. Crayne followed the lucky shot with one that shattered glass near the man's head. His next caught the man in the throat, leaving him gurgling as he slumped over the table. His dying finger jerked, and the gun exploded into the wooden floorboards.

As the greasy-haired man died, Jack fired again at Luke, lips compressed against the pain that radiated faster than the red stain on the white shirt. With two shots in his chest, Luke could not level the weapon he held. For a moment, Luke's arm was poised in the act of firing. Then the weight was too great for the muscles. It clattered on the scarred wood of the saloon floor as Luke slumped down in his chair, knocking it down as he fell to the floor.

Jack reached into the pocket of his vest. Half of the Jack of Diamonds went sailing, to land in the blood pooling next to Luke.

He clutched his side. Red there, too. Spreading fast when it burned the worst. For a moment, he rocked on his heels as onlookers wondered if this man, too, would fall to join the others.

Crayne's gun exploded again. "Don't think you really want to do that," he said to no one in particular, hoping that it worked as well in real life as it did in a story he had read years back.

Jack, wincing and gritting clenched teeth, moved quickly out the door. Whatever was in the glance he shot Crayne the writer never knew; he was covering the crowd.

"Uncle!" he heard Dawn scream.

She saw her uncle emerge, knew from the far-too-many shots something terrible had happened. He tried to grab the saddle horn and missed, almost falling. She helped him up and pushed him into the saddle.

"Go!" she heard Crayne call. "Get him out!"

Not waiting, she took the reins of Uncle Jack's horse. In moments they were down one street and through an alley, then another street and alley, and soon there were no buildings. She would figure the directions to right later. Now, she needed to find a place to keep him alive.

She wondered about Crayne, but there was no time. She had become close to the writer on their journey, but Jack came first. Crayne would have to take his chances.

Crayne was even more worried. He knew faces. And there was one familiar one moving towards him.

"Jed Loew, Circle I," Crayne said. "If I remember correctly."

"Nosy and interfering do-gooder," said Loew, "if *I* remember correctly. Don't really care about that fat, stinking 'breed, but Malachi Fairkins was a straight man when he wasn't drunk or actin' crazy. Wild, but good. Some of his kin ride for me."

"Now why is that not a surprise?" Crayne retorted. He knew Dawn and the wounded Jack had left. He had no idea if Luke was popular or not, or the greasy-haired man. No one else seemed to care. Loew was looking for an excuse more than he appeared upset. Whatever Crayne did, he needed to stop anyone from pursuing Jack and Dawn. He'd talk this thing out as long as Loew would let him.

"Got this affliction," Crayne said. "Poor innocent ol' me keeps finding myself mixed up in other people's troubles."

"Clever, huh?" said Loew. "Clever man from the East. Tell me, clever man from the East, what number comes after five?" He looked at the men behind him. Crayne could not remember how many shots he had fired or how many bullets he had left. Loew must have counted. One more thing to learn, if he survived.

Crayne knew where this was going. There was nothing to do but stall.

"Give me a minute. Let me think," he said, pretending to give the matter thought.

"Fifteen," he said. "Comes somewhere after five, doesn't it?"

"No old lady gonna save you this time, fella. Boys and I have a score to settle. Gonna enjoy it."

Loew had not rushed him yet. Crayne figured he must have at least one bullet. That should buy him some space. He moved away from the bar and towards the door.

"Can't run from all of us," Loew threatened.

"Happy to oblige; I only need a little room," Crayne said, covering the group with the gun as he moved to fill the doorway. He shoved the gun in his holster. Whatever happened, no one in the saloon was going to be running after Jack and Dawn while there was a brawl blocking the way out.

Now let befall what may.

"Need your dress fixed?" he asked Loew. "Or why else are you just standing there, holding up the dance?"

He recalled Loew charging. He recalled the pain in his hand when it connected with the man's mouth. The rest was noise and pain upon pain everywhere until there was no more of either.

He was floating. Everything was white. He briefly wondered if the news that he had reached Heaven would travel to where the Anglican minister was who sent the family—such as it was—packing when they showed up at a service the pink-jowled man insisted was for rich people only. He hoped so. It was a lovely thought.

"Mr. Crayne? Oh, you can open your eyes. I wondered if they would be swollen shut for eternity." The voice was familiar. Not English. American. A face came into view, quizzically peering at him as though he were a curiosity in a museum.

For a moment he was saddened; he could not have made it to Heaven if Mrs. Taylor of Laramie City, Wyoming, was frowning in his direction.

As he started to wake, he was assured he had not left this world by the throbbing pain that seemed to envelop him. His throat made noises that might have been words, but it sounded like an animal to him.

"Had I known, Mr. Crayne, you had a wish for a beating, I should have allowed you your way earlier in our acquaintance," she said. Her voice was kind. She could have been smiling, but his vision was not trustworthy enough to be certain. She held water to his lips. He swallowed and spit and swallowed. He breathed deeply. He was alive.

"Get away?"

"You are not making sense, which is reasonable given the beating you took."

"Jack. Dawn." Talking was beyond difficult. "Get away?"

"The other man with you in that horrible place did ride away with someone, or so I was told, but I think we can talk about that later. You have been unconscious for three days. You have cuts beyond counting; your face is swollen and will be for days; and I am certain at least two ribs are broken. However, if not for the size of the fight—for it seems your friends from the Circle I offended a few patrons in their pursuit of your demise and were themselves set upon as they tried to pound you to death—you might not have been so fortunate. I must say I was glad you picked another establishment to hold this event."

"Man. Shot."

"The man you shot?" She waved her hand. "A low-life prowler who might be beloved by his mother, but that is about all. They do try to have funerals for the dead, but I do not recall anyone having the time to attend his. The Circle I men were sent packing from town, having caused more than their share of damage—to the saloon, not you. We all take those things seriously here because cowboys can be mended cheaply, but our businesses cannot. However, for the moment, they are gone, and all is calm."

"Jack."

"This man the Jack of Justice as you call him? His calling card was found on Luke but not until after your little scrape. The sheriff thought you belonged in jail because some of the cowboys said you were involved in that gunfight, but I suggested you were simply in the wrong place at the wrong time and were the kind of man who simply could not resist joining in when there was trouble."

He was silent.

"You will tell me it all when you can talk. Rest now. There is a cavalry detachment that came here after they were told about this Jack of Justice, and there is a scribbler with them, so you may want to stay here."

"How—"

"I know because all the back copies—and Lord know how many other copies—of your magazine arrived," she said. "The last one explains that you were fired. It should be fascinating to hear why you are still here, Mr. Crayne."

She left. Army. Marshall with them. Had to be.

He could not sit, let alone stand. Everything hurt. He had to do it. Whatever Marshall was up to, he had to stop it. He braced himself for the pain and swung his legs down. As he rose, he saw the sun outside, the wall as it waved, and the floor as it came to meet him.

Mrs. Taylor was in focus when he came to.

"If you leave more bloodstains on the floor, I shall force you to leave," she said in mock severity.

"Ma'am." He could talk!

"You hit your head, fool man, and gave us two complete days of peace. Two more days of rest have helped. Your face looks almost normal now, although you look much shaggier than when we first met."

"Jack . . . I need . . ." It still hurt. "I need to find him."

"I shall come back, and we can talk," she said. "The army has come and gone. I should tell you that they informed me your friend, this man you call the Jack of Justice, has been proclaimed dead. I should go."

Dead. Two thoughts competed through his head. One that a man who was dying looked death in the eye and went out on his own terms. Death did not take him. He forced its hand. The second, the one with the power to make him all but cry, was that he was responsible, that without the chain of events that began when he christened a pseudo-Robin Hood–style man the Jack of Justice, Jack might be alive to this day. All for the sake of selling some magazines for a hateful, spiteful old man.

What a waste of a life.

"An entire issue?" Sullivan's voice was in the soprano register.

Southern was beaming. "Yes! Every word. Everything. Double the price for this. Call it a special. Use everything Crayne filed and everything we ever knew. Take Crayne's name off everything, of course. Commission Constantine to draw the final scene."

"He's expensive. No one knows what it looked like."

"Who cares, Sullivan?" chortled Southern. "No one here knows either. Tell Marshall to spend another three weeks there building up his material. Local color. Then the lectures start. We'll have a practice or two in Wyoming, to make sure the man can actually pull this off without getting drunk, but book a hall in Denver. Then Boston and New York City. We shall strike while we can."

"Marshall wired that there was talk Crayne might be dead as well."

"A bonus." said Southern. "Irrelevant. I want pieces on the army, too, Sullivan. You write them. Usual things I like. Controlling the savages. Like that. I want Sherman on our side in this one. I shall send him a box of those horrible things he smokes."

Sullivan grimaced, but acquiesced. With all the telegrams going back and forth, perhaps a couple to enquire about Crayne might not be noticed. But who in a wilderness of strangers would know or care? Crayne might well be dead, and everything might be over, but it was too neat, too quick and ignored the fact that, of all the things Crayne was, what he was the most was a survivor.

The next time Mrs. Taylor came into view, Crayne's vision had sharp edges, and the pain was not so all encompassing. He would live.

"You are not really a cowboy, Mr. Crayne, but you are a man, so I assume you will want this."

She held out a steaming mug of what smelled like very real coffee. She laughed at the speed with which he reached for it and gulped down a swig.

"Men who are shot to rags will sit up to swill that foul stuff; whatever you men see in it I shall never know." She took it from him and set it on a small table near the bed and helped him adjust himself. He reached for the tin cup again.

"Scald yourself while you drink it, then. I give up," she declared.

The door creaked open. A little face peeked in. Crayne first feared an attack, then he relaxed and tried to smile at tiny Amelia, in a light-blue dress with her hair in a long braid. She was scrubbed and clean—and very curious.

"Hello, Amelia, how are you?" She took that as an invitation to enter.

"No mud today."

"Well, Crayne, she remembers you."

"No. No mud, little one. I see a pretty little girl in a pretty dress."

"You hurt bad, Mr. Crayne?"

"No, Amelia. I was just sick."

"Stupid man stuff." Crayne coughed on his coffee. Mrs. Taylor blushed. "Miz Taylor told me." Amelia was now grinning happily the way only a child can when a small vocabulary has created endless consternation among the grown-ups. She approached Crayne. She touched his forehead.

"Grandma Four Elk had healing gift," she said. The child's hand was warm and soft on his forehead. She closed her eyes and spoke quietly in Sioux.

"It is a healing prayer," Mrs. Taylor said. "Amelia is teaching it to me."

The girl finished quickly. "There! Now Grandma Four Elk will watch over you and heal you. She only does this for the People, but because you are my friend, she will watch over you."

Crayne almost wanted to cry. In a world of misery and hate, if a child could share healing with a stranger, maybe—maybe—there was hope.

"Now I must go," Amelia said. "They will let me peel potatoes today." She was off, and he could hear feet slapping wood as she ran barefoot down the hall.

"I wonder where she left her shoes this time," sighed Martha Taylor. "She has been a gift, Mr. Crayne. Let me ensure the cook is there with her. I will also bring you more coffee. Then we can talk."

She returned shortly, another steaming cup in her hand. She handed it to him, and he drank deeply, feeling stronger from the smell alone.

"Is he really dead?"

"That is a funny thing. I assume you mean your Jack of Justice. The army made a big show of saying he was, but no one found a body. I know that men do not count much the reasoning power of women, but it seemed to me that all this was a show for this Hiram Marshall man, a terrible human being, who seemed to write down everything they said and was quite happy when they told him someone matching your description had helped the man and was also killed. No one found your body either—dead or alive."

Marshall would enjoy that, fumed Crayne.

"The telegraph man said he sent a long telegram, and that there were more coming from the fort when they returned there."

"What did he say?"

"I can't tell you that. It is private."

"But you know."

"Of course. I am only a woman." She smiled, looking thirty years younger as she enjoyed the groan he emitted. "It was all about the dramatic shootout in the saloon. I am confident that nothing of the like ever happened, nor do those men who frequent a saloon speak in such a fashion, but I suppose it is what writing does to embellish something after it happens. Two men killed the Jack of Justice and 'were themselves slain' before the 'outlaw' fled, 'leaving a trail of blood that ended in a stone-cold corpse.' " She stopped. "Is that real writing?"

"Wouldn't know, ma'am."

"The way that the soldiers told it when they were in my establishment was that they were ordered to search for this man and pronounce him dead; the news of the gunfire here came at the right time, so I suppose you and your friend have done everyone a favor. Your fellow scribbler seemed to take far too much delight in your reported demise. I gather you were not friends."

She could see gears grinding behind his façade as he sipped the coffee.

"Then he's alive," Crayne said at last.

"Why do you say that?"

"Sherman."

"You are speaking in riddles, or your head wound is acting up again."

There was a smile on Crayne's battered face.

"He was winning. Had to be. Had to be. Sherman in on it? Sherman want it quiet? Both? I have to tell him." He saw her. "Is Dakota safe?"

"Your horse is ready. You are not. One more day, then you may go. Why does all this matter? You came here to write. The story is over. Why not go back East?"

He told her.

"Well, if I am assisting a fool on a fool's errand, allow me to say I have rarely done so more willingly."

Riding had never been so much misery as it was today. Dakota, he was sure, hit every rock along the trail. He was dressed in clothes Mrs. Taylor had provided. Shame about the others. New clothes that were used until they were nothing but rags in only a month or two. Waste.

"You look like a cowboy now," she said. "You might as well dress like one."

She was right. He had stopped shaving days before the incident in Laramie. He now looked the part of scruffy range rider. He had the attitude as well. He carried with him enough guns for three men and not much food except flour for bread and coffee for survival, but he had learned the hard way. There was a package of cloth and medicine Martha Taylor said might heal someone shot, but she told him not to raise his hopes.

No one had seemed interested in him as he left Laramie. The Tanners might know something. Their trading post was the place where trails converged.

At first, they needed reassurance he was not a ghost, not riding with the army, and not out to ruin their peaceful—if not always legal—trade in all manner of things.

They had heard stories. The army was still unofficially asking about the man they officially said was dead, because he had created a new sense of pride in the Cheyenne and Sioux. Indians who thought they were strong were Indians who would not accept what the reservation held for them. Word from the soldiers was that as soon as they found the Jack of Justice for real, the official, public pronouncement that the man was dead would become reality.

The Tanners said that a few riders still combed the trails for Jack.

"Do you think he is dead?"

"If I believed everything the army told me, son, I'd be a bigger fool than I am now," Tanner said.

"You'll know for sure when you get to Top Hat," Mrs. Tanner

said. "If someone shoots at you, he's holed up there."

"Top Hat?"

"Guess you never made it all the way there before. One place we keep hearing he has gone to ground before. Rugged. Caves and such. Don't act like an Easterner, no one will know."

"Scalps. The truth this time. Not asking nicely again."

The look they gave him was venomous.

"You had best leave," Tanner told him. The disgust in his wife's face was complete.

"Who sells, buys, trades, obtains?" Crayne said, ignoring their reactions. They were quiet, eying one another. "I know that you know. *Who?*"

"Is that what this is all about?" Tanner said in wonderment. "Couple of fellas came by in the fall. Big money, they said. Indian scalps that went to rich folks in the East to hang on the wall. Didn't make any sense to me. Who puts another human being's hair on the wall? What kind of people live back there?"

Crayne knew. The fashionable. The kind who lived in the homes on Manhattan's Fifth Avenue and similar places. A fad. Killing for a fad. That was the kind of rotten society he pandered to as a writer. Then he thought less about the end result and how it could all be done. Like Jack said. A pyramid.

"Names," he said. "Who trades in scalps?"

They offered some names. A lot were guesses. One hit Crayne between the eyes. Now he had work to do. Someone else would write the story in ink. First, he would write it in blood.

CHAPTER SEVEN

Deriding himself for his pretensions, Crayne tried to look along the road for signs that Jack and Dawn had come this way.

None.

He could see wagon tracks in some mud here and there, and was highly pleased with himself for that, but it added nothing to what he knew. He pressed on, wondering, hoping, and fearing.

Top Hat was a grim sight; if anything had ever been painted, it was not so now. He'd seen towns like this in Dakota; they boomed when someone found gold or thought they did, then died a long, slow death waiting for something else to come along. Deadwood would combust some night with so much packed so tight and so much going on; Top Hat would crumble in silence unless the mountains held magic underground. Never know what the hills might hold, he thought—coal, lead. There were enough trees for lumber, but there was no river to float away the logs. Flatlands would be the better grazing, but who was he to tell.

He heard the blacksmith at work, the rhythmic clang of metal against metal. Then two quick strokes. Then the previous pattern resumed. For a second his hopes soared. No one sent out a signal if there was not someone or something worth hiding.

With one saloon, there was one place to start. Crayne was not Crayne. He was looking for a man and his niece, with most of the description focusing upon Dawn. If he was the only man that ever pursued her, he would be surprised. He had, in fact, missed her. If there were two more unlikely mongrels, he could not imagine it.

The expected rejection was nothing more than the first round of conversation. Crayne was sure of that after the man mentioned that there were steaks if Crayne was staying long enough to eat.

He was.

He took a table by the window, deciding that whoever might be looking at him, to report about what he looked like, he ought to make it easy for them.

Boots entered. He did not turn. They did not approach. There was a quiet conversation at the bar. The boots left.

"Pushin' on?" said the man named Lew when he brought Crayne his food.

"Tuckered," said Crayne. "Smith's stable down there let two-legged folks stay the night?"

"Only if you pay extra," said Lew. "Sam claims that is cuz critters don't like humans much. Mostly Sam figgers he can charge what he can any chance he gets."

"Know the feeling," replied Crayne.

"Trouble on the road?" Lew asked. The shaggy growth did not hide Crayne's red and lumpy face.

"Laramie," said Crayne dismissively, as though a few bumps were the price of a night on the town.

The man went back to the bar. Crayne polished off the food, left his money, and went to the stable, where he arranged to spend the night.

He did not sleep. He waited. Too old to learn patience. Too young to be cagey. Through a chink in the boards of the stable, he could see a light in the foothills. A small fire. Seen. Gone. Time to investigate.

Long after the last noise, he led Dakota out and mounted. The light was his intermittent guide. It was tiny, as though whoever lit it wanted it shielded. At times, it was invisible. A faint smell of wood burning grew stronger, telling Crayne he was near. A gun was in his hand as he left Dakota by a tree.

He crept closer.

"Gettin' better, Crayne, but you ain't good enough that I couldn't have killed you any time in the last hour," came Dawn's mocking and bemused voice.

Crayne flushed with both shame and joy. She was alive!

He moved into the light.

"What about Jack?" Perhaps all was well.

"Dyin' by drops."

The verdict had the force of a punch. He sat.

"I'm sorry."

"I took the bullet out, Crayne. Didn't damage him that bad. For a day he acted stronger. Then it went the other way. That disease, whatever you called it, that was eating him up inside, maybe, made him weaker than I thought. Something cut deep, could be. Ol' Jack bled too much. Fever. Ain't ate. Wondered if you were gonna come. Sent word. Didn't know whether to expect you after we heard you was dead. Heard he was dead, too, so we didn't know," She stood up. "Think he's been waitin'."

She passed an inch away. He touched her arm. "I tried, Dawn."

Her eyes glittered with brimming tears. "Told me. Told me you hit one of 'em, saved him from dyin' there. Think he was mad at you a while 'til I got mad at him."

"Sorry it wasn't enough."

"None of us can do more than God gives us to work with, Crayne. God, the spirits my kin believe in . . . been thinking of 'em a lot lately. Whoever's comin' for Jack, hope they treat him gentle." She sniveled. "Hated leavin' you, but it was Jack."

"Understood." The firelight was now full on her face.

"Pretty bad Injun, huh, cryin' to some Eastern writer. Not what we're s'posed to be, is it?"

"Don't know. Never read any of what they printed of what I wrote. Figured it might be bad for the digestion."

Her lips registered the joke.

"He knew you'd come."

"What about you? You glad I came?"

"Oh, Crayne, don't know. Wish we were all a life away from here. Wish we were in that land where nobody cares about nothin'. Wish me and Jack was going on forever. Wish I could take time and go backwards."

She was quiet. Her forehead leaned on his shoulder.

"Yeah, Crayne. Matters. Only man in Wyoming or anywhere to care. We will have time later. Better see him now. Not sure how long he has left."

Jack was in a small cave by a fire that was hidden from the entrance. The cave looped around, so his chamber was sealed from view.

"You could have stayed here. Inside."

"Knew you'd come pokin' and get hurt if I didn't make it easy on you," she said. "Lew'n the others said there was a man lookin' for somebody. Didn't look like you. They were sure it was some cowboy."

"Don't much feel like a writer anymore."

"Sure don't look like one, neither." She turned to the figure on the blankets. "He's here, Uncle Jack. Looks like a range bum and smells like a stable, but it's Crayne. Coulda shot him, but I didn't want to wake you."

The bloodless lips moved in what passed for a smile. His breath was in gasps. "Crayne . . . closer."

Crayne moved as close as he could. The fire was blazing to warm Jack, but the man's hands were like ice. His face sported crusts of blood—some dried, some fresh by the corner of his mouth.

"Man's old when he needs a scribbler to help him out of a spot."

"My honor. Sorry I didn't shoot them quicker."

"Chest been tellin' me it's time. Wanted to buy a little more, son." He grimaced. "Can't buy what God won't sell. Ride Dawn where she needs to be so she is safe. Down Cheyenne way there's family. She barks loud, but she's good people, Crayne."

"I know that. Whatever she needs."

"Bury me out here, Crayne, Dawn. Don't need no markers. Deep enough nobody digs it until some fool opens a mine and finds a surprise." The thought seemed to make him smile. He coughed up blood. Dawn went to fetch water.

"It's not finished," he said to Crayne, whispering as fast as he could for as long as he could until she returned. Talons grabbed Crayne's arm.

"Will be," replied Crayne, wondering at the way two men could understand each other when they knew each other for such a short time. "I know some names. One you know. One you didn't. Pyramid's gonna come a-tumbling down, Jack. My word on it."

There was something like peace in the urgent face looking back. Jack breathed a huge sigh, as though whatever had kept him alive could now depart from the wreck it was leaving behind.

"Do believe you."

More coughing. Dawn moved past Crayne with a tin cup brimming with water.

"Never had a daughter, Dawn. Wish, girl, we had . . . that ranch . . . more time . . . Wish . . . all those years . . . wasted . . . trade it for one more day."

Jack held her hand. Crayne could almost see him slipping away.

"Dawn? Fire going out?"

"No, Uncle."

"Crayne. No regrets, Crayne. Someday, you tell them. Tell it true. No fancy words. Dirt plain truth."

"I will."

"Dawn . . . I taught you the words. It's time, girl. Don't matter how it comes out. Say them with me?"

He could see the man's lips moving, but there were no words. Dawn held water to his lips. He swallowed at first, then gasped and spat it out. Eyes met eyes. He nodded at her.

Together, they talked in an Indian language Crayne did not know. Their voices were a hushed, braided whisper; then there was only her husky voice singing a song for those going home to whatever God they believed in.

Then she, too, ceased her singing. The fire crackled. The tears dripped.

The Jack of Justice had gone home.

Crayne dug the grave near two oaks that were landmarks. Someday, he knew, they would be gone, as would all of it. For now, it seemed appropriate. They might be back in a month, a year, or never. When it was done, they stood, wordless under a Wyoming sky that wore its deepest blue for the day.

"I promised him I'd see you settled," Crayne said.

"Not leaving today." She started weeping. "You had your life, your writing. Never had nothing. Uncle Jack, he stepped in. Made me feel proud. Not ashamed. Knew when I heard about Sally it was him. Made livin' matter. Nothin' matters now, Crayne. Why make half-breed kids for a world that hates 'em? Never gonna fit in a world that looks down on me because my skin is too dark. With all the fighting, never gonna fit in a world that knows how much white I got in me. Jack's sister is near Cheyenne. She don't really care much about what anyone says.

Good woman. But it ain't home. Got no home. Don't want charity. Want to belong someplace, Crayne. One place that's mine. Mine, hear? A place that is safe where the world can't sneak in and disapprove of me and look down at me and maybe even try to kill me. Can you imagine how that feels?"

A man who had been a writer most of the last twelve years, and a Pinkerton agent in the breach, knew well that life held no fixed direction except the one Jack had taken on his way to whatever home awaits restless souls. She needed a road that could bring her some peace. That was what she wanted.

Or was it? She had walked back to the cave. He took some things from his saddlebag and went up the hill, overlooking the prairie and the woodlands that stretched out in a pattern of tans, greens, and grays. He wrote every word of everything that was said, that was done. It might never be seen, even be read, but maybe someday, somehow, the truth would be told.

If they said ten words all the rest of that day it was a lot.

It was nearly dusk when Lew, the bartender, rode up. He was grim-faced when he heard Jack had died.

"Four men come to town this afternoon," he said. "Fellas named Danvers. Lookin' for a wounded man." He stepped back in surprise and alarm as they rose together and talked over each other as each claimed it as their job.

"Don't suppose you would listen to me if I told you this ain't a job for ladies of uncertain lineage that might have refined sensibilities somewhere hidden real, real deep in the background," Crayne said.

"Don't suppose *you* would listen to me if I told you this ain't a job for scribblers and such who don't know real life when it hits them in the face," she said.

"What do I tell them?" Lew roared after the argument showed no signs of abating. In the silence after his question, a partnership was formed when two pairs of eyes met.

"Tell them a fool man and woman workin' a hill country mine told you that they saw something. Tell 'em you rode out to let them know, and they will come in and tell them man-hunters about it in the morning when the miner and his wife come for provisions. Tell 'em they don't travel at night cuz she's half-Injun and superstitious. Tell 'em the folks wonder if there's money in it," Crayne said.

Lew looked at Dawn. She nodded. Her mouth was sliding sideways in a feral, ferocious grin of excitement. "Maybe you make stuff up better than I thought."

He stuck out a hand. "Partners?"

She took it. There was more than partnership on the wind; there was more than revenge. Whatever it was, it would keep for another day.

"Why?" she asked.

"You said it: nothin' much better to do."

"Nope," she said. "Can't think of anything I'd like doing better, Crayne. They hounded Uncle Jack for months. Must figger they got him bayed and treed. Maybe they heard the army talking."

"Always did like a good hunt, Dawn," said Crayne. "Tell me what's where. It is hardly Chicago down there, but I need to know more than how to find the saloon and the stable."

"Why?"

"If it was you, would you suspect that if you rode into a town sheltering an outlaw that there might be a trap?"

"I would."

"Then we should not disappoint them."

"This is the most ridiculous costume . . ."

"You're my wife, and I'm a miner, so you have to look like a woman," Crayne said, looking at Dawn in an ill-fitting dress that Lew had donated. It had belonged to his late wife, who had been about six inches taller than Dawn.

"I don't look like a woman to you, Crayne?"

"You have to look like a woman to them. And, especially, a squaw woman. They can't treat you with enough contempt. You dress the way you usually do, they won't take their eyes off of you. Like this, you will be invisible. Trust me."

"You learn these tricks at that Pinkerton place, Crayne?"

"Watched other people live their lives long enough to learn a bit," he said. "Maybe it's time we use their tricks for ourselves."

They rode into town, Crayne loudly berating Dawn for everything from the holes in his socks to a burned dinner.

"Man might not want to keep this up much longer; man is having too much fun," she seethed.

"Woman might just need to know her place," he said lowly with a broad grin still in place as he spoke without missing a beat of his critique of her ways. He wondered exactly what form retribution would take, but that was a thought for after this little adventure was completed.

Two men came out of the saloon as they passed.

"Hey!" said one. Crayne continued to assail Dawn for a mix of omissions, getting louder by the minute.

"Hey, you!" yelled the heavy-bearded man, He pulled his gun and fired in the air when neither Dawn nor Crayne seemed to pay him any notice.

Crayne appeared startled. "Sorry, sir; these days have been a trial. We are so near to finding gold, and all the complications that vex me. This woman . . ."

He rather rudely pushed Dawn off of Dakota; she stumbled and promised very swift retribution in eyes that immediately went downcast.

"Now buy the flour you were supposed to buy on the last trip to town and meet me here in an hour. A man has work to do." She walked away.

"Faster, squaw, faster!"

Oh, he was going to pay!

She moved away, an ungainly figure that no one cared to notice. Crayne wondered about the two who were so far hidden. She would find them. He was certain of that.

"You men had questions? Like to help, but it is hard to talk when your throat is so dry you can hardly speak," said Crayne to the men, knowing how those who sold information wheedled their way into getting what they wanted from those who bought it.

With ill grace, they moved into the saloon. They bought Crayne a beer. Lew took his time but eventually moved into the storeroom in the back, leaving them alone. Crayne was sure there was a shotgun there.

"What was it you folks wanted? That man with the blood all over him? I knew there had to be a reward. Is it big? I can use the cash money."

"Outlaw," said one of the Danvers boys. "We're trackin' him."

"Is there a reward? Not tellin' if you ain't sharin'."

One of the men grabbed Crayne's shirtfront. "Don't play with us," he rumbled. "Where is he?"

"No harm in askin'," whined Crayne, fussing over his shirt after the man released him. "Man's got a right to try to get what he can."

"You seen him or not?"

"Certain sure I did," said Crayne, bobbing his head a few times to appear sufficiently ridiculous. "Farm about a mile that way." He pointed. "Run down. Men hide there on the run all the time. Came through 'bout two weeks ago. Had a wagon. Supplies. Stayin' a while, I reckon. Nobody else stays. Only him."

For a moment, he was afraid he had overplayed it. Neither man moved.

"Told you the place had to be a hideout," rumbled one.

"Nothing left; let's go now and finish him."

One slapped a couple of coins on the bar and told the bartender to keep the change. They pushed themselves away from the bar and started for the door.

"Fellas?" called Crayne in his best whining voice, lifting a near-empty glass. "Gave you a lot."

One gestured with his head; the other moved and put a coin on the bar, disgust plain on his face. As he turned to walk back to the door, Crayne opened his coat. It had been way too quiet way too long.

Dawn did not disappoint him. He heard her rifle, other gunshots, and then a fusillade as she fired as fast as she could lever.

The two men in the saloon were torn. They knew instantly they had been set up but were unsure whether to go to the shooting or turn on Crayne. That hesitation was his salvation.

By the time they turned, he had his gun out and ready. It was possible they might give up; they might tell Crayne and Dawn something about who hired them. It was, still, the code he learned not to shoot first unless there was no choice. He waited a moment.

They dug for their guns. No choice indeed.

The weeks spent learning the ways of a Colt when he first joined the Pinkertons were his advantage again—that and the almost constant use of the gun these past days. They fired four bullets; none hit. He fired the same. None missed. He hoped.

They were slumped by the door. He was wary. He waited. If two bullets really hit them both in the chest, no matter how many thick coats and shirts they wore, there would be blood flowing soon. If they were wounded, it might be a trickle. Only one seemed to be bleeding enough. He was making noises. The other made none.

Crayne's boots sounded loud against the floor. He stopped behind the one clearly dying. He cocked back the Colt. The one playing dead—if he was—would need to see to be sure. The eye opened. It saw a gun lifting. The gunman tried to roll and shoot, but all that happened was that a bullet near the heart and one dead center joined the one that had nicked the man's side. The red stream beneath him answered all questions.

"Lew, I need your help before the floor is stained so badly you make me clean it."

The bartender emerged, looking behind the bar where, miraculously, the mirror had not been hit. He grabbed one pair of boots.

"Well, move," he said, taking one man roughly outside and dumping him in the street. Crayne followed, realizing that the indignities of the dead were much less than those of the living.

"What did you do, Crayne, have to dance with them?" called out Dawn, walking across the street. "Been done with my two for hours."

"Where were they?"

"One in that alley, one by the dry goods store. Shouldn't have made a mess in Lew's place, Crayne."

"Remind me next time to let you do all the entertaining."

"We squaws don't do that," she sniped.

He grinned. "Since you said you were gonna shoot whoever used the word, you have to shoot yourself now, too, Dawn."

"I'll focus on you for now."

"Let's see what they had on them."

There was not much on the men that was of any use. Some bullets and food. Spare clothes. Not much money. A clipping. Crayne recognized it. It was from the very first Jack of Justice piece.

"Can't have enough of reading what you wrote?" Dawn asked, looking over his shoulder. She looked at his face when no expected retort ensued.

He was quiet. His eyes looked at her; his mind saw something else.

"Nearest telegraph. Where is it?"

"Injun no know," she shot back.

"Quit the act. You are as smart as I am, maybe smarter. I'm not here to be a mark. Where?"

"Telegraph in Laramie City. Not giving any more answers unless you tell me what we are doing, Crayne."

"Not going there." She agreed Laramie had not been kind to them.

"The fort."

"Probably not the best idea we ever had."

"Telegraph lines follow the railroad, Crayne. Towns are where you can find operators and such. Cheyenne?"

"Where did Jack start? Place called Crooked something. Right?"

"Crooked Creek. About twenty miles north of Cheyenne. There's a line out to Colquitt Springs; it's near Crooked Creek."

"Good. You got family near Cheyenne, Jack said."

"He did. I didn't. Not going there."

"Why not?"

"There are white folks, Crayne, that think if maybe I put on a pretty dress and a bonnet and maybe stay out of the sun, and my skin doesn't turn too dark from the wind, I can fool some desperate cowboy into thinking I'm nothing more than a dark-skinned white girl. I speak English real good, so a man not interested in looking too closely because men are so desperate for wives out here might just snap me up," she said.

She paused and shook her head back and forth in anger.

"They mean well. I know they do. My Sioux family is on one reservation or another or maybe in Canada with Sitting Bull; the Cheyenne kin are down south from what I heard. I'm not really welcome there, and I don't want to go. They'd take me from obligation if I went, but I'm not going some place where no one wants me."

"Then you ride with me." He knew where this would go a while back, but it never quite seemed real. Now it did. "Deal."

"Crayne, you get shot in the head? Deal? Who agreed to what?"

"You agreed to ride with me."

"What? When did I do that?"

"Right this minute." He reached and touched her shoulders firmly. "Dawn, we're two people no one else in the whole wide world knows about or cares about. There was a woman I was going to marry. In the East. Long time ago. She took up with another man. Married him. Was going to kill him; then I let it all go. Never saw her again. Never went looking for women again. Not my life. I got no money except what we've stolen. I can't do much that earns money except write, and now I've been fired from my last chance to do that. There is something that hurts to finish, and I can't do it alone. This might end good; it might end bad. I don't care. Whatever it is, I want to face it down together. Two mongrels nobody wants. How can it go wrong?"

"I left you in Laramie in a fix where you could have died." He wondered why her eyes were all wet.

"Kind of hoping you don't make a habit of it," he said. "You saved the man you were bound to try to save. I heard you call my name. I heard what you said. You kept faith. All I can ask for. Keeping faith."

Her hands gripped his arms. "Crayne . . ." She never finished. His arms had encircled her, and the kiss was intense and long.

"Gonna leave me to bury 'em?" came the sound of Lew's complaining voice from behind her. They separated with flushed faces to see his grin. "Your uncle would be happy, girl. Worried, he did, you never finding a man. Said he figgered if you found the right man and have enough kids you could defeat the Sioux nation and the whites combined."

Now she was coughing and choking.

Lew, a rare smile on his face at the havoc he had wrought, spoke to Crayne. "Figger you two have some things you plan to do. Welcome to come back here. Any time. Jack was a friend. Don't get many in this life. Now grab a set of boots and give me a hand so I can get this trash buried."

"You never told me what you are planning," Dawn said as they sat close by the fire near the cave where Jack died.

"Guess I think I know the answer, but when you even the score, do you want them to know it was you, or do what you need to do on the quiet-like and they never realize it?"

"Someone done wrong, you mean like to Jack, and I'm the one who makes it right, I want them to know where it came from."

"What about if doing it out in the open gives them the chance to stomp you flat?"

"Especially then, Crayne. Especially then. I want them to know before they died that I was better."

"Then what I am planning to do next will be exactly what you wanted."

Chapter Eight

"You think this will work?"

"Has to."

"You aren't him."

"The ones we have to fool won't know." Dawn looked upset. They were waiting in a grove of trees not far from Colonel Anderson's ranch.

"What's wrong?"

"Crayne, getting used to the thought there's maybe somebody I want to stay alive, and maybe something like tomorrow is worth seeing, and I don't want you dead right away until I decide."

"Don't mean to inconvenience you." The look stopped the sarcasm. He reached out for her. "Not going to be shot dead. Only way this works is if we do this. Otherwise, the wrong folks win."

She nodded. They rode up to the gate of the ranch, confident they could fulfill Jack's wishes. Too confident.

The gate appeared unguarded until they were within fifty yards. Two men with rifles appeared, two more to either side of them. On another day they might have stopped to have a word with Crayne before they opened fire. But what they saw was Crayne wearing a white shirt and a black vest—no matter how ill-fitting—with a shaggy beard. Knowing someone was coming to kill the rancher, only a far more cautious lookout would have thought of something more than firing first and asking for polite introductions later.

They turned the horses and were running before the first bullet flew. Dawn's horse could not match Dakota. Crayne was well out in front. He turned back again. She had been five feet behind. Now she was twenty-five feet. Her horse was riding in the wrong direction, and she was slumped on his neck. From the calls of triumph coming from the ranch gate, they knew what had happened better than Crayne.

They would be coming for her.

They would not kill her.

Dakota had rarely felt a kick in the ribs before. Crayne could feel the surprise in his stride even as he responded by galloping faster than even Crayne had ever known. He pulled on the reins hard. Dakota was not of a mind to stop.

There was blood on Dawn's jacket; she groaned and flailed weakly but did not fight him as he pulled in the reins of her horse. The horse did not like the idea, though, and it all but bucked Dawn off. She lolled.

The horse realized the arm hauling on its reins would not be denied. It stopped. Crayne dismounted.

"Dawn?"

"Give me a gun, Crayne," she muttered. "Dropped mine. Face them. Not in the back. Face the devils. Face them down."

He gave her a rifle. She was good with one; he was not. He briefly deliberated. He could not control her horse with her on it. She could not ride alone. He once again was lifting her onto Dakota's back, but this time she did not resist. She openly moaned when he touched her side, then clung to his horse's mane. Her eyes were drifting in and out of focus.

He opened up the saddlebags of Dawn's horse. There were two leather pouches within that he knew were all Dawn owned in the world that mattered. He jammed them in Dakota's saddlebags, then grabbed the trailing reins of her horse, mounted Dakota, and moved off.

He had been too slow. He could hear and feel the running horses before they appeared.

Run? Fight? Only one choice. He turned Dakota to face the pursuers who would be coming into sight soon, then he dismounted to stand next to her.

"Dawn?"

"What, Crayne?"

"Guests arriving for the dance, Dawn. Tell you when, you fire every round you own. Aim by the rotten tree stump. Then hang on. Don't fall off."

"Girl has to do everything in this outfit," she said.

"Squaw should do what she's told," he said.

"Remind me to shoot you when I'm done shooting everyone else," Dawn said. She tried to smile, but it sagged in pain. "Mean that."

"Promise," he said.

There was one chance. Timing was everything. Too soon and it would not work; too late and it would not matter. Now . . . no. Wait. Wait. Wait.

"Now!" he called out. He slapped Dawn's horse on the rump, and it galloped off. For a moment, the colonel's men were uncertain whether to follow that animal or continue the way they were riding.

From Dakota's back, Dawn's rifle worked faster than he would have thought possible, given her condition. One down. The others came closer.

Crayne had stowed four handguns on belts across the saddle horn, courtesy of the Danvers boys. Now he used them, one at a time—firing, cocking, firing, cocking, as fast as his hand could go until there were four guns on the ground and at least two of the riders coming after them lying there as well. They had bought themselves time.

He mounted fast, grabbing Dawn when it seemed that she would tumble from the motion of the horse. Then he kicked Dakota one last time and grabbed the reins with one hand and Dawn with the other as Dakota's muscles responded with a lurch and leap and a gallop that no other horse could match. Rifles were firing, but Crayne, who had grown used to judging such things in the past weeks, could tell nothing was flying past him. Soon, they were nothing more than distant noises.

There was not much near but scrub and prairie. There were far too many hours until dark. Dawn was whimpering at almost every thump of Dakota's hooves. He had no idea which way was which, but he headed for the roughest ground he could find. Through trees; rocky outcrops would deny pursuers a way to find his trail. Make it work for them, at least. His hand was wet from Dawn's blood. No choice.

Orange was starting to tinge the sky. Dawn was almost openly crying. Even Dakota was tired. Here would have to do. A thin creek trickled through a deep cut. Some brush that grew wide from the creek's supply of water spread on the bank. Not much, but it would suffice; he hoped they had left the colonel's men behind.

He gingerly maneuvered Dakota down the bank, fearful that Dawn would pitch off. Dakota was happy to drink. He eased Dawn down from the horse, laid her in the sandy fine-ground rocks and silt of the creek bed and looked her over. He slid off her jacket. Blood had soaked through her shirt from her right shoulder to her waist. He tore the sodden cloth. She had been half asleep until that moment.

The bullet had hit her under her right armpit from the back and hadn't quite exited. It looked like a lump under the skin.

"Use my knife," she said, whispering. She had been looking at the wound with him, looking at his face as he spoke. "It keeps moving. Hurts, Crayne."

"You spit blood?" She did not know, but she shook her head. Then she felt dizzy from that and put her head back.

"Quit talkin' and do what has to be done, Crayne. You have to do this, and then we can find a place to hide."

"I've never . . ."

"One writer whines more than ten squaws. Now do what I tell you. Cut it out before I grow tired of waiting and do it myself."

He had washed the knife in the creek's waters, then heated it in the small fire he built. Fire did something that stopped pus from forming. So did whiskey, but there was none to be had, or he may have had a swallow before trying to do what his old London mentor would have done without even looking.

She lay on her jacket, with her eyes glittering with tears she blinked away as she promised herself not to cry out for mercy and not to show weakness. Not in front of Crayne. Never.

He hesitated. She flinched as the heated knife touched her skin.

"Crayne, quit bein' a girl about it," she said. "If it don't come out, it kills me. It's gonna hurt. I'm gonna scream. People scream when you cut stuff out of them. I'm gonna scream loud. I might black out. If I cuss you in Cheyenne it's because it don't fit in white. Now before I get real sick and make a big mess, do what I said, and *get it over with.*"

"Don't die, Dawn."

"You'd starve without your squaw?" She tried to laugh, then coughed. A faint tinge of red made him feel weak and puny, unable to do more than watch this woman who meant his world die by inches. He was lost.

For a second, there was no sunset, grass, or wind. There was the smell of wet stone and soot. Old Alehouse Annie, the closest he ever had to a mother, looking matter of factly at the wound as the blood was pouring from the leg where the soldier's bullet had struck him.

"Don't be afraid," she had said that day. "When it's your turn, lad, do for others what was done for you."

Today was his turn. He asked God to add another to the pile of favors Crayne owed. He cut.

There was a touch of a breeze on her face; water gurgled near her ear. She could smell a horse; a bear had been near not that long ago. Floating. She must have floated too far. Into the fire. It was burning her. She turned; the vision went to black as roaring filled her ears, and a little girl screamed her name.

Darkness. Alertness coursed in her veins. The place of the dead was a place of tricks. She would be ready. Shapes were moving. Coyote, closing in. She waited. Waited. Now! Her leg lashed out.

Amid an exclamation water poured all over her face. She was now fully aware. The darkness had a fire—stars across the night sky. And a man muttering something that sounded a lot like cuss words.

"Crayne?"

"And is it that kicking your only friend hard is an old Sioux ceremony to mark the moment a squaw returns to the land of the living?" he asked.

"I'm not dead?"

"Not yet, although I might be reconsidering my options now that the water for my coffee is all over your bandages." His white teeth shone in the semi-darkness. Behind him, a full moon rippled across the plains. She was alive. She was alive! Memory returned. She looked around, then regretted it as her right side flared in fire.

"The colonel's men?"

"Nobody rode this way, not yet anyway, so I hope they gave up. Been dark a couple hours or so." He squatted down next to her and softly touched her face. His fingers went through her hair. "Thought for a minute I lost you."

"Squaws are tough."

"That word again." He reached out his hand. She took it. He looked at the bandage. The red area had grown for a while, then stopped. The less she moved the better; the faster they moved the more likely they would live.

"Think you can ride?"

She knew the same thing he did. A full moon on the water would be a path to someplace other than where they were. If there was a search on, and sooner or later the colonel's men would put their minds to it, eventually their hiding place would be found.

"Gonna navigate by stars, Crayne, until we are good and lost?"

"If we're lost, they can't find us."

"White folks say stupid things," she muttered, weaving as she tried sitting up.

They waited until she was sure she would not pass out. She walked a few steps. The world went side to side, but it never fell over. She was ready.

He gave her a spare shirt to put under her bloodstained jacket and walked off to look for anyone moving in the darkness. She washed in the creek. Water. Her hair was dripping; there was blood who knew where, and she knew the pain was only going to grow worse. But she was alive.

Crayne returned after a few moments. She held his hand tightly as he lifted her to Dakota's saddle, then mounted behind her. The rhythmic clopping of Dakota's hooves on the rocks, and the gentle swaying of the horse as he walked through the creek, lulled Dawn's senses from wakefulness into a trance and, after a few miles, into sleep.

Crayne kept Dakota moving. The night was pleasant, cool

after the heat of the day. The creek shown like a living silver highway. They had ridden northeast from Cheyenne toward the colonel's ranch. Best he could tell from the moon, they were heading south. Dawn was warm against him. Once he stopped when he thought her breathing had ceased, but there it was—soft and regular. He wondered, irreverently, whether it was the God of the whites or the Great Spirit of the Sioux and Cheyenne who kept her alive, but he thanked both, wondering if some day men would decide they were one and the same. No matter now. They were alive. Some other day, they would be back to take care of Jack's unfinished business—no, their unfinished business, now. For the moment, living was enough.

By morning, Dawn was burning, but they were far enough away after riding all night that they could stop. It took two days, but fortunately Dawn's fever broke after spiking to the point where she was almost delirious.

They camped by a run-down shack Crayne was afraid might tumble around them. The brush and scrub trees had grown up past where the windows would have been if it had them. Ten years of dust and dirt were on the dried, unpainted floorboards; sparkles of sunlight lit the inside where the planks of the walls gaped. It was shelter. Dawn lay under blankets, hair damp with sweat from the fever. She had come and gone in the past two days, sometimes herself, sometimes a ghost. A few times she talked in one Indian language, a couple in another. Once she made a pointed observation about Crayne's intelligence that made him smile. She held his hand a lot, squeezed it hard in one fevered dream. After one, she cried. She often touched the small carved buffalo that hung on a rawhide thong around her neck.

Now, as he looked at her, he could see the haze gone from her eyes.

"Quite a palace, Crayne."

"Fit for a . . . Well, I won't say it."

"Better not, scribbler." She shifted, grimaced a bit, but only pushed harder as she struggled to sit up. "Where are we?"

"Maybe twenty miles from the colonel's place. Cheyenne's west a ways, I think. Or the ocean is. Or maybe it's north. Or somethin'." He was smiling; one of the few times she had seen him fully relaxed and happy.

"Frontiersmen all over Wyoming flirting with a girl, and I end up riding with a writer who don't know east from south."

Crayne grinned. "Steering by the stars is an Injun trick, and you're the Injun. Can't expect me to do your work, woman."

She grinned. Alive was good. Whatever the last days had been, they were done. She was back. She felt strong. She kept grinning at Crayne; he kept grinning back. Wherever they had been together, they were coming back to life stronger.

"What now?"

"Back to Cheyenne. Want you healed before we do that again. Anyhow, Dawn, we have to watch better, plan better. We're lucky we were not killed. Colonel knows we're coming. Only good thing is that with me dressed this way, he might have thought it was Jack. Might not worry about some writer coming to talk about the West and marauding Indians and all that. I can charm my way in to see him."

Dawn snorted.

"We'll see. We will find a way to arrest or kill or stop the colonel and the rest of them, but I'm not losing you in the process. I still have some money, so we can eat for a while, long as you don't eat too much or too often."

She understood the meaning behind the banter. They had been naive and overconfident. The next time, they needed to do the job right. She would wait. As a girl, she knew from the

Sioux that patience was the hardest skill for a hunter to master. She would try.

With all manner of people going and coming, no one paid much notice to them as they entered Cheyenne. He wanted to tell Matthew he was alive. The young man who kept the stable didn't seem to care if two stray people wanted to stay there, too, as long as it was extra money. Dakota was enjoying his first grain in weeks as Crayne and Dawn went to go find the Western Union office. She had been trying to tell him not to say a word; they were safer dead than alive. He told her Sullivan was trustworthy. She knew no one was trustworthy when money was at stake.

They both jumped, startled, as a voice in the press of people walking down Cheyenne's main street called his name.

"Keep going," he said. His hand was down by his gun.

"Too many people," she admonished through clenched teeth.

Feet pounded on the duckboards behind them.

She turned faster than he did. Her knife was at the throat of a short, round, gray-haired man whose fringe was long and curly around a bald spot that was bridged by one stray strand of hair. Incoherent sounds came from the wide open mouth beneath the iron-gray mustache. His eyes behind the spectacles bulged large with fear.

"Let him go, Dawn," said Crayne, not believing the apparition in front of him. "I know him. Let him go!"

She was reluctant but obeyed. The knife remained in her hand as she released him.

The man recovered the derby hat that had fallen from his head and clapped it back in its accustomed place to restore some semblance of dignity, then straightened his clothes elaborately, as though an extra wrinkle among the hundreds of ink stains would make a difference.

"I see you have become one with the natives," he said in an accent Dawn could not place. "I am charging Matthew double. I should have known you would descend into a career as a ruffian." The man was trying hard to control a smile.

"What are you doing here? You had a plan to open that place in Chicago; you left New York to go there."

"The newspaper folded. Young men, they always find jobs. Everyone wants young men. Old men? Not so much, Crayne. Anyhow, Chicago was a lot like New York. Busy people. Rude people. Too many people. I moved to Kansas. I was a printer and ran a small newspaper there. I moved to Cheyenne a few months ago, and then I bought the printer's shop in Colquitt Springs. It is a very small place, but it is a very nice one for me. I come here to buy that which comes by train—my ink and my paper."

"You mentioned Matthew. Is he well?"

"Oh undoubtedly. I am out here risking my life among the heathen, and Matthew is sipping . . . well, something . . . in his genteel home with his genteel wife. He and I have stayed in touch off and on. You know Matthew. Two words after six months is a lot. I sent him a letter once. I received about four lines in return."

"Why did you mention him?"

"Ahem." Dawn was giving Crayne a look that suggested he might introduce her quickly before she took it even worse. He flushed and touched her arm.

"I am sorry, Dawn. The surprise of a friendly face. Franz Schultz, may I present Fire Buffalo Dawn, if you like her Cheyenne name; Red Coyote Dance, if you like her Sioux name, or Blanche, if you prefer her white name. For some reason I am not given to understand, she answers to Dawn." Crayne paused. "Mostly. And she doesn't bite." Pause. "Mostly." Pause. "Kicks like a mule, though."

"Want to find out again right here, Crayne?"

Franz was grinning widely.

"Miss, I am sorry for your misfortune in taking up with a ruffian whose ways have been molded by the gangs of Five Points instead of finding a man whose breeding in the academy of Berlin gives him superior tastes," said Schultz.

"And who was thrown out for saying things about the government."

Schultz smiled. "Your friend and I fail to always contain our true feelings."

"I noticed."

"Dawn, Franz here was the best printer I ever knew; many times he could make anything look pretty, even some of the slop I wrote in the early days. Six months? Why didn't Matthew tell me?"

Indeed, thought Crayne, why not? He would have confided everything in Franz, unlike Elezial Newsom. Franz would have dropped everything to help. He was so deep in thought he bumped into Dawn when she stopped walking.

"Need help breaking in the feet, Crayne?"

"Here," said Franz. There was a wagon with barrels of ink and bundles of paper. "Come and meet Clara. See my shop. This Cheyenne, it wants to be everything I left behind. From Colquitt Springs, I can live there and print there and deliver the papers here, and people actually buy them."

If it kept Crayne from doing something stupid, Dawn was all for it. They collected Dakota, and soon she was next to Franz on the wagon seat, trying not to wince as it bounced along the trail.

Colquitt Springs was small but busy. Franz must not have been the only one who wanted to be near Cheyenne without being in it. They pulled up beside a shop with the sign PRINTER.

"This is mine," he said, waving his arm toward the place. "The owner ahead of me ran a newspaper. The *Territorial Courier.* He was much like you, Crayne. He offended almost everyone to the point where no one would buy or advertise in his paper, so I bought the press and his business, and here I am. Come inside and see. The press came from my homeland. I think it was made before I was born, and it has certainly done a lot of traveling, but, with a few repairs and modifications, it will last for years to come."

The smells and sights were a slice of the past. It had been about three years since Crayne had been around so much ink in one place. He saw Dawn watching him. So familiar, and yet so strange now. Some days he felt the whole of his life before Wyoming was someone else's story.

"Matthew had sent me a telegram a while ago asking to keep an eye out for you, and so I have indulged in forays into the masses to see if you would appear. I have devoted hours to this endeavor, and the soles of my shoes are worn thin from the effort," Franz said.

"First time you went looking?" Crayne said, smiling.

"Third," Schultz replied with a laugh.

"A letter from Matthew arrived yesterday, so I know what he knows. He had a suspicion you were dead, actually, and was trying to find out what happened after some incident in Laramie City. I followed your series. You ran afoul of the Old Man again, I take it? I don't know which gift you covet more, writing or biting the hand that feeds you. Matthew seemed very anxious, unusually so."

"I tried to tell them something they didn't want to hear," said Crayne.

"You have not changed. Come in and talk. Clara will be—well, surprised—to see you. Or perhaps she will assume that when everything is settled again, along you come to unsettle it all."

Clara Schultz had always been certain Crayne would lead her husband astray in the wilds of New York City, where they had met during the early 1870s, when Crayne was no longer the wild man on the Plains but a writer sent hither and yon on assignments around the teeming city.

Clara never understood that his wildness has nothing to do with alcohol and women, but with throwing aside the strictures of society that chafed his spirit. Franz, who had been nothing more than a printer, was one of the few who set type to care what the words said and suggest, demand, or ignore the writers altogether and make changes he thought needed to be made. One such change triggered a huge row with Crayne, whose opinion of himself at the time was far greater than it would be in the years to come. When they were done arguing, they decided they had enjoyed their spat so much they became friends. It was an unlikely friendship between the younger Crayne, to whom printing was nothing more than a slow and unreliable way to lay his words before the public, and Franz, who loved the mechanics of his machines and believed most of what the magazine printed was best left unread.

"I tell him you were not dead; and you turn up on my doorway, skinny and filthy again," Clara Schultz exclaimed. Whatever the past, she was clearly happy to see him now. She hugged Crayne.

"My friend, Dawn," he said, forbearing to recite the litany of her names. Dawn exclaimed in pain as Clara gave her a giant, forceful hug.

"What has happened?"

"She was shot," said Crayne.

"Because of you," said Clara, casting a withering glance at Crayne as she wagged her finger at him. "Heathens. Children.

Doing whatever you did that resulted in this nice young lady being shot. Shame on you! How could you do that, Crayne? How many times did I tell Franz you would lead him down the vegetable path."

"Garden path," interjected Crayne, watching Dawn smile amid Clara's outburst.

"Word games. You and your word games. It is all the same, and see here what you have done to this nice little girl. The poor girl. We shall leave these foolish men, and you can tell me about it." She put a hand in the middle of Dawn's back and started to steer her out of the room as Dawn looked back and smirked over her shoulder at Crayne. "And, Franz, you do not go anywhere with this man." She then smiled at Crayne. "It seems like yesterday since the last time I said that. Now behave, and I will see to this sweet child."

Dawn was pushed away by Clara to some distant part of the print shop that must have served as their home. The sound of female voices faded.

"She missed you," remarked Franz. "She only scolds the people she likes."

"Tell me what you heard from Matthew." Franz outlined it as Sullivan had written it, from Crayne's proposal to change the story to the change in writers, and the role of Sherman and the army in ensuring that the Jack of Justice series came to an end. Sullivan noted that it was fortunate for them all that, in this case, real life imitated the journalism world, and the man they had written about was dead. He asked if Franz had any proof of Jack's death and said he would make it worth his while to find information to prove what the *Reporter* had already published, which led Franz to wonder what game was being played.

"I told him the man was dead," Franz said.

"What makes you so sure?" asked Crayne. He chided himself for not letting an old friend have the truth, but he and Dawn had an obligation to Jack. He was not sure quite where it led, yet, but, until he was, and until he was sure that, in a world where everyone and everything changed, an old friend had not, he would keep his cards close. There had also been, on the ride to Cheyenne, the windy tendrils of a plan to build on Jack's efforts that kept taking shape but reached no definite form.

"The army said so."

"The army, Franz, says a lot of things. There is talk he is still out there, lying low until the extra patrols cease."

"Where did you hear this? Can I print it?"

"There is a lot of talk on the trail, Franz, far from town. I can't tell you if it is true or not, but I would bet there have been sightings even after the army said he was dead."

"Do you know where?"

"Heard something about a Colonel Something . . ."

"Anderson. Colonel Anderson. Big rancher. Very hard man. Not a very nice one. There was a fight out at his ranch a week or more ago, or so I heard, when Indians tried to raid him. I was told there were about a dozen, but that his men killed them. I do not know if this was true, but ranches constantly have riders looking to see what they can steal."

"Maybe it was more. Don't really know." He was manipulating Franz; he was not quite lying. He had whetted Franz's curiosity. Let the process finish the rest of the work.

"There is supposed to be some big event with all the ranchers. Perhaps I can ask him then. In the meantime, let me see what more there might be to this," Franz mused aloud. "Even if it is all as substantial as the air, Crayne, it is something different to write about."

"Seen Newsom?"

"Part of my competition," said Schultz. "Mean old man. Each newspaper in Cheyenne tries to devour every other one. They do not think I am competition, because they do not see me very often."

"Tell me about Newsom and Southern."

"Knew each other in the war. Newsom is a real business man, Crayne. He has his fingers in all manner of pies. There was talk he was going to retire and move East because he had made so much money, but when I asked him about this, because I wanted to buy some of his printing equipment, he denied everything, was very rude, and all but threw me out. Out here I know there are very few rules, and almost no law, so people like him do what they please."

"So there must be something to it."

"So you writers would say."

Crayne drummed his fingers on the side table next to the overstuffed chair where he sat. He was impatient. He did not want to be indoors waiting; he wanted to be outdoors doing something. He could not explain why, but he felt the pressure of time to complete Jack's work. At the very least, he should telegraph Matthew so his old friend would know he had survived. If Matthew had thoughts, he could put them in a letter to Franz. He explained to Franz where he was going.

"Be careful," said Franz. "Some of these people you are dealing with are important, and they have many connections. If Matthew can ask me to look out for you, so can someone else."

"They all think I'm dead," Crayne replied.

"Matthew did not," replied Franz simply. "I think he expected you would turn up somehow, in some unexpected place. I do not know, Crayne. He seemed very anxious to locate you. Your Jack of Justice is a legend. You are part of that story, Crayne, whether you see it or not. If someone wanted him to go away, they may want you to go away. Once you reappear, someone may want you to disappear."

"Who are 'they,' Franz?"

He shrugged.

"It was the army that was involved, but we all know the army has to dance when someone else calls the tune, Crayne. Find that someone else. There are people like Colonel Anderson who the territory thinks are important and the army thinks are important. There are probably people with connections to the East who are important—at least to themselves. From the little you told me, if your Jack of Justice felt there was some organization behind the atrocities he was pursuing, it might go East, it might go towards Denver, but it would be beyond the people here. Even Colonel Anderson is more concerned with wiping out anyone and everyone who might be a threat than he is with pursuing anything like what you suggest might have been happening. You know it could have all been a coincidence."

Crayne saw Jack's face in his mind.

"It wasn't," he told Franz.

Crayne had learned how to more or less navigate the prairie using the sun, the moon, and the stars; he could find his way through the alleys of Five Points without a misstep as he had through the maze of Whitechapel as a child. Cheyenne eluded him. There were only a few streets, but a few buildings were clustered apart from the main street. There had to be more than one Western Union office. The only one he knew of was across from Newsom's establishment, a place he did not want to go. Dawn had insisted he stay out of sight once she realized she could not talk him out of a trip to Cheyenne. She and Franz both made sense. That was what worried him.

In desperation he asked a passing boy.

"Folla the lines, ya tinhorn," whooped the boy.

So much for feeling he looked the part of whoever he was supposed to be.

There was a shadow by the edge of the row of buildings across from Western Union. Crayne waited there to see if Newsom would emerge. Newsom meant Southern, and, although he was unsure exactly what that connection entailed, it wasn't good. If Southern wanted the Jack of Justice stories stopped, did he know something more about what triggered the Jack of Justice in the first place? Was he the powerful presence behind the scenes? Crayne did not want to find out right away.

Newsom eventually emerged, with a fancy coat and a small black hat, walking with a silver-tipped cane through the crowd that seemed always to be moving in this place, as though it were a city and not a raw, incoherent frontier collection of baked wood, dust, and flesh on the edge of civilization.

The Western Union man had no interest in Crayne's claim that his friend would cover the charges. That pile of hard money Crayne once possessed had dwindled, and Crayne was loathe to part with any coin he could keep. The man was flint.

Crayne kept the message short.

NOT DEAD CAN YOU HELP
STAYING WITH FRANZ

The telegram would go to Sullivan's home. Perhaps tomorrow there might be a reply. Crayne realized as he turned to leave the office that, despite the dangers and fears when he and Dawn were on the run and hiding, there was an uncomplicated simplicity in existing without fearing that life was a narrow track through a dusky swamp with missteps readily available. Perhaps they should go back to Top Hat, find something that kept their bellies mostly filled, and let the world scheme and seethe as it would. Something to think about.

He was so lost in thought that he failed to notice a young man studying him as he left the telegraph office, walking alone a few feet before mingling with the noisy clomping of miners, cowboys, and railroad men jostling along through Cheyenne.

★ ★ ★ ★ ★

"That was a real pie," marveled Crayne, wiping his lips after having eaten far too much. Clara's dinners had been legendary back East. Some things did not change.

"She only brings out the wooden ones when it's only me and her," laughed Franz.

He and Clara had marveled at how much food their two guests had packed away. When their long-grown children were young, they could eat. Nothing like that. He and Clara insisted on cleaning dishes afterward.

"It is what we do, and it is the time we talk about things we need to talk about," he said. "You will learn about this in time."

In truth, he was curious to find out what Clara had learned from Dawn about Crayne, whose diffidence with women was notorious. How the man could land in Wyoming with a woman who—while clearly a blend of races—was strong, proud, and wild. Not pretty in the drawing room, cloying sense, but striking—a face no one would forget. Crayne himself had changed. Franz had last seen him in early '76, before the Custer column, when Crayne was a man on his way up. Now, it was hard to square that man with the grim-faced man across the table who sounded like his old friend, and looked like his old friend, but had changed below the surface in ways Franz knew he had barely glimpsed.

The back door to the printing shop let out to an open space. Crayne and Dawn slipped out, past the small pen where Franz and Clara kept chickens. Behind them, there was the tiny tinkling of a piano from one of the bustling saloons that testified to the fact that Colquitt Springs was a growing community.

The west was bands of grays and oranges as the long-set sun crept deeper behind the horizon. Smells of cut hay, cooked food, and wood smoke drifted along as they stood in the gathering dimness, for once not doing, but being . . . not running, standing still.

"Amid all this doing nothing, you come up with a plan yet, Crayne?"

"No," he replied honestly. "Sounds like we can kill the colonel in a couple of weeks when he comes here for something or other, but it doesn't sit right. We could snipe him, backshoot him, or risk it in the middle of town and likely be caught. Don't like either choice. Killing a man from an ambush might make him a hero. So crowded in town I worry a gun would kill the wrong person. Jack took people straight up. I don't know how to do that. I can fire a gun; I can probably draw one faster than this colonel. I can hit what I shoot at most of the time on good days, but I get the feeling he never travels alone." Frustration was curling across his words.

"Crayne, you scheme as pretty as the day is long when you set your mind to it," she said. "Somethin' will come to you."

"Can't let them win, Dawn. I promised Jack." He had also promised to keep Dawn safe. Could he do both? "I have to," he finished out loud.

"You'll figure it, Crayne. Maybe you can take some time from all this thinkin' about tomorrow to think about something for today?"

They were shoulder to shoulder. She had turned to face him as he spoke.

"Such as?"

"Crayne, you Eastern writer people ever do anything without talking it to death?" She put her arms around him and pulled his face to hers. There was an exclamation of surprise and then, for a time beneath a sky that threw stars to the four corners of the globe with wild abandon, there was no tomorrow, no yesterday, only a moment for two people to hold onto all that was real and celebrate living.

Chapter Nine

"You miss this, don't you?" asked Dawn later when they returned inside. Crayne closely examined the press and poked at its workings.

"Yes and no," said Crayne. "Writing was most of my life since I came to this country, for all that it seems like it was someone else's story."

"You never told me how it started."

"I knew my letters and could read and write. Some minister who worked among the poor taught me. I guess I was his best pupil. One day he stopped showing up, but by then I could read and steal books or read discarded newspapers. When folks in Whitechapel or the docks needed letters done, even when I was young, I did them. There was a match seller who would talk all day. Stories and tales. I started writing them down for him to sell with his matches. They sold. We found a printer who would print them cheaply. Soon he made more on the stories, so I wrote more and more. It was one of the few things I could do well, and, if it brought in money for the people in the place where I stayed, it was good because it meant we survived."

"Will you go back to it, when this is done?"

The door slammed open.

Two men with guns entered. One wore a badge in the shape of a star. A third hung behind—Paul Hartsfield, Newsom's employee.

"This the man?" the one with the badge asked Hartsfield,

who nodded. "Run along." The man waited.

"Crayne, I'm Ben Fairweather. Marshal. This is my town, and I keep it clean. My office has received an official complaint about you. Seems you took money from a man name of Southern back in New York City to do some work for that man and never did it and never gave the money back, so you are now being arrested for theft, unless you have that money right to hand here and can give it to me so I can pay your debt."

He could not. It had been spent all over Wyoming. Southern. Long reach from New York City. How could the man have known? Of course—that's why Newsom's lackey was there. Crayne must have missed him in the crowd on the streets.

"Man make this complaint himself? Don't I have the right to talk to who charges me with something?"

"Elezial Newsom bore witness, and he's a solid citizen. His man here came to identify you. Haven't had it happen more than once or twice, but you got to go to jail until New York City sends someone to take you back there or I get the piece of paper that says I have to send you in shackles. Week or so, usually. I think it was the last time; might be more. Should not take money from people, Crayne."

Crayne could not go back. He could not resist. His mind bounced as thoughts careened through his head. Not revenge. Southern won. Something else. Something bigger. More important. What? What could an outcast writer have done while stumbling about Wyoming Territory in some Quixotic quest to make things fair that would matter to a man who had more power and money than any ten men?

"Son, you can go quiet or you can go dead, but you got to go with me."

"Crayne!"

"Can't fight this one, Dawn. When the odds are too great, there is no shame in giving up—for the moment."

Dawn blazed her fury at Fairweather. "You should be ashamed doing some man's unlawful bidding."

"Tell your squaw to shut her mouth," said Hartsfield. Crayne was quick. Dawn was quicker. The heel of her hand caught the man full in the mouth. Something broke, and there was blood.

Crayne wrestled her away and shoved her roughly into the confused arms of Clara, who had come running with Franz.

Fairweather, who had been jostled in the process and knocked aside, cocked his .45.

"Accident, Marshal," said Crayne. "Dawn was saying good-bye, and I was surrendering, and we hit this fella in the mouth by accident. Awful sorry."

Fairweather's face was stone. "Stand up, Terry," he told the younger man. "Now, miss, you stand right there, and Crayne you come with me, and, Terry, if you bleed on Miz Schultz's floor you are gonna have to come back and scrub it, so step lively, because these are respectable folks."

Crayne moved quickly before Dawn could do something else. Fairweather gripped one arm and escorted him to the jail, a frame building with two metal-barred cells and metal bars on the windows. He sent Hartsfield to have his mouth looked at, because the bleeding did not stop. He then escorted Crayne to a cell and locked the door.

"Crayne, the law is a funny thing. I got cause to lock you up, and it don't matter if I like it none. Thing smells, but it's by the book. Sorry about Terry's talk back there. I was born here. Figure maybe someday it will go back the way it was—people trying to get along—but now there's too many whites being too pushy over Indian land, too many Indians who think they can shoot one white and the rest of us will all run back to Momma, and it won't be pretty for a while. She your wife?"

"Friend."

"Wife you say? Then she can visit. Only wives can visit. Nothing funny, Crayne. Last man tried to escape—three-four years back—was hung by vigilantes. There are rounds I have to make. I am usually here in the evenings. When she comes 'round to the window, tell her that." He turned away. "One other thing. Bars in that window might let you pass stuff from the outside in. Thing is, there's most nights drunks in the alley who want a free drink by telling tales of what they see. Hard to do much they won't see and want to tell me about so I can buy them a bottle. Let the law do its job, son. When we start deciding whether to obey the law or not, things go sideways fast, and it gets ugly. Don't like ugly, son." He left.

Fairweather was a wise man, Crayne decided, when Dawn was outside the window in an hour telling him she had a gun. When he mentioned she might be watched, she told him there were five or six men in the alley. She stalked off.

She came in the marshal's office with a meal later, when Fairweather was back. He brought her a chair and let her sit on one side of the bars while Crayne ate on the other, after Fairweather had inspected the plate Dawn brought and suggested second portions of the pie might have been nice for the man with a badge.

He stayed at a desk, close enough to hear most of what was said but far enough away to be decent about giving them as much privacy as a man in a jail might be allowed.

Dawn pushed a moccasined foot through the bars. "Talk," she whispered. He did, explaining whatever foul thing he could think of that Southern might be up to. He kept his eyes on her face between bites, glancing down here and there to see she had slipped off one moccasin and with her toes was extracting a knife from the left moccasin. She put the moccasin back on as he covered the knife with his larger boot.

"Time, folks," said Fairweather, walking over.

Dawn thanked him profusely. Fairweather showed her out

and locked the door behind her. Crayne used the time to tuck the knife in his pants, where it would be hidden by his jacket. He was not sure when and how. Fairweather was a good man. Hurting good men never did anyone any good.

"Door to the street squeaks," Fairweather said. "I don't fix it because I like it that way. If you break out of your cell, you'll have ten drunks on you in a minute when you hit the street. Get some rest instead, son. I'll wire New York about you tomorrow. I have to head over to Cheyenne, but I'll arrange with Earl at the saloon to feed you regular." He paused. "God comes out on the side of the folks that deserve, son. Don't seem that way sometimes, but it happens every day. Have a little faith, son."

Crayne was wide awake in the darkness. If he left Wyoming Territory for New York, it was over. He might be able to make it back to the West . . . he might not. Jack would never win. He could not see himself leading Jack's life either, even if he found a way to escape. He was not an outlaw. There had to be a way out, but every idea that sprouted withered quickly.

The door rattled, creaked, then was flung open. Crayne could feel the breath of the air and see the square of darkness beyond the doorway. It had to be Dawn. He waited. Boots moved on the floor. Keys jangled. A man whose face he could not see and whose shape he did not know was walking towards him. The one thing Crayne could see was a gun in the man's right hand as he walked between Crayne and a window.

"Move back," said Hartsfield. "You ain't goin' to New York. Back. Lift your hands so I can see them against the window. Now!"

"If this was a charade, you could have told me," retorted Crayne.

"Law had to believe it," replied Hartsfield. "Move!"

Crayne complied hesitantly. He did not believe Hartsfield was there to help. He was trapped. No noble thoughts suitable for a hero filled his head. Only fear.

Fear abated a pulsebeat as the man turned the key in the lock. "Out of there."

Crayne's racing mind realized why he was not already dead. He could not be killed here. It would be murder. Caught escaping, it would be justice. Hartsfield would want him calm until there was a bullet buried in him. He had from the cell to the door.

"Hands up," said the man. Crayne did so, expressing feigned outrage and surprise.

"You should have kept runnin', fella. You really think they were going to let you live with what you know? They want you dead. No hard feelings. This is only business."

"I need my hat," he complained, wondering what the man knew.

"Not where you're going. No tricks. March." The gun jabbed his back.

"This isn't legal."

"Shut up or I shoot you here."

The knife was still in the back of his pants. All he needed was one chance. The door was closer with every step; his options were shrinking equally as fast.

"Stop." The pressure of the gun left Crayne's back. The man moved around to the side, where he could be sure Crayne didn't reach out his hand for the door. Crayne's eyes, well accustomed to the darkness, saw the gun gesture toward the street.

The air was cool on his sweaty face. One chance. He stepped through the doorway as the figure shadowing him moved confidently behind him. Crayne heard the door squeaking as it prepared to latch. One hand on the gun, one on the door. Best odds he could hope for.

Hartsfield's divided concentration gave Crayne the chance to slam back into the man, knocking the gun aside as he bounced into the door, rattling the glass. Hartsfield's hand cocked the gun and fired, but the flame that shot from the barrel at Crayne's hip and singed the leather of his belt was the only damage done.

Crayne had barely enough space. His hand reached behind him for the knife. He turned, slashing. The man yelled as the blade Dawn had sharpened slit his cheek. He was trapped against the door. Crayne head-butted the man in the face. The pop of cartilage told him it worked as well here as it did in London.

But in London there were no guns. Crayne swung down with the knife. He hit the jacket, and it glanced. Another swing and he hit flesh. Another.

The man shoved Crayne away with his left hand; Crayne stumbled. The gun hand was now free to move.

The man's gurgling choking cough was muffled by the sound of the gun firing twice. Crayne heard the bullets, but they missed. The knife had not. The man was staggering. Crayne watched a moment, then realized as he heard distant voices that the gunfire would bring the curious in moments. He ran back inside, collected his hat and jacket. Looked at Fairweather's desk. There was a piece of paper on it. He felt for a pencil. Quick. Scribble. Go!

He ran down an alley to the back side of the street's row of buildings, then ran until he found the stable. He lit a lantern. He idly wondered what Dakota thought of all this as Crayne hurriedly saddled the horse. The rifle was still in its scabbard. Good. There would be spare shells in the saddlebags. He opened the rear door of the stable and led Dakota out.

Angry voices. Loud voices.

He heard a call for the marshal. Men running like chickens making almost as much sense.

He mounted Dakota and moved farther from the buildings.

There was no time. There had to be time. He dismounted and led Dakota down an alley. The street was clear where he was; the commotion was at the far end of town. He crossed the main street, half expecting a challenge or a shot. Neither came.

When he reached the edge of town, he tied the horse to a tree behind the stores and ran until he found the printer's shop. The rear door was not locked. They had dropped their guns in the hall. He was no gunfighter, but riding unarmed would be suicide. He buckled his around his waist, leaving the extra one in his pants.

"Dawn," he whispered loudly. The first night, she slept in a room with the Schultzes. He moved that way.

A gun clicked. He was sure Franz never slept Indian-light.

"Dawn. Please do not shoot! It's me. Crayne!"

"How'd you escape?"

"Wasn't going to New York—was set up to be killed. I need to leave town as fast as possible, but I wanted you to know I was leaving. Follow me when you can. I'll leave signs. Those rock things you told me about."

"No," she insisted. "No trail. You don't know what you're doing, and you will lead them to you. Don't. There's a place five-six miles southeast. Hills. Ride to the hills. Creek almost forms a knot; swale and a space of two outcrops make a shelter. Rocks are brown there. Sacred place. Safe there. Brown rocks. Remember. Go."

Voices were coming. "Go!"

He ran. No one was behind the buildings.

"Stop!"

Wrong.

The rifle fired, but marksmanship in the dark with a running target was only good in the babble writers wrote to please readers. He reached Dakota and jumped into the saddle. There was one more thing to do to help ensure his getaway.

"Meet you in Cheyenne," he called.

He took one quick look up as he rode away. Whatever the stars wanted to say about direction on this moonless night, it did not matter. He had no idea which way they were going, but, for now, away was enough.

Fairweather was livid. Crayne was gone. Hartsfield was wounded so badly he would probably die within hours. Hartsfield had a gun on him and had been stabbed by a knife that Fairweather was pretty sure he knew was slipped in by Dawn. As best Fairweather could interpret what he saw, there was a struggle, which made it seem more likely to him that Hartsfield did not enter the jail with the intent to set Crayne free.

Nothing made sense. Newsom was hand-in-glove with that Eastern publisher who wanted Crayne arrested and sent back there for some fool reason that, Fairweather was sure, had nothing to do with money. Why would Newsom's lackey then sneak in with a gun? Some deeper game was being played than Fairweather could comprehend. There would never be a straight answer. Hartsfield did not breathe without Newsom's permission, and with men like Newsom, the truth was always murky. Adding to Fairweather's confusion over what took place was the note on his desk where it looked like someone had scrawled what looked like "No choice" on a list of supplies.

"He must have come upon Crayne escaping," Newsom said, after making it clear that the town's council of leaders counted him as one of its valued members. "Hartsfield is an employee, Marshal. I do not keep track of where he comes and goes as long as he is ready to work in the morning."

Weasel was a word used for many men. Never did it seem to apply more than to the man in front of him, Fairweather mused. He let it go. What kind of lie a man utters never matters when a man knows it's nothing more than a stinking lie.

There was little help at the printer's shop. Fairweather hardly expected Crayne's friends to tell the law where he went. With Newsom there as well as a few members of a self-appointed posse who wanted the dollar wage given out when there was a hunt for somebody important, he was denied the chance to ask what was really going on.

"I have to look for him," he said. "It's the law."

"Your law," said Dawn. "There is no law for people like me, and people like Crayne who ride with me."

"Law isn't perfect," he said. "But if you go up against it, be prepared for the consequences, miss."

Dawn waited for the marshal to mention the knife. When he did not, she wondered what lay beneath his words and decided that she would say nothing to him about Crayne's visit.

Fairweather knew that his talk was bluster. Crayne was no cowboy, but he knew all the tricks. He had emptied the stable of its horses last night before riding out. Not only did it take precious hours to recover livestock that owners prized more than someone wanted by a New York City rich man, there were so many trails leading out of Colquitt Springs that he had no idea which was the one to follow. He was pretty sure Dawn's claim that Crayne told her he wanted to get to Cheyenne on some urgent business was a trick to throw them off, but it gave him an excuse to start looking where he was sure Crayne would not be found.

The law said he had to look. He was going to look. But something told him that Crayne would be back in time, and that whatever the business was that involved Crayne and Newsom, the accounts were far from settled. The law could be patient.

When he had been in the East, everyone said that the prairie was flat. Endless. Crayne had come to know the rugged land much better. What looked flat at a distance was carved by creek beds that flowed once a year, broken up by rocks that poked through the thin soil, and filled with scrubby trees and brush that were interspersed with the tall, waving grass that, some years, could reach to the belly of a horse. A man moving through the sea of meadows could leave a trail any tracker could find, then have that trail go cold when the dirt gave way to nothing but rock. Crayne took his time and worried more about leaving the hardest trail to follow than which way he was going, making it as hard as possible for the pursuers he knew would come sooner or later.

He'd spent the balance of the night by a small stand of oaks. When light dawned, he oriented himself by the sunrise and rode northwest a while. By mid-day, he felt safe turning back the way Dawn wanted him to go. Twice he thought he saw horsemen, but no one came close enough to be a concern. As the day slid into evening, he realized he had no firm idea of where he was. He knew he had not ridden past that rocky formation in the morning, but it looked a lot like one he had seen before. Put him in London, and he could find his way through the warren of alleys. Out here, he was far too easily lost. He camped and waited for morning.

When the sun rose, he rode for the place Dawn told him to go. What Dawn described would be near hills. When he reached them he would turn south. He did. There were usually trees to screen him, but that meant riding very carefully to ensure nothing scratched Dakota or knocked him out of the saddle. Time did not matter. Remaining unseen did.

He stopped as the sun was sinking. It was not what he heard, but what he did not. No birds. No skulking of small mammals underfoot. Dakota's ears were at attention, as though the horse was trying to find a sound that wasn't there. Tired as he was, he could feel it. Something different. Wrong? Deadly? He sat atop

Dakota. No noises. None. He wished Dawn were here to explain it.

There was a small rise. He wanted to whoop as they reached it. A creek that sure looked like a knot to him. Only a couple of days to ride five miles. A reminder, if he needed one, of what he could and could not accomplish on his own in this wild land. He found the space she told him, where the rocks enfolded him like two arms, and made camp. He'd find out in the morning if the rocks were brown. His saddlebags still had flour and a few carrots. There were enough sticks for a fire. The creek had water. It might not be a feast for a king, but he was alive and free.

And ready to get even.

Chapter Ten

He'd been watchful long after the sun went down. He'd seen the early stars wheel through the sky on their paths. Then, after not sleeping since his escape, his eyes gave up the unequal contest.

He knew as he opened them that he was not alone. He had camped amid the rocks where he could not be seen and Dakota would be mostly hidden. He had leaned back against them by his tiny fire so nothing would be behind him. Now they scraped his back as he stumbled to his feet, almost falling. He straightened himself up and reached for the rifle that had fallen from his drowsy hands to the ground.

"You dance well," came the voice. He blinked the haze away from his eyes that turned the men before him into glowing figures wreathed in gold from a fire that had now become bright with flames. His eyes cleared. It was not good.

About a dozen men stood behind one leader. Long, black hair fluttered in the breeze as the dawn turned grays and blues into browns and yellows. All Indians. Most appeared to hold rifles. All men. Young. Behind them, there were horses. Not a saddle among them.

He ran his hands across his face and through his hair. No escape. Show no fear. His heart was pounding as his mind raced.

"I would invite you to get down and come in, but you have already done so," he said by way of a reply. "There is almost half a carrot to share if you are hungry."

He kept his hand at his side, near enough to give him a chance but not so close that it would touch off a gunfight. "I would share the rest with you, but I ate breakfast for supper last night. There might be more dirt in the coffee than there should be, but some say it embellishes the flavor."

The leader did not move or react. It was as though Crayne had not spoken. Having been told more times than he could count that his mouth would be the death of him, Crayne wondered if this was, indeed, that long-expected event.

"Tell me, Circle Rider, whose horse moves as if you were lost, what are you looking for? What bring you to this place? What do you hope to gain? Do you come to rob?"

Someone had been watching. Someone was always watching. "Looking for a place to stay. Didn't mean to trespass if this is your camp."

"Do not lie," scolded the leader, coming closer as those behind him took several paces forward as well. "You rode in circles to hide that you were seeking this place. This is not a place a white man would dare to seek."

Crayne looked at the menacing ring of foreboding. The young, hard faces could have been made of stone. No two were dressed alike in castoff clothing that combined shirts that hung low beneath jackets on some, unbuttoned vests and leggings for others, and open-fronted coats on a couple. They all had rifles that looked new and were clearly comfortable in the grips of their owners. If they had been watching, there was little he could say they did not know. But he would not beg.

"I am a white man. You are a Cheyenne. This is Wyoming Territory," he said, lifting his arms wide in a gesture that prompted movement of rifles. "Am I not required by law and custom to lie?"

One of the men behind the leader laughed. "Raccoon Eyes has a sharp tongue, Red Bear."

No, thought Crayne, knowing that only one person had ever named him that based on the dark circles that stood out under his eyes when he was pushing beyond his body's limits. The man walked closer, and Crayne could easily see his features in the morning sun. Yes, he realized. One of the Indians who had tried to rob him weeks ago. Were the others there as well? Yes. The rounder one by the horses and the thin one at the far edge of the line watching the drama unfold. Sioux and Cheyenne riding together? For a moment he felt fear. There had been rumors Sitting Bull's warriors would return from Canada to be joined by Cheyenne and Sioux from Kansas to sweep the plains of whites. Crayne had dismissed it as idle talk from the drinkers who assumed Indians would do vast, impossible feats. Now, he wondered if he had been wrong. They would not see weakness.

"Wet Britches."

The Sioux warrior's lips pursed as a small titter of laughter echoed behind him. "You insult me before my brothers?"

"Never were what one might call properly introduced," Crayne replied. "Never made it past insults to real names. I'll answer to mine if you answer to yours."

"I am Wolf Thunder," the Indian said proudly.

"I am Crayne. Now that we have obeyed the rules and the social graces, maybe I'll be on my way and leave you your place in peace."

"No," said the leader of the group, motioning the Sioux to move back. "You will tell us why you are here."

"You saw me. Lost. Tenderfoot. Easterner. No offence."

"What happened before what we saw?"

Why not? "I'm running from the law because I killed someone in Colquitt Springs, that little town near Cheyenne. I needed a place to hide. Simple."

"How did you find this place? Do you know where you are?"

"Wyoming Territory, last I looked."

The leader strode angrily toward Crayne.

"This is Cheyenne land!" He reached out to grab Crayne.

Crayne was faster. He had the knife out and at the leader's throat as he grabbed one of the man's arms and thrust it painfully behind his back.

"Don't want your land, friend. Tell your friends to back off and let me go." The final word was the last sound Crayne made before he was riding the leader's back en route to a hard landing on the dusty grass of the prairie. The knife was now, in turn, at his throat.

"This is a sacred Cheyenne place where spirits gather," the leader said. "The spirits gather the lost ones to shelter them and protect them. You ride here to hunt us down. You will bring others. There are places we will never surrender to you."

The knife moved. Crayne felt it slide across the skin of his neck to where the whiskers stopped growing. He looked at the leader's face as it was animated by some powerful emotion. Crayne vowed not to die begging. The Indian's arm moved quickly.

The rawhide loop around Crayne's neck was sliced cleanly through. The leader grabbed it and looked at the small figure of a buffalo hanging from it. The tip of the knife was now jammed under Crayne's chin.

"Where did you obtain this, and from whose dead body did you take it, white man?"

The menace in the words was unmistakable. For a moment Crayne was sure he was dead. He tried moving; the knife jabbed again, insistently. He looked in the face of the man who was going to kill him.

He saw the answer.

"She gave it to me. Your sister, or whoever she is to you, gave it to me. Fire Buffalo Dawn gave it to me." He kept recounting her names. "Red Coyote Dance gave it to me. Blanche gave it to me. Whatever you call her. Girl kicks like a mule at the word 'squaw' gave it to me. Points her rifle at strangers for what I believe is entertainment. Girl rode with the Jack of Justice. She's alive. She's in Colquitt Springs. She's my friend. Friend. She sent me here."

An impassive face registered the words.

"Half sister."

Crayne exhaled. "I recall that it was complicated. I cannot remember which parent you might have shared. But I know your name. You are Red Bear."

Red Bear looked down at him. The knife remained in place.

"Want to kill me later?" Crayne suggested. "Take some time to think about it? She might get awful mad if you kill me without asking first. Girl likes being asked. That one especially. Small things might not matter, but killing is a little different. Not saying she might not want it done, because there have been a few moments, but if she does, she will want to do it herself. You know her. Am I correct?"

Red Bear leaped to his feet and walked away, issuing a stream of orders to his followers in a language Crayne did not understand. He then came back to Crayne, who was now sitting on the ground, heart pounding and still expecting to die.

"Come," he said, walking toward the rocks and the shade of an overhanging tree. When Crayne caught up, Red Bear spoke. "Talk."

Crayne told it all—from his assignment to his most recent escape. He tried to gauge the effect of the tale on Red Bear, but it was hopeless. The Indian leader was flat faced. With a red piece of cloth binding his hair in place, he wore a buttonless, black, frock coat that was stained and worn over a bare chest marked with some color of tattoo. The sleeves had been hacked off near the elbow, revealing a length of muscled forearm. Red Bear wore buckskin leggings like the ones Dawn wore when he met her. Barely Crayne's height, he was broader and moved with the grace of an animal and radiated a powerful personality. He had a full, strong face with a prominent nose, strong chin, black, burning eyes. Around his neck was a rawhide thong with a similar charm to the one Dawn gave Crayne, done by the same hand, but it was of a bear.

"Jack was a very strange man," he said at last. "The Jack of Justice. Clever, you white men. Did you know the story when you named him that?" Crayne shook his head. "Very clever. Our whole family is a series of men and women who did what they pleased and left the tribes and white society behind. Before the whites came, when the Sioux and Cheyenne would fight, my family bred children neither wanted. Jack stole from whoever he felt wronged him. I heard some of this when we were in your Kansas. I thought there was hope. The ones there, the Arapahos and the rest, would not ride here. These are my family, my brothers. You shall come to our camp. It is not far."

"Dawn told me to stay here."

"We shall watch this place. You do not know where you are, do you?"

"She said it was sacred."

"Old ones from long before rest in the dirt. They guard this place; those who must flee can shelter, but not long remain. She sent you here to have the spirits look over you. Perhaps she knew I would pass this way because it was a refuge for us as children." Crayne thought of little Amelia's Grandma Four Elk. "She is well?"

"Last time I saw her." Crayne could not resist a smile.

"You are her man?"

"You trying to get me to say the word 'squaw'?" Crayne asked. Red Bear roared.

"You know my sister," he exclaimed. "Are you?"

"Not sure how we left things," said Crayne. "I was in a rush.

She hung that around my neck and sent me here."

Red Bear nodded. "All is well, then, Crayne. All is well. You said she will come?"

"I cannot imagine your sister sitting out this dance," Crayne replied. "The way I see things, I would imagine they are watching her to see if she will lead them to me, and she is being cat-patient waiting."

Not quite that patient.

It had now been a week since Crayne escaped. Dawn had tried to busy herself by working with Franz in his shop. He knew where everything went, but his fingers were stiff. Hers were nimble but unfocused.

Still, when a broadside warning patrons of one of the saloons not to randomly spit on the floor was printed with no help from Franz other than directions here and there and some startled gestures when he was sure it was all going wrong, all six copies with about twelve words each, she was quite proud of her accomplishment.

Franz caught her looking out the back door, watching the watchers who were out of sight. "Patience."

She shook her head. Franz had been kind. He and Clara went out information gathering for her. Newsom's assistant had died. The marshal seemed concerned, but there was no posse out riding the plains. There was no trace of Crayne. There was work to be done. The printing work was clean. But something else needed doing. If Crayne was waiting, she needed to go before he gave up and went to the colonel's ranch and ended up getting his fool self killed doing some half-witted thing he would think was noble. She would not let that happen. She had lost everyone she planned to lose.

"I'm going."

"A few more nights," Franz advised. "The moon appeared

again last night. You would be seen. Wait a few days until there is no moon. Then we will help."

"No. I am going tonight."

Franz long ago gave up battling those with stronger wills than his. After all, was this not why he and Clara had been surreptitiously plotting?

"Do what we tell you when it is time," he said.

She impulsively hugged the man. She had never had a white man be so kind, and there were no words. She tried anyhow. He shushed her.

"If Clara and I wanted to plod through life, we could have stayed in Prussia," he said. "Come back to us when this is over."

He left soon after. He returned once, briefly, and spoke to Clara and left without another word. Clara had spare clothing, food, and new blankets ready for her.

"These . . . we have more than we can use. It is cold at night," she said. "Crayne is a lucky man."

They extinguished the lamps and all but one candle on the floor. Clara sat near. The watch in her hand read ten o'clock.

"Go out this door," Clara told Dawn as she pointed to the front. "Stay in the shadow. When you hear the noise, it is your chance. Do not worry. More noise is better." She hugged Dawn. "Go with God."

Dawn heard the rear door shut and heard Clara talking, as if to someone. She wondered who. Franz was not around. She did not stay to investigate but did as directed—this once. She was in the street in seconds, the door closing silently behind her. She noiselessly crept along the duckboards as far as she could go. There was a saloon up the street still lit. Noisy. She could not risk going further, even though the stable was only twenty yards away on the other side of the street.

She jumped at the gunfire. Not one shot. A rifle and a pistol.

Shot after shot. Men started pouring out of the saloon. Dawn gathered her bundle close and ran.

Clara Schultz was laughing as she fired the rifle in the air over and over. She and Franz had each gargled with whiskey, splashed each other about the face with the stuff, and they had each swallowed a bit. Perhaps, in deference to nerves that refused to be quiet, more than merely a bit.

Franz was firing the pistol he usually kept on the floor of a closet, over and over. She had not seen him misbehave with such abandon since they left Prussia in 1848. This Wyoming land did things to men.

She giggled. It did something to everyone. She idly wondered how far Dawn had gotten, then fired the rifle toward the moon one more time. She could hear men yelling, and she was going to have this fun while it lasted.

The same sliver of a rising moon that shown down upon Dawn as she took the trail illuminated a disgusted collection of posse members who found a printer and his wife in some drunken game about shooting the moon, walked them back to their shop, and then went back to their posts to wait.

Not the least abashed, the couple lit the shop brightly and laughed until the sun rose. What was a headache from a game like this. A serious game, but a game nonetheless.

Red Bear and most of his riders had left the camp some time during the day and returned when the sun was setting. The sizzle of grease and smell of meat told Crayne they had been hunting.

"Eat with me," Red Bear said. "I have thought much upon this. The spirits want me to help, or you would not be here. Did you and Dawn have a plan?"

One had been stirring in Crayne's head as he watched Red

Bear's riders effortlessly leap up on the backs of their animals. But there was a question to be asked.

"How is it you ride free without pursuit?"

"Red Cloud, and men like him, have accepted that they cannot win the war against the whites. Perhaps if we had fought like you do—to kill and not for glory—and all the nations as one, it would have been different. Some of us have no homes where the Sioux are penned; the Cheyenne have been marched away. Tribal politics can be brutal, Crayne, and most of us here have had arguments with the leaders of the tribes. Some of us want to be free, even if it means a hungry belly. Some of us have no place that matters, except on the back of a pony. The army catches a few. They do not know how to catch us all. If we take a little, hurt as few as we can, and avoid riding under their noses, they can pretend we are not here. We bring families meat; we sometimes scare those who need it. We cannot wage war; we cannot live under the terms of what you people call peace. The leaders of the Sioux and the Cheyenne wink and ignore us and in their hearts wish they could ride with us."

"Did Dawn ride with you?" he asked, having noted the women and children with the men, all clad in a collection of rags that were clearly discarded by whites.

"For a time, a short time. Dawn is white in an Indian world and Indian in a white world, Crayne. She has seen both so much that she belongs in neither. She and Jack shared a soul. I fear she will be lost without him. We heard he was dead; I have tried to find her. Even one who wishes to be alone should not be left alone by herself in the world."

"I expect she will be along. We will wait for her, because I don't want to hear about it if we do not."

Red Bear's eyes crinkled. "She has you trained. Then we must be ready. What is it you want me to do?"

They talked until the food was gone and the sunlight, too, and into the silver and blue shades of evening.

Dawn had ridden carefully in the moonlight. She knew the way to the sacred refuge, but there was no need to hurry and push the horse into a hole he did not see. She wondered if Crayne had found it. He was a tenderfoot in some ways, a survivor in others.

She knew she was nearing his camp when she first smelled wood smoke. Crayne clearly did not know how far smells carried. Closer still when she could detect the smell of cooked food.

"Crayne!" she called out as she could see the tiny flames. "You better have left some for me!"

The only answer she received was a mechanical sound of a rifle being cocked.

Red Bear had looked askance at Crayne when the white man jostled him awake. In a camp filled with Indians whose lives depended on hearing noises, it was hard to believe no one heard a shot except for a white man who was so clearly deeply rooted in the East despite acquiring many frontier ways.

"Red Bear, I've been up all night. I know what I heard. Sharps rifle. Different sound from a Winchester. It was hushed, but I know what it was. Look, man. I was a Pinkerton for two years. I know what I'm talking about. Either someone found your trail or mine. Either way, we're not alone out here. The shot was that way." He pointed south, toward the place where they had met him.

The camp was awake now. There was little to be lost by investigating. Red Bear looked harshly at the sentry who was supposed to be on watch. He was a new rider of whom Red Bear remained unsure. Putting off a reprimand until they found his sister, he gave the command, and, in a moment, eight riders were gone, mounting their saddle-less horses with an ease and grace Crayne knew he could not have mastered with a thousand days to practice. He watched them go, graceful riders skylined against the horizon—a scene these plains had witnessed 10,000 times before and one Crayne knew was nearing the end of its time.

"You are sad."

"It is a sad time," Crayne replied. "In these weeks, I have wondered often how two peoples so different can exist in the same place, in the same time, without one uprooting and destroying the other—not simply in battle, but in everything."

"It ends the way it ends, Crayne," replied Red Bear. "I cannot see that. I never think of it. What this place becomes when I am dust like those who rest in the sacred grove is not mine to control. I am given what I am given. I will give it up when I am dead." He looked intently at Crayne. "And I will fight who I choose when I choose where I choose until that day, and my spirit will rest happily when I meet my ancestors. What I do matters, Crayne, not what I wish I could have done. White people think too much, Crayne."

Four quick shots in succession rang out to the south.

"They have found something. Let us see what is there."

"Took your time," Dawn said as she greeted Crayne, who had ridden ahead once he could see her profile in view. "See you met some new friends." Red Bear's men were dismounted, waiting. Watching.

She was astride her horse. One of Red Bear's men was on the ground on his knees with a piece of leather binding his hands. The men sent ahead surrounded him, arms folded across their chests.

Dawn looked past Crayne. She swallowed hard.

"Brother," she called. Cheyenne women did not run up and embrace men. Not in full view of everyone.

"Sister." Cheyenne men did not shed a tear at seeing a favorite person in the flesh instead of only in dreams and memories. "Tell us."

When Red Bear's riders had come upon them, Dawn was being led toward Cheyenne, her hands bound across her saddle horn. Stone Bear was leading her horse.

Red Bear dismounted. He walked to Stone Bear's horse, where a gun lay on the ground. "Sharps rifle. Are you sure you are not part Cheyenne, Crayne?" He picked it up and aimed it at the Sioux who not long ago had come to him for food and a place to belong.

"Why?"

No reply.

"I can shoot you anywhere and let you bleed for hours, Stone Bear. I can make it quick. Why did you betray me?"

"They search for these two. They will pay money. Money buys food. You ride like a warrior, but the people starve. I can feed many with the price on her head. She is not of my people or yours."

"The price is put by those who sell the hair of our people."

"If a white man scalps a drunk, am I to care that it is a Cheyenne? If my sister starves in the hills while you ride and tell them on the reservation how brave you are, I must act—like a warrior who does what must be done and not a proud child."

"She is my sister," Red Bear said.

"She is part white," countered Stone Bear.

"She is more loyal that you will ever be," hissed Red Bear, cocking the rifle.

"No!" called out Dawn, walking over to put her left hand on the barrel and lower it as she glared into the eyes of her brother. "I'm the one he wanted." Her face glowed in savage anticipation. "He talked about the things he would do. Let him have the chance." She drew the knife Crayne had given back to her before he fled. "If he has the courage."

They stood watching each other. Neither one was in a hurry. Dawn's eyes flicked towards Crayne. The message was clear: stay out. He thought about how fast he could reach his gun if it all went bad. He could do it, but there would be a high risk of killing someone who, if not innocent, was at least not his intended target. He nodded back, not liking it. Then her eyes locked on the big man.

The big Sioux looked confident. Dawn looked nervous and afraid. Her eyes kept darting around as if she expected help to waltz in and rescue her. She backed up every time the big man moved and kept moving away until she started to run out of open space to run away in. Dawn backed away a little more. The big man's smirk grew as Dawn moved closer and closer to the circle of onlookers. Her eyes darted from side to side, as if now that she was confronted with what she had asked for, she was looking for a way to escape.

When her room was all used up, the big man closed, not taking any precautions—counting on size and strength to wipe out the woman he thought was afraid of him. The man moved fast for a large hulk, blade slashing towards Dawn's body in a sweeping cut that ripped her jacket. That was too close. There was no more room to back up. The large man's eyes telegraphed the next slash. Dawn steeled herself; Crayne knew what she was planning. The blade flashed, and a gash opened up on her left cheek, sending blood streaking down her face.

The blade had barely finished gouging its thin, red line, and the onlookers were still gasping when Dawn grabbed the hand that swung the knife and pulled it down even as she brought her foot up, kicking the big man square in the gut, ending the roar of triumph in a howl of pain. The big man staggered in pain and surprise. He forgot to move. She threw one punch at his unguarded face, sending blood and teeth spurting from his mouth to spray her and the dirt with red mist. Dawn kicked a second time, with one heel landing on the bent-over big man's nose.

The man writhed. Dawn lost her purchase and landed with a thud. The partially blinded man swung a backhanded slash at her body as she rose, cutting her jacket again but giving her the opening she wanted. She grabbed the hand and twisted the wrist, sending the knife clattering to the ground. Dawn reached for it, but a foot in her ribs slammed her hard. The big man grabbed down and pulled her up, slamming her in the face with a fist. He put his hands around her neck. Crayne was yelling for her to move. The man squeezed. Then he contorted in pain. With her knife jammed in his unprotected ribs, Dawn head-butted the broken nose, breaking the intensity of the grip. The man flopped to the ground. Dawn rose to stand over him. He rose with one last roar, but the wound in his side was too much. He was slow. She was quick. She kicked him behind one knee. He fell a final time. She pulled the knife from his ribs. Blood spurted. With the man's arms flailing she reached under them for the unprotected throat and ended it with swift efficiency.

During the fight, the circle of watchers had contracted as they gazed on the spectacle. Two had hung back—the other two who rode with Stone Bear. Wet Britches was reaching for something under the blanket slung over his shoulder. Crayne had seen enough to know what was coming. "Down!" he yelled.

Red Bear sent a knife toward one of the renegades as he shrugged aside the blanket over his shoulder and lifted a rifle. The knife missed, but the renegade had to move aside to miss it. Crayne fired four shots fast. Two hit Wet Britches, one in the chest and one lower. He was staggering from the impact, doubled over as he made a wobbly circle.

The lone renegade now confronted eight rifles pointed at him. He lowered his rifle.

"This is my sister," said Red Bear, walking to him. "You would betray me? You would betray the hospitality I offered you? You would do this?"

"She is not one of us," said the remaining renegade. "It is as Stone Bear said. A man will pay money for them. We heard this at the fort. A man in Cheyenne. Money buys food, Red Bear. Money buys guns."

"What is this man's name?" asked Crayne, moving forward. "Tell me his name!"

"You are a spirit, Raccoon Eyes," said the man. "Spirits belong back in the spirit world. Ask me then."

He was raising the rifle when eight guns spoke.

Crayne knelt by the dying Indian. "His name. Tell me his name so the ghosts of your people will not hunt you down for all time."

Noises and red emerged from his mouth. Then nothing.

Crayne angrily jammed his gun back into its holster. He had been close to unraveling the mystery behind the scalp trading. Now he was back to guessing in the dark. He would think about it later.

Dawn's cut had stopped bleeding. The light of combat was still in her eyes as Crayne touched her unwounded cheek.

"Had to, Crayne. You didn't hear what he said."

"I promise never to complain again about the stew," he said lightly. "Ever."

Red Bear joined them.

"This is what has happened from all of these wars of your people, Crayne. They were lost; their people went with Sitting Bull to Canada. They rode alone these past years, or with others like them. My people, your people"—he looked at Crayne—"they are all alike when they ride beyond where the People should go. You asked before about us. There are dozens, hundreds, of people like us, Crayne. Indians left behind by the treaties . . . white men who never found the gold they wanted. The land was once like a beautiful bowl, Crayne. Today that bowl is shattered pieces. It is not for me to know; perhaps one day it will become a beautiful bowl again, but I will only see the pieces." He moved off to join his men and oversee the disposal of the bodies.

"Are you badly injured?" Crayne asked Dawn.

"Got hurt worse as a kid. Mostly with that one there. Jacket needs mending." She shrugged, wishing to put behind her any expression of the disapproval she was sure was in his face. "Don't expect you to understand, Crayne, but there are things I can't let go. Won't let go. Taken all I'm going to take."

Justice. It was all about justice, whether with rocks in the streets of London or knives in Wyoming. "You're wrong, Dawn. I do understand. I do."

She moved in closer to him. He could smell the blood that was now staining his shirt as she leaned into him. "What do we do, Crayne? You planning on riding with him?"

Crayne shook his head. "I'm not native to here, Dawn. Not an Indian either. I understand not being able to walk away from your own fight. Don't like seeing you put your life on the line."

"Unless you are doing that with me?" She had that look on her face he had come to know.

"Something like that, Dawn." He put an arm over her shoulders. Tomorrow could wait for a few minutes. "Once you regain your breath from trying to accomplish your death, I shall tell you how I plan to risk both our necks."

"You writers have all manner of fine words for a girl, Crayne."

"I do my best." They walked away, hand in hand.

Red Bear watched. There would be a fight soon. They were born to battle, Dawn and her man. It was in their souls; it was on the wind. He was grateful the spirits sent her a partner with whom she could fight the world.

He shouted for his men to prepare. When they rode, he was sure, they would need every gun. He did not expect they would be idle very long.

The dead were buried. Red Bear, out of caution, wanted the day spent in waiting to be sure Dawn was not followed.

"Do I look that stupid?" she asked her half brother.

"I am responsible to my friends for their lives," he replied placidly. "If these three knew there were men looking for you, there are others. I do not care, but do you know why you are of such interest?"

They summarized what they had done and where they had been. "My best guess," said Crayne at last, "is that, although Jack thought this colonel was the man at the top of whatever has been going on in the scalp-trading business, there is someone else who knows we know about the business. I sat in jail and tried to figure it, but I couldn't."

Red Bear asked Dawn about her life with Jack. She talked about all manner of things, including her work with Franz in the printer's shop.

"When he bought the shop, he acquired this thing called a camera," she explained. "He let me use it. He said that what they call 'photographers' in the big cities can take the photographs and make thousands of them. When I told him there was a fear among our people that the picture captured a piece of the soul, he let me take his picture. Then he ripped it up. Nothing happened. It was nothing more than paper and some things he put on it."

"Pictures."

Dawn and Red Bear looked at Crayne.

"That is how we will do it," he said with a smile that she

knew meant he had resolved whatever had been on his mind. "Someone in New York City has been manipulating us. It is time that we returned the favor. Red Bear, I need you to wait here for a while. Can you?"

The Cheyenne nodded.

"Dawn, I need Franz and his camera so that we can tell the world something very, very important. Once I think this through, you need to take the risk of riding into town to bring him here. My friend is going to cover the story of his life."

Chapter Eleven

Red Bear and his men edged north toward rougher ground, fearing they might be found. Crayne could not believe that rugged hills and flat prairie could exist so close together. Some of the lane seemed like the giant top of a rough-hewn table with dotted grasslands waving in a wind that never fully died away. Crayne wondered if anyone ever grew tired of looking at Wyoming. He didn't.

Guns!

Crayne was suddenly the last one in line as Red Bear and his warriors kicked their horses to an instant gallop.

"Ride, slowpoke!" Dawn called over her shoulder.

Crayne did not understand. One minute, caution was all there was in the world. The next, it was discarded for a mad dash to who knew where.

He rode.

The country they were riding through was rugged. Red Bear seemed to know a path around the jagged rocks that poked up with no apparent pattern. He waved and pointed, and the group split as the sound became clearer—a small and ragged volley of guns and a very hesitant reply. More guns in the volley than those firing back. One side had rifles; the other, rifles and pistols. More than that, Crayne could not discern, and he was proud of himself for that knowledge.

"How do you know what to do?" he asked Red Bear.

"Rustlers, thieves, or someone fighting a small rancher or

farmer," said Red Bear. "It does not matter who it is, because whoever is being attacked is the one we help. These are very good people. They are Basques, from across the great water. How they came to be here I do not know, but they open their home when my men and I are near. They hurt no one. They raise sheep. They make things from the wool to sell."

Crayne was unable to learn more, for, at that moment, the side with the rifles began to fire in a volley that did not seem as though it would end.

"Hey-hah!" called Red Bear. He, Dawn, two others, and Crayne, who lagged behind, rode for the guns.

Crayne could see that a group of cowboys, whose horses were behind them, had attacked a ranch. Several bodies lay on the ground in a corral. The attack must have brought about some kind of response, because three or four people, who were using the corner of the house for cover, were firing at the dozen or so cowboys.

The cowboys turned to meet the threat from Red Bear and Dawn. Rifles fired as the Indians lowered themselves to the necks of their horses to present as small a target as possible. Crayne, aware Dawn was scolding him to do something, wondered how they could do that and not fall off.

Crayne belatedly realized he was now the most visible of all targets. There were no trees and no fences to hide behind. He had no hopes of hitting anyone with a rifle from the back of a horse.

The only weapon he had was the one he was riding.

"Let's go, Dakota."

He could hear Red Bear and those with him firing from his right as he spurred Dakota for one of the few times in the horse's life. It responded by leaping forward and charging at the men who were torn between taking the easy shot at him and firing at those trying to kill them.

Crayne was now up to them. One man tried to stand in front of Dakota to have a good shot at Crayne, but he lingered too long after his first shot, which hit Crayne in the right ankle, failed to stop the horse and rider. His scream was all Crayne heard as the horse pounded over him.

Crayne passed the men and was now among their horses as he tried to rein in Dakota. He pulled his revolver and fired it up in the air. Again. The horses, between Dakota's charge and the guns, spooked and began to gallop away from the fight, which swelled in volume behind Crayne.

He was able to regain control of Dakota and turned back. The fight was over. The men whom Red Bear had sent away had circled around and come upon the cowboys from behind. No one had seemed to want to surrender, or no one was asked to. Not one cowboy was standing as Crayne dismounted. He realized then that the pain in his ankle was from a wound as he saw the flapping hole in the leather of his boot.

He stopped cold.

"I know this man," he told Dawn and Red Bear as they approached.

"Are you crazy?" called Dawn. "What were you thinking? Most lame-brained thing I ever saw, and, with everything this one ever did"—she jerked a thumb at Red Bear—"that's saying something. You want to be dead, or you forget that this ain't some little scene you wrote?"

"I've seen him," Crayne repeated.

"Who cares?" Dawn exploded. "Are you listening to me, or do you have no explanation for how you almost let someone kill you because you still don't understand how to fight out here?"

Red Bear was moving away to the lumps on the ground. Some men and women who had hidden from behind the house were now running there as well.

"We're alive, Dawn. We can fight later," Crayne said as he

limped over as well. He missed the look she gave him.

"Are they dead?" Red Bear said as he rose from one body, looking at the cowboys.

"More or less," replied Dawn.

Red Bear fired a bullet into the mass of bodies.

"Brother?"

"See this, sister? See what they have done? See what has been allowed to happen here? See this horrible thing."

Red Bear pointed to the body of a girl, perhaps twelve. She had been shot several times through the body, but that was not what had driven Red Bear to anger.

Long cuts had been made across her forehead and down her hairline on each side. Even Crayne, who knew the least of any of them, knew that someone had wanted to take the little girl's scalp. Other warriors with Red Bear were kneeling by two others who were dead—a woman and another girl.

"Dawn! They can't see this." Crayne pointed to the onrushing family members.

"You can't hide all the white man's ugly, Crayne," she snapped but along with Red Bear walked over to meet the onrushing collection of older men and women. "Happy with what you see? You talk all philosophical, Crayne, and you mean well, but this makes me want to kill and rip every one of them to pieces. Killing every one of them five times would be too easy on them. And you? You stand there and worry about being proper. When you gonna care? When you gonna get mad enough to get even like Jack did?"

The agony and anguish from the Indians was almost more than Crayne could bear. At first, he had privately condemned Red Bear as a savage for firing blindly into the pile of the dead. Now, he understood.

Ernesto Ortega, who had come from the hilly regions of the

Spanish peninsula to raise sheep in peace, explained what had happened.

"We were tending to the sheep. Maria, Donna, and Christa were watching the house and feeding the chickens," he said. Crayne looked at the slaughtered birds. Vicious.

"We heard shots. A lot of shots. It took time to get here, because we had walked to the pasture. When we arrived, they were already dead. They were . . ."

Red Bear's face was a study in rage as the old man stopped talking and gestured emptily with his hands. Dawn glared at Crayne.

"I don't understand," Crayne said. "Why?"

"Their hair, Crayne!" Dawn was screaming. "Want to touch it? I want to kill them all. I want to put a gun to them and kill them. Whoever buys these."

She saw Crayne's blank look.

"Spanish, Mexican, whatever they are they have black hair that is straight, Crayne. Close enough to Injun hair for some scalp hunter. They've killed so many Indians now they need other people."

Crayne's mouth hung open. That had never occurred to him.

"Red Bear! Cowboys!" One of Red Bear's warriors rode hard into the ranch yard.

Red Bear put his fingers to his mouth and whistled. His men ran to their horses.

"If we are found here, Ernesto, they will kill us and blame us for this. We must go. We shall return and keep watch, but we must go." He turned to Dawn, who had looked toward Crayne but seemed unsure what to do. "Sister?"

Dawn was stroking the hair of one of the dead girls, face twisted in misery and rage. She looked at Red Bear uncomprehendingly.

"We must go."

"Go with them," Crayne told her.

She said nothing.

"We do not know who is coming, but, if they catch you here, they may kill you. I can talk my way out of anything. As you keep telling me, I'm a white man. Go!"

She ran for her horse as Red Bear's men swept from the ranch yard. She did not look back.

The riders were a group of neighbor ranchers who had heard the gunfire. Disregarding almost everything Ernesto said in his flawed English, a portion of the group went riding after the Indians who they were sure were responsible.

For the first time since the Washita, Crayne knew this was something he could write without notes. This was not simply war between peoples, but murder for the sake of gain—and a sick, twisted purpose was behind it. He understood Dawn's rage. He battled for her, not because of her cause, but because it was her. Until this day he had thought that would be enough.

Crayne did not dare take off his boot, for fear the ankle would swell so much he could not put it back on. It did not bleed much, but it ached. He helped build coffins. He had done it before. They laid the two girls in one, for that is what the family wanted. The ceremony to bury them was simple. Ernesto read a few words from a book in their language. One by one, family members and friends stepped to the grave to speak. Then it was Crayne's turn.

"I do not understand this," he said. "I do not know how, or when, but I know that one day the men who are behind this will be caught and punished even as those were who did the terrible killing." He looked across their faces. "I will not rest until that day."

When the graves were filled, he saddled Dakota, but, before he could leave the ranch, a posse led by Fairweather filled the ranch yard. Crayne thought about running, but it seemed pointless. The posse knew there had been a massacre, and its members wanted to shoot somebody, and anybody would do.

"You!"

"Marshal."

"What are you doing here? No. Don't tell me. Guidry, Morris. Watch him. He moves, shoot him."

Fairweather spoke with Ernesto and the family, and then some of the ranchers and neighbors who had stayed for the funerals. Then it was Crayne's turn.

"You killed Newsom's man."

"Self defense."

"No witnesses to say otherwise."

"Marshal, I can't go back to jail." He tried to explain about what had happened to the Basques.

"Save it, son. First jail, then conversation. And if you try running, much as I hate to do it, you will be shot dead. Law might not be what we want, but it's the law, son, and it is what I live by. Maybe you want to try living by it this once, since you have no other choice?"

A crash followed by extended cursing broke the limping staccato of inexpert hammering. Crayne limped to the window of his makeshift cell in the back of Hiram Overby's store, leg still smarting from the wound he had received. He pulled himself up by the window's recently installed bars for a look-see. At least the view was better here than the jail. Fairweather had told the town fathers of Colquitt Springs that he refused to use the old jail until it could be properly cleaned of Hartsfield's blood, meaning Crayne was locked in a room that smelled like onions and potatoes.

Sure enough. When the dust cleared, the gallows was toppled and its platform shattered. Another construction mishap. He didn't know whether to smile or not. Maybe he should volunteer to see it done right. That would be a first for Colquitt Springs.

Events had moved at lightning speed when Crayne returned from the massacre of the Basque family. Judge John Calhoun had come out from Cheyenne, given Crayne a fifteen-minute trial, and said he should hang for murder and inciting Indians. Newsom was smirking in the background of the saloon that offered free drinks when the entertainment was over and had shaken hands with the judge afterward. The judge seemed to know Newsom well.

Fairweather was irate but kept saying there was nothing he could do because the law had spoken.

Then Crayne sat for two days while they built a gallows. He knew he should try to escape. The bars on his cell were loose enough, being barely set in the stone before he was plunked there to await hanging. He hadn't ever tried. Even if he escaped, he was limping so badly he would be quickly and easily caught. Time was not on his side. One of these days, the folks of Colquitt Springs were going to grow sick of trying to build his gallows and shoot him. He shouldn't find it amusing. It was.

Today was not that day. Slow feet were coming down the warped wood floor of the hall to his cell, preceded by the smell of strong coffee. Crayne lowered himself gingerly, wincing as he hit the floor, to prepare for whatever might be breakfast in a friendship that had been an odd byproduct of his confinement.

He waited for the noises. The wooden chair across the hallway scraped along the floor. It was used by the guards. At first, they watched him all day when they thought he was more energetic than he was. They gave up watching out of boredom except for old Henry Watkins in the afternoon, who liked to play checkers. Then Henry found better things to do. A key turned in the lock of the door to what had been Hiram's storeroom until commandeered by the town until such time as they could hang Crayne.

"Take this before I burn my hand off," grumbled Fairweather, holding a cup of steaming coffee. Crayne grabbed the cup and looked. No food today. Yesterday there were eggs. Maybe later. He had the time to wait.

He sat down on the edge of the cot that was the room's sole piece of furniture. "Boys aren't doing too well with my gallows, Marshal. Might die of old age here waitin' to be hung." Fairweather grimaced. "I'll help 'em if you want. Get me out of this cell. Somethin' different to do. 'Town Hangs Man on Gallows He Built.' Maybe I could be written about in a newspaper story from some place that don't ever have anything happen much. Maybe the *Global Reporter* will take a first-person account. Can't go faster than an old dog right now so I'm not much of a risk to run. Gettin' tired of waitin'."

Fairweather had no retort. Usually, there was banter with the coffee.

"Somethin' wrong, Marshal? Jennie isn't worse, is she?"

"Matter of time or so they tell me," Fairweather said, not wanting to talk of his fading wife. "Matter of time." The marshal sighed and took off his hat, running his fingers through his gray hair that retained islands of its reddish-brown color. His big, drooping mustache twitched. It reminded Crayne of a cat's tail when he did that. "I want the straight of it, Crayne."

"Told you a few times."

"Tell me again."

"That man was going to kill me. Those Basques were killed by white men. Someone out there is murdering people to sell their hair. Newsom is involved."

"How do you know?"

"Because I'm here."

Fairweather kept staring at Crayne, as if his mournful, dark eyes could distill the truth. Then he stared through him and spoke.

"An old Cheyenne called One Wing came in to town yesterday. Scared fella. Told me about some things. Guess whoever has been attacking families has been busy. Didn't know the half of it. Seems more than one family's been attacked. Cowboys put it down to not liking sheepmen. There were maybe five-six attacks in the past two years. Few Mexican herders' families. Dead are all women. Scalped. Couple men, but they had long hair. Seems something out there is really happening, Crayne."

Being right was not much consolation. Still, he felt his pulse race.

"Don't fret on it, Marshal, unless you worry that gallows is going to take a few upright and law-abiding folks with it who come out for the entertainment of a hanging." The lopsided grin emerged.

"Crayne, I was born eight miles down the road. Never been out of the territory. Never gonna. This is my land, my town, my home. My kids' home. Seen the cavalry ride through. Seen good Indians and bad whites. Other way around, too. This don't set to rights."

"Appreciate the sentiment, Marshal. Don't say that too loud, though. They hang folks like that."

Fairweather looked at Crayne a long time in silence, as if making a final judgment.

"Crayne, if tonight the door down the hall ain't locked, rickety thing it is because the Buford brothers never set it right, and this here one ain't locked because there's marks on it like you picked it, I suppose you might go for a stroll." Crayne wondered if he had a head wound he didn't know about.

Fairweather continued. "Your horse is in the stable because we can't sell him legal like until you're dead. If he happened to be all saddled and ready and you were escaped and such, I'd be the first to lead a posse after you and bring you back, because I know you said you were heading east to Missouri."

Eyes met eyes. Crayne got the drift now. "I did say that. Certainly did. Forgot it. Remember it now. My Great-aunt Maude in Missouri. Do need to ride to see her, now that you mention it."

"Good." The marshal rose, anxious to make the visit quick now that he had done the deed. Privacy did not exist in a small town. "Long as you don't ride around in Wyoming. That woman, them Injuns, they gonna end up dead one day, Crayne. Only one winner when you fight the world."

Crayne knew that well. He had not expected to see Dawn again after his trial. Maybe on the other side.

"Why, Marshal? Why?" Nobody gave Crayne a break. Never.

"Crayne, there's the law, and there's justice." Fairweather looked pained. "They give me this star and said to be the law. When the law don't bring justice, then the time has come for the man who is the law to fix the way the law does its work. What with Jennie and all, a man gets to thinking about a lot of things. Dyin'. Livin'. Right and wrong. Things that keep us from doin' what's right. When death itself don't matter, because whatever life holds is goin' away, it changes how you see this world, Crayne. Then there's you. Scribbler. Franz tells me tales. Pinkertons tell me tales. You ride on both sides of the law at the same time. For a man who don't seem to care about which side of the line you ride, you have a lot of people on the right side think all this is a raw deal and that you ought to not die for being dropped in the middle of whatever it is that is going on out there. Guess I'm one."

Fairweather rose with a slight groan.

"Not comin' to tuck you in tonight, so take the cup when you're done. Don't need to advertise the service or every drunk will want it." He turned away. "Forgot. Told my brother-in-law that gallows needed to fall at least three times before he could be done with it, but it's hard watching him build that badly on purpose. And one more thing, Crayne. Don't really care if the jail smells of blood. But if I locked you there again, we never could have played this little game. So you owe me. You know I have rules. Think on those rules when you get out of this town. Good Book says to pass on what gets given to you, so, when the time comes, Crayne, be there for somebody who maybe don't deserve it but maybe does."

He turned and walked away. The door shut. The lock never clicked.

Hiram Overby was a trusting man. He closed up, never looking back to see if the storeroom was locked. Crayne waited. The cell seemed more airless than usual. Darkness fell. Noises! A key turned the lock on the hallway door. A hinge squeaked. Feet receded. A tiny bell jingled as the store's outer door shut.

The voice in his head warned of a trap. A man lived or died on trust. Did he trust Fairweather? Another voice asked if it mattered: waiting to hang or being shot down trying to run? One choice.

The indoor hinges squeaked a mite too much for comfort. No one was there to hear them. He was in Hiram's store. He took his time, taking the things a man on the run would need. Not much moving out on the town's street. He watched a long time. He opened the outer door a crack. No bell would advertise his leaving. Outdoors. For a moment, he breathed free air. The stars through his window had been one square; now the full majesty of night enveloped him. For a moment, the thrill of the night flooded him like a fever. He waited and listened. The town of Colquitt Springs was small enough to only have a few buildings. The saloon was two doors down from the store and the stable on the far side. Only the saloon did much business in the dark. Lamps were lit inside. The direct route was a risk. He looped around behind the buildings, fearing his boots would make noise.

A creaking one-word sign moved in the light breeze. The stable doors were closed. There would be noise, and he was still slow from the ankle wound. He waited again. Patient wolves lived; impatient ones didn't.

Now! He pushed open the bolt; it positively shrieked.

He looked in the dimness. Sure enough, a saddled horse was waiting near the door. It was Dakota, the only friend Crayne was certain he had left in the world.

The scraping of a match and its flare into light were simultaneous. "Not so fast. Hands high."

Vigilance Committee Chairman Buck Hartsfield, with a shotgun in one hand and a lantern in the other, was regarding Crayne. Another man stood to his side, pointing a gun at Fairweather, whose hands were in the air and whose look of shame and defeat moved Crayne to pity. Hartsfield and Newsom had been grinning with the judge when they hauled Crayne away after his trial.

"Delbert here said there was a long powwow this morning. Been paying him to listen. He heard some from the outside of your cell. Here we are," Hartsfield gloated, pointing at the young man, who Crayne recognized as one of the vagrants who hung around Overby's while he was jailed there. "Wasn't sure until I saw the horse had saddled himself. That right, Marshal? Or did the horse have help? He focused on Crayne. "You murdered a good man, and you are going to pay."

"Man I killed was worth less than what a man cleans out of a stall," spoke up Crayne, in a long, lazy affected drawl. He looked defiance at Hartsfield. Made a guess. "Blood do tell." He looked alert, not defeated. "Not feeling repentant. Your brother was worthless trash."

"Put those hands up," commanded Hartsfield. "Then turn around."

"Can I shoot him, Buck?" asked Delbert. "Can I shoot him now? Please?"

"He's all yours, Delbert, once we take him outside," spoke Hartsfield. "We want it clear Crayne was trying to escape, and we happened to be here to kill him after he gunned down the marshal. Not gonna let the family know you were a turncoat, Marshal. Owe poor Jennie and the girl that much. Owe you nuthin'."

"Went looking for something to eat and ended up turned around, Buck," replied Crayne, buying time with phony words. He found himself slipping into the speech pattern of the men he wrote about. "Thought I'd see how the horse is eatin'. Don't know what the fuss is about. Told the marshal today I'd help the boys with the gallows since all them boys have so much trouble. Seein's how they're your kin I shouldn't be surprised."

"Laugh now, Crayne. I'll laugh over your body in a minute. Now, Delbert." Delbert chortled. He shoved Fairweather. Crayne moved at the same time. He stumbled.

"No tricks," yelled Hartsfield.

The light shimmered; it could have been a trick of the eyes. Then they heard the noise. In the circle of light from the lamp, a large-handled knife Hiram Overby never was going to have the chance to sell was poking out of Hartsfield's chest.

"No!" exclaimed Delbert, shifting his gun to sight on Crayne. The lantern swung wildly as Hartsfield pitched and gurgled. It fell to the straw along with the shotgun as Hartsfield clutched at the knife. The weird dance of shadows on the stable walls and the flaring of the light made Delbert fire wildly. Fairweather tried to wrestle the gun away.

The shotgun in Hartsfield's dying hands went off as the man

writhed. Fairweather tumbled. A revolver barked. The vigilance committee leader stopped moving. A shiny new smoking .45 was in Crayne's hands, pulled from a stiff leather gun belt Crayne had liberated from Overby's store.

Crayne now had the gun trained on the vigilance committee chairman's toady. "Give it up, boy," he said. "Give it up."

Delbert held his hands high. He gestured with his chin behind Crayne. "Crayne, we got other things to worry about. Look behind you."

Oil and flame from the lantern were mixing with dry hay. Fumes said something had caught. Dakota whinnied. Crayne risked a quick look. The young man saw his chance and took it. He should not have. Crayne's new gun shot a hair to the left, but it didn't matter. Delbert crumpled to the ground, moaning until the fourth shot hit.

Sparing barely a look for Hartsfield and Delbert, Crayne knelt by Fairweather.

"C'mon, Marshal, let's get you out of here," he said. Fairweather's head flopped as Crayne lifted his body. The flickering light showed a lot of wet around the wound from the shotgun's slug. Dead? Crayne still had to save him. He dragged him outside.

He deserved to be laid out proper. He looked around hoping someone was near, but either no one heard the shots or no one cared enough to leave a card game to investigate. He had to go.

First, he needed something more than a gun. Crayne patted down Hartsfield. A jacket pocket had a wad of green folding money. Another had a small purse that was heavy with coins. Hartsfield didn't need them. He did. The flames were spreading.

He mounted Dakota. There was an acrid smell. Straw and hot oil. A good man would take the horses out first. A desperate man would ride. For a second he thought Fairweather moved.

Trick of light.

He fired his brand-new gun two times in the air, reloaded fast, and repeated the noise-making, then ran inside the stable and untied every horse he could find.

Horses were going every which way as some loud voices approached.

"Fire!" one yelled. "Fire!" He pointed toward the stable. Men ran to rescue the horses. A couple of faces turned as they passed Crayne as, at the edge of the fire's glow, he mounted Dakota. Then they pointed.

Someone identified him. "That writer! He's getting away," yelled a voice in the crowd. There was a smattering of gunfire, but he was well beyond pistol range.

Then the noise was left behind, then the glow of the fire, and soon there was nothing at all under the stars but a free man who had cheated death looking at the stars to find his way.

Chapter Twelve

The New York City offices of the *Global Reporter* were a dangerous place to be; when Southern's rage grew beyond words, he threw whatever was nearest. Ink pots could not only be deadly, they could ruin a suit of clothes that cost many weeks' pay.

The telegram still lay on Southern's desk, the worse for the many times it had been balled up and thrown against a wall or whoever might have been in its path.

The telegram explained that the seven words were found in a note stuck to Franz Schultz's printing shop door. Schultz, in a rare bit of friendship to a competitor, had shared them with Newsom, who shared them with Southern.

"*Global Reporter:* I am coming for you," were the words of the message. The telegram said that a crude J was underneath. Half of the Jack of Spades was attached to the note, which was being sent by mail.

"Schultz did not say a word about this to anyone?" Southern asked again.

"Newsom made it worth his while not to," Sullivan said, repeating the message for the tenth time, while wondering what had been in the other communications that had come from Wyoming. Newsom was shifty.

"Better be enough. Man could ruin us with an exclusive."

"He no longer has the note," Sullivan said.

"What? No one told me."

"Newsom did," Sullivan said levelly, trying to shut the old

man's mouth. He had forgotten that Newsom told that to him and not Southern.

"Need the army to know. Sherman. No. Not yet. Out there. Fort Laramie or whatever is closer. Reward for these men—Crayne and this Jack."

Sullivan then asked a bland question, trying to keep his voice neutral. "Dead, sir, or alive?"

"They are a menace, Sullivan. A menace. See to it, Sullivan. Dead or alive."

"You let them hang him?"

Franz Schultz was dreaming of a night in Germany many years ago when the police prodded him with their clubs, only to awake and find a very cold rifle barrel poking into his side through the thin cloth of his nightshirt.

Franz could barely hear Clara's muted response, and the words "Should have."

"Do not move!" Dawn said harshly. "You were his friend, and he's gone and dead?"

"He is gone, young woman, but very much alive," Clara said with asperity. "You may either put down that weapon or leave, because I do not allow this behavior in my own home." Franz could almost see wills battling in the semi-darkness.

Dawn lowered the rifle.

"I shall make tea," Clara said, rising. "I will not have coffee at this hour." She glared at Dawn as she passed her. "Did you wipe your feet? No, of course not! This is a stable. I told you Franz we should have moved to San Francisco."

She walked down the hall, naming all the places she knew they should have gone to instead of Wyoming. Franz watched her go with a smile, a dark figure in the dimness of the night—the light of his life.

"As I told you, he is alive," Franz said. "May I have a moment to dress, unless you fear an ambush? You can wait in the kitchen."

By the time Franz emerged from the bedroom, dressed, he was greeted by his wife's long summary of all the evils visited upon poor Dawn by "that rogue and ruffian Crayne." Franz smiled broadly. He wondered once that, if Crayne had not existed, he would have had to invent him, so Clara would have someone to scold instead of him.

He kissed her on the cheek. "I married well."

"You did," she replied. "There are some who cannot say this."

Dawn saw their eyes lock a minute and felt envious that any two people that old could still care so much, when no one seemed to care for her at all.

Franz ran through Crayne's arrest, confinement, and eventual escape. The marshal, he said, was now expected to live, but with his body badly burned he might never be a lawman again.

"Where is Crayne?"

"I thought he might be with you," Franz replied.

"We did not . . . I said things when we found the girls," she said. "I was angry, and he . . . he doesn't understand."

"That was upsetting," Franz said. "He left me this to print, along with a message to the *Global Reporte*r that I have already passed along. I am not sure whether to print it or not."

Dawn looked at the paper by the light of the flickering candle.

"Death roams the Shadowlands," it began. "It preys on the weak, the defenseless, and those no one who has the power to stop it cares to know exists."

The article then listed killings, some of which Dawn knew nothing about, ending with the deaths of the little Basque girls.

"And who will be next?" it read. "The girl whose hair can be sold, the old man whose fingers can be trinkets, or the child to be slaughtered with impunity to please those hypocrites in the East who—if the just God in which we believe were to come to

Earth this moment—would be put in a fire to which Hell would be as a cool breeze.

"Death begets death. The circle still turns. Tomorrow, or the tomorrow after a thousand tomorrows, the man on the top will be the man at the bottom. For the dead will be avenged. –The Jack of Justice."

Dawn's eyes were wet when she handed it back.

"Yes," she said. "Print it. He wants them afraid that Jack is hunting them."

"Then I shall print it," Franz said happily. "I shall sell dozens of newspapers!"

"I never knew what he felt about anything," Dawn remonstrated.

"He speaks little," Franz said. "He only really communicates when he writes. The rest of the time he is like ice and stone."

"Tell me where he is!"

"He came here briefly right after he escaped, about two weeks ago. He left this, another note, and some instructions. I burned the instructions. I do not know what he is doing. For a while, I know we were watched, but I do not think so now. I do not know."

Dawn said she was sure they were not. She rose.

"Stay," said Clara. "Have a meal. A bath perhaps. Maybe a few meals. Then see how you feel and what you want to do. You look like you have been an outer law for days."

"Outlaw," corrected Franz.

"He fixes my words. Mr. Scholar. Ask him to fix an egg, girl, and see what a mess there would be. Listen to Clara!"

She could hardly not. Dawn agreed. She would spend two days in Colquitt Springs and then go back to where Red Bear and his men were hiding.

For most of the first day, she slept. The second, she ate. Clara packed her a sack with bread and meat—more than Red Bear's men ate in a normal day.

"Crayne survives," Franz told her as she prepared to leave. "Civilization goes only so deep in him, child. He ran wild on the streets of London when he was a child, and for all of his words and all of his writing, there is still that wild person in there. He will find you, and you will find him. In time."

Dawn wondered as she walked to her horse if he was watching. Only a fool would return to a place where he was still a wanted man, even though Fairweather was healing much better than expected.

"I have some very pointed things to say to him when you find him," the marshal had gasped to Dawn when she went to his house to see him. "Want to find out for sure if he tried to fry me or save me, girl. Been hearing it both ways. Everybody is looking for him and that Jack fella. Find him first."

That would not be easy, with self-appointed posses roaming the plains and a five-thousand-dollar reward issued by Crayne's former magazine. Crayne was too much an Easterner to survive, she thought. Then she realized he had already fooled everyone for two weeks.

She put down the sack and tossed the red blanket over the back of her horse. A paper fluttered out.

"Flat ridge east end box draw."

Dawn looked around. No one appeared to have seen the paper. She tucked it in the sack Clara gave her, threw it and the leather bag she had brought with her that carried her ammunition and a few other things over the horse's back, and rode west out of town.

She tried to think of the landscape. The rough country was to the east and north. She would head west a while, then drift north before doubling back. Other than a few stares, no one in

Colquitt Springs had bothered her, but she was not taking chances.

Her opinion of Crayne's skills started to fall when she saw the thin column of blue smoke that was highlighted by the early morning sun. She had camped on the plains the previous night. She would be patient. The longer she took, the more chance she would spot anyone.

Why bother? She shook her head. The fool might as well have stood on the hill and screamed his location. The plume went high. Anyone ten miles away could see it.

She rode towards it, wary. That beacon would attract anyone hunting Crayne. She crossed a creek bed that in spring and winter flowed, but now was dust. There must have been water underground, because the grass grew thin on the banks with some scrubby little bushes nearby as well. The growth was thick enough that it all but choked off the path she was following, forcing her down a steep-sided bank, which was strewn with dead branches and twigs that snapped loudly as her horse walked over them, picking its way along.

Dawn's brain finished telling her that this was not natural at the same moment she heard the click of a gun.

"Took long enough. Good squaw would have had my food here days ago."

"Tenderfoot directions," she replied. "Ain't your food."

He stepped out from the area where he had hidden himself, tossing aside branches he had cut. She saw a ragged beard and gaunt features below vast dark circles that framed his eyes. He was hatless, with windblown hair. He reeked of fatigue.

She nodded.

"Progress. Not a bad trap, even though I knew it was one from a mile away. Might be as good as a ten-year-old Cheyenne pretty soon, if you keep learning."

"Fooled you."

"Knew it was you."

"He didn't." Crayne gestured with the gun toward the boots that stuck out from under a bush. "Probably good thing he came along. I was down to seven shells and no water. We better move along. Not safe here."

He mounted Dakota. Looked back.

"Good to see you. I was not sure you would come."

Dawn hated apologies. They were rare and uncomfortable. Crayne seemed to know what was coming. He waved at the air.

"Talk later. Ride now."

Watching this man who now seemed to have all the veneer of his Eastern ways peeled away, a man who had fooled her and killed a man while traveling alone, she wondered exactly who—and what—she was riding with.

They made camp for the night in a crevice in the rock wall of the small canyon. The place allowed them to see anyone coming. Dawn built the fire behind the rocks where it could not be seen easily.

Crayne started with her departure and, leaving out things he did not want to share, explained how he came to be on the run.

"You used me," she said after a time.

"A little," he admitted. "Someone was watching Franz and Clara's shop. I thought it was better that they think they had everything as they wanted. If you came to see them, someone would see you. They would rifle whatever you brought. All I had to do was wait. I also had left Franz and Clara a description of the place so if someone came and tried to force an answer from them, they could give it. I wasn't sure when he came by which had happened."

"Still does not set right, Crayne. Why do they want you dead?" She paused. "Other than the obvious reasons anyone could give." She tried a small smile.

"I don't need a list of those," he answered, grinning. "And not from you, young lady, in particular."

He stretched. Anything anyone else cooked was better than everything he could prepare.

"Best I can guess, Dawn, someone thinks I know something about who was behind those scalp hunters. That someone is willing to kill to stop whatever it is I am supposed to know from being shared. Problem is, I don't know anything. No, not right. I have a lot of guesses, but nothing certain."

"Plan to share?"

"No. Not yet. Not until I'm sure. You know the Rawhide Butte post where the army patrols the Cheyenne-Deadwood stage route?" She nodded. "Lieutenant I knew from Deadwood out there. Kyle Phillips. Good man. Rode up there and talked to him a bit about this scalp thing. Far as he knew, no one complained to the army about it. No one." Dawn shrugged. Neither she nor Jack ever thought of turning to the army for help.

"You don't understand, do you?"

"What, Crayne?" she asked. He had acquired some burr and needed to rave about whatever it was.

"All the time Jack was killing people, best the army knew was that he was a wild man killing to kill. No idea why. Maybe if you had told them, maybe someone would have done something." He wanted to tell her that if they had, perhaps the Basque families would not have been killed. It was true. It was also too cruel an honesty to share. He kept it to himself.

"Crayne, you don't understand. Army, law, nobody does things for people like me. None of 'em."

Crayne sighed. She still did not understand Jack.

"Dawn, Jack was a man who did a lot of things in his life that were outside the law. Don't even know how much of his life he was a good man." He could see her start to bristle. "I know at the end he was, but before, when he was robbing coaches and stealing from the army. Never told me how you met him."

"Trading post those cheatin' people run," she said. "Three men thought they could push around a squaw. Do whatever they wanted. Understand, Crayne? The ones that run the place didn't want to see or hear. Jack was there. Told 'em once to stop. They didn't. He shot 'em. Right there. Right then. Dead. All three. Never had anyone stand up for me. Went to thank him, and he coughed blood. Not much. Not like the end, but enough to know he was sick. Rode with him that day until the day he died and never rode with a better man."

"He ever say much about likin' Indians?"

"Took a while before I figgered he liked anybody," she replied. "Tough cuss. Then after a while he started acting like I was his own. We hid out. Then he started hearing things. Guess he wanted to do something good."

"And then he killed Dirk Rawlings."

"So what?"

"Dawn, Jack was never on a crusade to save Indians. He was out to save one. Only one. You. He was afraid your hair was going to be the prize one day and wanted to stop it before he died. That's why he never went to the army. It was always about protecting you."

Dawn touched the hair that flowed down her back.

"How do you know?"

"He told me. Near the end. Wanted you in a place where folks would protect you. White folks. I think he knew he had started something that was growing bigger but didn't know what. He thought it might grow out of control. He was worried about you."

"You sayin' because he stood up for me that all this started?"

"I think it made someone worried, someone who is in charge

of this business, that this was going to blow up soon, and they wanted to acquire as many scalps as they could as fast as they could. I know this subject is not something you want to hear about, but I have tried to look at it like the man running it—like a business. He wants to make money. He wants to keep it a secret. He is nervous. Somehow I fit in, but I do not know where or why. The *Global Reporter* sent me here to find him, and I have wondered about the men in New York City, because New York City is where people buy everything, and they are the ones who sent me."

The small fire was now fading red edged in black. Dawn had a revelation.

"You're afraid," she told Crayne.

He nodded. "For you. For me. Phillips said the forts keep being told the Indians are running wild, when they all know it is not true. I guess they have stopped telling Washington the truth and go out on patrols knowing there is nothing to find to say they obeyed orders. But if someone that high is peddling lies to start the army killing Indians, then this is not something small, but big. And I do not know how big it is."

"They haven't gotten us yet, Crayne."

Crayne touched the hair that moved in the soft sunset breeze.

"I don't want to lose you trying to save your life," Crayne replied.

"My life. My rules," she said. She looked into a mournfully serious face worn from time on the run. "No tell squaw what do, white man."

She watched the expected smile briefly flare at his mouth, but the shadows never left his eyes.

"Maybe, Crayne, just maybe you been swatting at this thing so long you are distracted trying to stay alive. Maybe if these folks out here are like puppets, you need to find a way to swat at whatever hand has hold of the strings. Don't know how that happens, being a lowly squaw and all, but you are the famous Eastern writer with those fancy words and thoughts up there, so maybe it will come to you. Last time we were together, you sounded like you had some plan that you probably forgot by now while you were tryin' to be the featured entertainment at a hanging and amuse the town. Maybe you ought to remember it, whatever it was, unless it ends up with us being shot at again. We done that enough."

She stopped and regarded him. "Now move over. Not sitting next to you if it means sitting on that rock."

He shifted to his right. She sat next to him and placed her head on his shoulder. They were quiet a long time.

"Crayne, I . . ."

"It does not matter," he said. "You are here."

She wondered if he had gone to sleep.

"Not giving up, Dawn," he said after a time.

"Never," she replied.

He was quiet. She began to talk, then looked up and realized he had drifted off to sleep. She moved off of his shoulder, threw a blanket over him, and watched the plains sleep beneath the stars.

CHAPTER THIRTEEN

Hiram Marshall was sleeping the sleep of the just in a Laramie City hotel. He had finished rewriting the text of the lecture he would give in the East. He kept revising it because each version seemed, to him, to shower him with insufficient glory for the demise of the Jack of Justice.

He had enjoyed his time in Laramie, much more since it had been published that, prior to his lecture tour, he would be staying at Laramie's Grand Hotel, where he would be working on his reminiscences. Certainly many ladies had been impressed. He did wish fewer smoked and more had all their teeth, however.

The time where he was feted was coming to a close, though. Southern would be coming West for the first few dates of the tour to be sure it met his expectations and bully everyone in sight until it did. He had not understood the reasons why Southern, who never left the city, was coming West.

Those reasons were, in fact, known only to Southern, who had received a very small brown paper–wrapped package from Wyoming. After its arrival, he had emerged from his office promising a variety of dire fates to the Jack of Justice, Crayne, and anyone and everyone remotely connected with the fact that at least one of them, and perhaps both, might still be alive.

Sullivan had tried to ease Southern's wrath by distracting him with the Mystery Trunk murder case in Boston, or the Atlanta crime where a couple was decapitated in their sleep. At other times, they would have been front-page stories for weeks.

Now, Southern waved them off.

"We are going to Wyoming," he declared to Sullivan several days after the package's arrival. Sullivan appeared horrified at the thought.

"That is too dangerous," he remonstrated.

"Whether this is all Crayne, or whether this fool Jack is alive, I am not running from any man, or any legend, or any anyone," Southern thundered. The package had been a challenge he could not ignore. "You will find that wretch Marshall. Wring the liquor out of him. We will begin lecture tours in every one of these towns where Crayne might be hiding. We will show him that we are not afraid."

Sullivan argued about the cost, about the lack of decent accommodations, about this and about that until Southern declared that one more objection and Sullivan would be fired. Sullivan then went to the nearest Western Union to begin a series of telegrams to Wyoming. Before he did so, he was able to see the contents of the package Southern had received. A blood-soaked Jack of Spades was there, clipped to a calling card of Southern's.

Marshall had mixed feelings about Southern's impending visit. He feared the old man might try to take away his own glory. For that reason, Marshall was sitting once again with a piece of paper, revising the text of the message he would give. He had practiced his oratory, with sweeping gestures and dramatic flourishes. He would rivet them to their seats. But he still needed to be certain that what he said made it clear that he was the one who had rid Wyoming of this Jack of Justice. He needed to be more than a narrator of the deeds of others. He needed everyone in attendance—especially those women looking for an attractive, eligible man of bravery and courage—to see him as a man who helped bring justice to the wild, untamed West.

Southern had made it clear that talk of the Jack of Justice being alive was someone trying to copy the dead killer. When Marshall had fretted once about Crayne, who seemed to have vanished, he was told that the man was most likely dead and was to stay that way.

In spite of that, there were times when he thought of Crayne, but if the man had not surfaced by now, the rumors that he had been killed must be true. He thought of his luck. He had worried about writing the Jack of Justice's death—something very clearly ordered by Southern—if the man was alive. Southern had no real idea of what men out here were like if their reputations—as flimsy as they might be—were compromised. There had been talk the man was someone who could not die, but the Indians had legends like that.

They were doomed. This wild frontier had little longer to live, and those living on its edges seemed oblivious to the fact that with every step of progress they pursued so assiduously, they were ending the world in which they thrived. A world of marvels . . . a time when a man could be famous overnight. As he was on his way to being. He slept soundly, without the gun by his side that had been there when he was worried about outlaws and others.

It was his undoing.

The iron hand that clamped across his mouth smelled of bacon and straw. The figure that cocked a rifle at his head was dimly menacing, more so as the sleep cleared from his eyes and he could read the intent in her eyes.

"Hello, Hiram."

He turned his head to see the figure on the other side of the bed. Crayne! Words caught. He gasped. He was going to die here!

"Meet Dawn. Dawn, say hello to the nice writer."

"Move and I kill you," she said.

"She has style, Hiram. Not the kind of style you have when you write about things that never happened, but style. Did I tell you she rode with the Jack of Justice? Her uncle? Really more like a father."

He gurgled in terror.

"She and I, Hiram, . . . I guess I have to tell you we have had some very deep discussions about your fate. She seems to be very set on having a Sioux ceremony where they pull a man apart piece by piece starting with the softest places. Or maybe it is Cheyenne. I forget these things, like I forget how many times I have been waiting to meet you again."

Hiram could not see the look Dawn gave Crayne in the semi-darkness. He saw white teeth. Was she grinning at the prospect of some fiendish ritual? He had heard tales.

"There's also a Shoshone ceremony where you sweat the truth out of someone over a fire built in a lodge of rocks. Takes days, though, and we're in a hurry."

"What . . . what?"

"What do I want, Hiram? Three things. First, it was real kind of you to post all those notices about you staying here while you prepare to tell the world what a great man you are. Took a while to find you, but we did. Shame all that practice was for nothing because no one is ever going to hear a thing you planned to say. You are going to go to Western Union and send a telegram. First thing. I have the text written out so you don't need to worry about writing something . . . never were very good, you know. Next thing, Hiram, you are going to hire a horse and head for New Mexico or some place far from Wyoming. California might be good. Leavin' today. Dawn here will make sure you buy a good horse and don't lose your way. You are never, ever, coming back to Wyoming or getting in touch with Southern or anyone else at the *Global Reporter*. I will know when you do, because I have someone on the inside who knows everything. If you do, I will kill you, unless Dawn beats me to it the way she likes to do. Understand?"

Marshall nodded.

"Dawn, you hear anything? I didn't. Go ahead and kill him."

"I said yes. Yes, Crayne. But you said three things. What is the third?"

"That one, Hiram, we are both going to enjoy."

"Crayne . . . they forced me."

"Tell me."

Hiram told about Southern and Sherman. It was as Crayne had suspected. He gave Hiram's tale a single grunt in response. Hiram was clearly disappointed his revelation would buy him so little gratitude. He began to invent.

"Dawn, he's lying now. Shoot him, skin him, I don't care; but end all of this nonsense."

The girl moved closer. He was sure she had a giant knife in one hand.

"No, Crayne," Marshall whined. "I'll do what you say."

"Then you live; you keep the money Southern sent you, and you know you did one thing right, Hiram. Get dressed."

The Western Union operator knew only that Hiram had been an important guest at the hotel. He looked at the text and, when told it was urgent, promised to send it without delay to the places on the list.

"I have other business, Hiram," Crayne said after their next use for Marshall had been completed. "If I see you again after today, I shall kill you."

Marshall looked from Crayne to Dawn to the smirking Franz Schultz. For a moment, he thought they were going to kill him.

"Dawn, take him out of my sight. If he gives you trouble, kill him and be done with it. It won't matter for the picture either way. I'll meet you in an hour or so by that tree where they hang criminals. It ought to be light enough by then."

"You sure this is going to work, Crayne?" Dawn asked as Marshall cowered nearby.

"No idea," he replied. "Never tried it. Whoever is the next rung on the ladder in this outfit is too high for us to see and too smart for us to catch. Maybe we need to grab their attention. Maybe we need to spread the word."

"You say so. I think killing them all and hoping the right one is somewhere in the pile might work better, but I'm only"—she looked at him as he looked back in anticipation—"the working half of this outfit."

Crayne watched the shaking scribbler walk down the street with Dawn walking a step behind and to the right. Like a squaw. Or a guard. One very primed and loaded.

The bartender remembered Crayne when he went to find an ally he needed to make his plan work. In time, he and Dawn were sitting with Martha Taylor once she had seen Marshall's pitiful figure shrink in the distance after leaving Laramie. Crayne and the older woman were urgently talking about telegrams and freight wagons when Dawn noticed a small girl watching from the hallway outside the office. She was Sioux!

"I am Dawn," she told Amelia as she left Crayne and went into the hall to find the girl.

"Are you Mr. Crayne's wife?" Amelia asked. Dawn tried to explain, but the girl seemed bent on drawing her own conclusions. Amelia frowned. "Are you Cheyenne?"

Dawn smiled. Whites only saw Indians in one form. Each people knew its own. She explained. Amelia told her about Crayne and how they met—a tale Crayne had never told her.

"You are very lucky, Amelia," Dawn said at last, trying to find the right words she wished someone had told her.

"Why?" asked the little girl.

"You are very important," Dawn told her. "You are Sioux,

and you are being raised white. When you are older, you will know everything about both worlds, and you can be a bridge between them. So that good people can understand one another. Some people do not understand, but you and I know that, without a bridge, everyone ends up stuck in the mud."

The girl giggled, but looked happy. Dawn felt a bit guilty. She had never felt like a bridge as much as a misfit, but she also knew that children can grow up to become what they believe. She wanted Amelia to have the chance.

Then Amelia squealed.

"Are you two going to conspire all day?" Crayne asked. Amelia held up her arms, and Dawn's question about children that she had never asked was answered.

It was late on a summer day. The air in the *Global Reporter*'s offices was stuffy, smoky, and stale. Matthew Sullivan morosely stared at the drivel sent his way from a writer who was certain that his abundance of cleverness in saying the same things over and over would mask the dearth of content. The work that had been the joy of his life had turned into a humdrum series of bad stories by worse writers.

Sullivan stared at the telegraph room. They would leave for Wyoming the next day. He was hoping something would come that would change Southern's plans. He knew the telegraph was working. He would know if anything came. The page told him when telegrams for Southern came in from Wyoming. Daily. Sometimes twice in a day. He never asked the boy for the contents. One had just been delivered. That would be three this day. Whatever the news, it prompted a burst of outrage from the inner sanctum that was Southern's private office.

Southern's feet made the floor quiver as he stomped to Sullivan's desk.

"Tell me the truth, Sullivan," roared Southern.

"I always do," replied Sullivan coolly. He had recently spoken to his wife about finding other work. Deep down, Southern was a bully, but, until recently, that side of him had showed itself but rarely. In recent weeks, corresponding roughly to the time since Crayne had been sent on his ill-fated mission to Wyoming, the mood was constant. There were other magazines. There were newspapers. He had hoped to wait until everything he was working on had properly matured, but perhaps sooner would be better than later. Sullivan was a loyal man, but that loyalty was fraying daily.

"Have you heard from Crayne?" The hatred and intensity Southern radiated repelled Sullivan.

"Not since he was fired. We were professional friends, colleagues, sir. Is there anything else?"

"There is a railway express package coming for me. The minute it arrives in this office it is to go to my home, if I am not here. Is that understood? It is not to be opened, by anyone. Not to be opened!"

"I shall give the instructions."

"You will see to it yourself. Do you understand? Carry on, Sullivan."

Southern then stalked off, exiting the offices with a door crashing on its hinges and Sullivan mentally hearing the glass shatter.

Sullivan absently looked at a few more pieces by writers whose hopes were uniformly in excess of their talents, packed some papers to read at home, and started for the door.

"Mr. Sullivan, sir?" It was Randall, the janitor, who had come back from the War Between the States with only one hand and a leg that was balky. Southern took him on out of pity and never let Randall forget how much he should be grateful.

"Are you well, Randall?" asked Sullivan.

"Me and Scotty . . . well, you been askin'. Found 'em." He

pushed a wad of crumpled yellow pieces of thin paper into Sullivan's hands. "If you go, sir, there's some that want to go with you."

"I'm not going anywhere, Randall."

"We know the signs, sir. Say the word." He shuffled away. Sullivan jammed the papers into his jacket pocket and walked out of the offices, taking a detour on his usual walk home to be sure no one had seen him and no one was following him. He found a bench and carefully withdrew the papers, fearing the gusts of sooty wind might take the flimsy things from his grasp at any second. Then, as he saw what they revealed, he decided he needed to brood upon these in private.

He came in the door breathless and moving fast.

"What is it, dear?"

"Answers. I need to sit by the lamp."

"Shall I hold dinner, dear?"

"Bother dinner!" he snapped. Truly the woman did not have a clue about what went on outside the doors of the house. He went to a bottle holding an amber liquid and splashed a generous amount into a glass.

He did not know all of what he had, but the telegram from Laramie, Wyoming, that had arrived this very day had five simple words: "Jack Justice alive. Have proof."

Dawn was sweating fast as she and Franz worked the press. Crayne had to remain in hiding, but she did not. It was a good thing she had returned from Laramie when she did. Franz could set type easily, but working the machine was hard. They had been printing nonstop for what seemed like a month but was only a week.

The sensational edition of the newspaper that reported how the Jack of Justice and a gang of wild Indians were raiding through eastern Wyoming was in so much demand that Franz expected he would use a month's worth of paper on that one week's edition.

There was also a strong demand for the exclusive pictures taken by Franz after he was kidnapped at gunpoint by the Jack of Justice and forced to take pictures of the outlaw and his men.

Next to one man who looked quite dead, and whose chest bore the Jack of Justice's trademark ripped playing card, could be seen part of a man, who wore a white shirt and black vest. Crayne had been pleased with Marshall's performance as a corpse and offered him a return engagement as the real thing if he ever breathed a word of the deception. The flour that had lightly coated Marshall's face to ensure a proper pallor had also been in Crayne's beard, making the piece of his face that was visible seem as old as Jack. As deceptions went, it was all Crayne could wish, although it did mean he needed to return to the now-unwelcome routine of shaving daily so that the deception would not be revealed. The picture had been redrawn by Clara as a woodcut so the old press could print it. Artists at newspapers and magazines would redraw it in a more dramatic fashion as they liberally copied and adapted the tale.

The piece of fiction that passed for a story had been written by Crayne in haste before he fled for some place he never quite said, telling Dawn there was one thing he needed to do.

Franz and Dawn had sought out Fairweather with their report of Jack of Justice and his gang. The marshal had been expected to die but refused to cooperate. His wife, also written off for dead, had similarly proven the local gossip mill wrong. Fairweather said little, other than asking Dawn if it would come out right in the end. She gave him the truth.

There had been odd moments when she was sure their tale was perceived as the falsehood it was, but Crayne had been right. Gullible people could be easily fooled. After reading about Indian raids, many of the men rode out to go fight back, not knowing that there was no one to fight. The report was picked up by other newspapers, spreading its sensational claims.

"Why did Crayne want us to do this?" asked Franz. "For a week I will be the most famous newspaper man in Wyoming, and when the truth is learned I will be vilified as a fraud, but I think he had something more in mind."

Crayne had explained it all in a rush of words before he left. It didn't make sense to Dawn, but she did her best to summarize Crayne's scrambled thoughts and words.

"He thinks somebody else is behind all this. The colonel is mean and old and ornery, but no one ever said he was smart. Crayne thinks that making someone believe Jack is alive and hunting will make whoever it is do something stupid, and then Crayne can find him."

"What do you think?"

She stopped work briefly, knocking hair from her eyes with a swipe of an arm that left ink staining her forehead.

"If it isn't an old Indian saying, maybe it should be. Anyone who sets himself up as a target usually gets his wish." She paused. "He's on the trail of something more than I know, Franz, and I don't think he cares what happens as long as he reaches the end of that trail. Live or die."

"You pointing a gun at me?" Crayne called as he walked up to the trading post.

"Yup," called Tanner.

"Smart man," replied Crayne. "The way I see it, you have to either shoot me now or listen to me. I think you need to listen, because Canadee is too young to be a widow."

"Thoughtful, Mr. Crayne," she called from the stable behind him.

"Folks, I have lost count of how many people I killed lately. Whether I shoot him through the window or you by the doorway, I will kill one of you before you kill me, if you are even able to do so. That does not have to be. I don't feel compelled to kill you. Yet."

"Listen to him, Jackson," she called.

Tanner came out, gun down.

"Let me make this very quick. You told three Indian loafers who do some dirty work for you that Dawn and I were worth money. You had set me up for them to rob me, but it didn't work out so well for them or you. You protected Jack, sort of, but Dawn and I were something else, especially me."

"Nothing personal," said Tanner. "You had hard money."

"Not anymore," said Crayne. "It's gone. So are they. I know you dealt in scalps. Do not deny it the way you did before. Too many roads lead here. I can call in the army to find out, if you want."

"Never liked it," said Canadee, moving closer. "Never did."

"Never killed nobody," Tanner said. "Here and there, men turned them in. Mostly folks who took them from the dead. Heard tell about people being killed for their hair. Never did that; never knew a man who did. Colonel paid high. Man has to eat."

"Man does not take scalps from Wyoming to New York City without help. Tell me how. Then I'm gone. I have no quarrel with folks who try to survive even when they make the wrong choices. But I want to end this. Only way you see me again is if you start up again. Then we settle this."

They talked. Then he rode.

Southern hated travel. The bouncing was bad. The disrespect was worse. The frontier was a place where people congregated who were misfits everywhere else. Skulkers.

He was irritably waiting in St. Louis along with Sullivan, whose company he detested but knew was necessary. The man was going to help his business grow, but he needed to spend more of his life out in the world and not whine behind a desk all day. Sullivan had been testy about this trip, insisting he had business in New York, but Southern insisted Sullivan needed to at least see the West once before he retreated to his office. If the man did not have the guts to be out in the field, Southern would need to find a new successor to run his businesses.

For all St. Louis tried to pretend it was civilized, it was at the edge of the frontier, and, to a man like Southern, this was clear. Still, Marshall's last telegram made it obvious the man was falling apart. Why he was in Laramie City when he was supposed to be in Cheyenne by now was not the least clear, and Marshall was going to hear about it. Southern knew Marshall was up to no good on the grounds that this was the man's usual habit.

Newsom said this man Schultz was a busybody trying to sell papers and that the pictures he was selling were obvious fakes. Marshall seemed to swallow it, as though the fact that someone was telling tales even taller than his own made the man cringe.

There was too much on the line to let this unravel. Southern had no choice but to go West. Sullivan, of course, knew none of this. Best to keep the man in the dark until he conferred with Newsom. There had been something lately in Sullivan's demeanor—something like a swagger. Something that at a very distant level Southern had perceived as a threat. It was new, this change, and it might have been the weather or his dyspepsia, but Southern was afraid it might be something more.

Sullivan, aware that Southern's moods were blacker than usual, gave the Old Man room and kept conversation to a minimum.

Southern observed with distaste his fellow travelers as they waited in the hotel lobby for the carriage that would jounce them to the train station for the next leg of the trip. A lecture tour had to start somewhere, and Hiram Marshall was not a big name. Yet. Work up to New York and Boston. He had this arranged, but he mistrusted Marshall. The man would drink too much, or cavort with some woman. Why else would he have been in Laramie?

"Mr. Southern. Mr. Southern." A Western Union man was moving through the crowd calling his name over and over.

"Here."

The man delivered the telegram, telling Southern he had been walking through crowds for two days waiting for Southern to arrive. Southern had no interest in the man's problems. No tipping. If the man didn't like his wage from Western Union, he could work some other place. The message made him gasp.

URGENT MEET SHERMAN CHEYENNE. URGENT SAID FIX MESS J O J.

It was from the New York City office.

What Sherman was doing in Cheyenne never went through his head. He would have Newsom deal with Marshall. He was four or five days from Wyoming. There was a week until the first lecture. Crayne might have resurfaced. Who knew? If it was this urgent, he needed to keep Sherman on his side. With Sherman, there was never any telling how the general would react and what he might do, so the only thing to do was obey without question, the way it was in Georgia during the war. He crumpled the telegram in his hand and let the crushed paper fall to the floor as he pushed through the crowd, gripping his silver-headed cane. He did not see Sullivan retrieve the crumpled yellow ball.

Elezial Newsom hated penny-ante printers like Franz Schultz. There were stacks of his own newspaper unsold as Schultz's sheet was read, sold, mailed, re-read, and consumed by every person in Wyoming and who knew how far East who could read.

Every newspaper liked a dash of sensation, but this was too much.

"I am Elezial Newsom," he told the obviously half-breed woman behind the counter after entering Schultz's shop. How could Schultz allow her to appear in a place where she was seen by the public, if he did keep a squaw?

"I ain't," she said, not looking up from where she was reading a sheet of paper. "Guess that means I am the lucky one here. Unless you come to sell out, there is nothin' anyone has to say to you, you mean old man. Git."

"I wish to speak with Franz Schultz about a matter of importance," he insisted.

She slammed the paper down and called the man's name, adding, "Franz, you owe Clara. You said he'd be here tomorrow. She picked today. Don't see the fuss myself. Nothing to write home about in the looks department."

"Coming, coming. Tell him to wait."

"Keep your scalp on," she said, glaring at him malevolently and enjoying his reaction. "Not that anyone wants to buy it. Sit in one of them chairs against the wall so I don't have to smell whatever you put on your hair."

Newsom thought for a moment about rapping her with his cane. He saw her eyes. She was waiting for him to do something. Schultz would need to be told she was a danger. The savages must be kept in their proper place.

"What is it, Elezial?" asked Franz, wiping ink off of his hands on a rag so soaked with ink the process produced little result. The man moved around the desk and chairs in the cluttered office with a practiced ease of navigation.

"Your Jack of Justice piece has stirred up feelings. These Indians think their savior is alive. The army has said he is dead.

You have either fabricated this or been foolishly taken in by someone who has been prevaricating."

"He speaks pretty," Dawn loudly said to no one. "Smelled a fish like that once, though. Dead fish, it was, if I recall right."

"Tell your squaw . . ." The hand on his neck stopped his speech. She had vaulted the low counter effortlessly, like a mountain lion. Newsom's heart pounded, and fear raced down his weak legs and gathered in his buckling knees.

"Dawn," said Franz reprovingly, mimicking the way Crayne often joshed with her. "You swore off killing the customers, remember? Clara does not want to clean up more blood."

Dawn looked at Franz. He could see the stoked-high anger within. He nodded, unsure how much of this was an act and how much was real. She released Newsom and roughly pushed him by the neck against the wall. "You were lucky. This time. Say it again, and I'll risk cleaning up the mess." He could feel her eagerness to attack. "I might like causing it."

Newsom was taken aback. "Have you lost your mind?" he demanded of Schultz.

"Possibly," said Franz. "Now that you have insulted my staff and questioned my sanity, will there be anything else? There are discoveries from the attack of those marauding Indians that have not yet been reported, and Dawn and I have much labor to do to finish our work and produce another extra edition."

"Schultz! I warn you! You are playing with fire by publishing anything. Some of them can read!"

Dawn took a step toward the quivering Newsom. "Can I please throw him out? I might break both legs doing it, and maybe I'll cut his head off, but I'll make sure all the pieces are picked up, promise. I even asked nice this time."

"Mr. Newsom is leaving, Dawn. But if he returns, I will be too busy to see what transpires."

She opened the door. "In that case, come again soon," she sneered.

The flustered Newsom fled in haste.

A pair of hands clapped. They turned to see Clara inspecting them.

"I assumed it was Crayne that led you to act like a child," she admonished, looking not the least upset. "I now see it was the other way around, Franz. When you are done with your playtime, there is food, children."

As she turned and went into the kitchen, Franz and Dawn exchanged a handshake. "Crayne would be proud of you," he told her.

Wherever he was, she thought. The last time she saw him, he said he would be back once he had made things right for all the souls who had been violated. She recalled the sadness in his face when he told her he would never be able to do what her uncle did. She wondered what he was doing. Any time he said he had a plan, any time he made it sound like he was playing it safe, she knew he was doing something foolish. Without her.

Chapter Fourteen

The plan was foolish. It could result in somebody killed. It should, in fact. She had told him that a thousand times. At least. For all the good it did. She had been glad to see him at first, then wondered if he had been hit on the head. Now she had to watch.

He had returned covered in dust from riding, but with something burning behind his eyes that would not let him rest. Now, everything would unfold. Dawn had a pocket full of shells in her coat pocket and was hoping for an excuse to use them. Patience, she told herself, patience. He had said she didn't come on stage until Act Two. She often wished he would make sense, but it was usually simpler not to ask.

Crayne rode up to the ranch gate, knowing there were eyes upon him the entire way. He had different clothes than the last time, was clean shaven and wearing something more respectable, if not quite Eastern. He rode the same horse. It was a risk. What was not?

"Stop!" A man moved out from behind a snake-log fence. "What's your business?"

"Here to see Colonel Anderson. My name is Hiram Marshall, and I write for the *Global Reporter.* I am writing about the Indian depredations in Wyoming, and I was told he might be someone to whom I should speak."

"He's busy."

"I have come from Cheyenne to speak with him. A Mr. Newsom suggested Colonel Anderson was the best person I should speak to."

"Newsom? Well, wait here."

Crayne waited, wondering who was observing him and from where.

"Hey!" A man at the door of the ranch house was calling. "He can give you a minute or two."

Crayne was profuse in his thanks as he led Dakota to the rail by the house. The hand asked him if he was armed.

Crayne opened his coat to show the gun belt buckled high on his waist, where no one but Eastern fools ever wore it. The hand made a sound, but no comment, and showed Crayne in.

Colonel Thaddeus Anderson was a big man. Not as old as Crayne expected for having ridden with the Colorado troops that fought at Sand Creek in 1864. Gruff and grizzled, he told Crayne that he was very busy, asked about Newsom enough to be sure Crayne had really met the man, then settled in a massive, carved-oak chair.

"Marshall, you say? Hiram Marshall? Know that name."

"I've written for many years, sir," said Crayne, asking Anderson all kinds of questions about ranching that gave Anderson the chance to expound on how hard it was to run a ranch the size of the empire he dominated. Crayne affected not to know much of anything until he was sure the rancher was comfortable talking to the writer. Then Crayne asked about Indians. Anderson replied by making it clear that, on his range, no Indians were allowed, and they were shot on sight.

"A bit extreme, Colonel? I mean, some might say so. You know what we hear back in the East these days."

"Boy, it is the way it is. As long as one of them lives, they are gonna want their land back. I'm not giving it up. Kill 'em quick is more a mercy than starving 'em slow on government land.

Makes more sense. Don't want them fed. We want them dead. Period."

Crayne made a show of writing down all the rest of the sermon Anderson delivered about the wisdom of exterminating the Cheyenne and Sioux. Crayne then lied and, telling Anderson it was the largest ranch he had ever seen, asked to be shown around. Anderson bragged as they walked about what he had built. Crayne noticed a small shed not far from the house. It stood out not by its location, but because it was the only thing that bore a lock.

"What about selling scalps? Is there such a trade?" asked Crayne innocently. "We hear many stories."

Anderson was quiet, looking hard at Crayne for a long moment. "*Global Reporter.* Hmmm . . . I guess you know what you're about," Anderson said thoughtfully. Then he spoke.

"The way it is, those people back there have the strangest ways. They want scalps. Maybe it makes 'em feel like a man. Don't know, don't care. I want those Cheyenne and Sioux and the rest gone. So it's like this, sonny: when I'm performing the righteous work of cleaning the prairie of what don't belong, I receive a recompense for conducting this campaign, which is what I want to do anyhow. Life works that way some times."

"But how do you acquire these items, now that the Indians are on reservations?"

"I think I'm done. Got a ranch to run." He called for a cowboy to "escort" Crayne out, which clearly meant to be sure the man was gone.

Crayne waved stupidly as he left. Things would be different when he returned.

The short late-summer night would be ending soon. There might not be as much time as he had wanted. It could not be helped. The colonel's cowboys had been loud and drunk late.

Crayne waited. He needed the darkness, but also to have the ranch yard to himself.

Dakota was tied a ways back. Crayne had ridden around over the hill behind the ranch house, then gone on foot to wait in the trees that had been planted to screen the house from the scorching summer heat. It had been some time since the last hooting and hollering of drunken cowboys staggering to the bunkhouse. He walked carefully, on the lookout for passed-out drunks or other debris. The lock on the shed was so rusted it was little more than a decoration.

The air inside was heavy with the stench of some kind of varnish. There were gaps in the boards that made up the walls; he could see stars. He could sense more than see objects hanging from the beams that spanned the shed. Fifteen, twenty? Maybe more. A drying shed. He reached out. Hair! Damp. Whatever had been put on it was not quite dry. He sniffed it.

Red Bear had been clear that, in his world, there was only one thing to do. Giving rest to souls took priority over punishing the guilty. The rest could wait if it had to. This could not. He'd better do what the Indians wanted done first. This once, they ought to come first.

Shutting the door behind him, Crayne lit a match. There had to be thirty scalps hanging. He shuddered. He held the match by one hanging scalp that was very wet. The flame all but leaped from the match to the strands of wet hair.

Paper. Paper would help the flames accomplish their purpose. There was some. He used up every match he had. Then he slipped out quietly and shut the door behind him as the flames were starting to catch. Crayne moved back to his lair to wait. There was no light sleeper awakened by the first plumes of smoke. There! The flames had started on the walls of the shed.

"Fire!"

The shed was now burning on two sides. Whatever was in it

would be charred in time, but for other purposes he needed a big, blazing fire. Crayne ran through the brush to find Dakota.

The east showed the thinnest band of gray denoting the start of a new day as Crayne mounted Dakota and pulled the rifle from its scabbard. The yells from the ranch yard were louder.

He moved down the hill until he was near the trees, then fired toward the flaming target the shed had become as fast as he could, sending men with buckets tumbling to the ground. He reloaded and fired again. The shed was now engulfed by fire on all sides. It was hopeless. Already some of the colonel's men had come to that conclusion and decided if they could not save the shed, they would kill the man who burned it.

Crayne fired some shots their way, then kicked Dakota hard as the horse raced through the ranch yard.

"After him!"

By now, the light was spreading in the east. Crayne rode south, retracing the route he and Dawn had taken weeks ago. He could hear the sounds of his pursuers. He waited and fired one final round of rifle shells, then jammed the gun in its scabbard and gave Dakota his head.

For a moment, it seemed he had waited too long. All of the colonel's men, including their leader, were chasing him. The fastest horses were almost within pistol shot distance. Dakota had hit his stride, but, with twenty riders on his tail, there seemed to be no chance he could escape. The Colonel's men scented victory. On they came.

At that moment, Dawn, Red Bear, and his men came out of the trees, screaming loudly and firing wildly. The screams of Indians always struck fear into whites. This was no exception. The colonel's men had their flanks exposed to the Indians and were no match for them. The Indians did not have the disciplined volleys that were the hallmark of the army, but they had been waiting all night for this chance to fight back at a rancher and his men who had committed atrocities upon them. The fight was short and brutal.

The colonel and a few of his men broke off the unequal contest and fled.

"Mine," screamed Dawn, turning her horse to follow. Red Bear and a couple of his men followed her. With the milieu of men and horses between him and the retreating colonel blocking any path to pursuit, Crayne had no choice but to watch.

Dawn galloped her horse as fast as she could. If Anderson and his henchmen reached the safety of the ranch house, they could hold out. Every ranch was a fort waiting for an attack. She could sense more than hear a horse beside her. Red Bear!

The trail was straight here. He did what she dared not. Red Bear let go the reins of his horse and fired over and over with his rifle. They had been close enough that the horsemen being pursued heard the gunshots and tried to move back and forth along the path to avoid being hit. That slowed them a bit. Red Bear now dropped back, having lost speed as he fired. Another round of shots. He hit one rider.

The colonel's men were riding faster than he was—lean riders on good horses. He was a heavy burden on his mount, and it was telling. He was dropping back. Dawn was gaining. Gaining. Her hat sailed off. The colonel looked once. She could see his fear. He looked again. Each look cost him ground. He called for his men to slow down for him, but they were riding for their lives and did not obey. Again Anderson turned; this time he held a pistol. The shot went wide.

She did not know how she looked, pursuing him as she called on the spirits of every ancestor she ever imagined, lips parted in rage and now savagely grinning as she watched him try to gallop faster while looking behind.

The horse knew more than its rider and swerved to avoid the tree at the side of the path. Anderson turned to look ahead in panic as the horse moved, hauling on the reins as he did so. Soon horse and rider tumbled in the dirt.

She dismounted with a leap. Anderson rolled and staggered, trying to find a way to stand on legs that were shaking with a head that refused to stop spinning. He reached his feet, turning to raise his pistol towards his pursuer.

Dawn slowed her dead run as she reached him. His gun rose toward her face. She slapped his arm aside, pulled the knife from her belt, and slashed at him with brutal accuracy.

His free hand went to cover the thin red line at the left side of his throat. His eyes were wide. His mouth made noises.

"I should leave you like this," she told him. "I should let you know what it feels like to have someone take your hair while you are still alive. I should let you die inch by inch out here while I watch."

She knew he heard. The fear of retribution showed. Again he tried to raise the gun that was turning heavier by the moment.

"You ain't worth it. Anyways, I ain't you."

She buried the knife deep in his chest with a single thrust.

For a moment he stood, took a jagged step, then fell face down. She watched as the blood pooled. When the pool had stopped spreading, she flopped him over and pulled out the knife, wiping it on his pants. She closed her eyes and thought of Jack. She hoped the dead truly saw everything. She hoped that half-smile he gave her when he teased her was on his face now.

Red Bear at last rode up beside her.

"The work is done?" he asked.

"This part," she replied.

Crayne was anxiously awaiting their return. Of the twenty who had chased Crayne, at least a dozen were killed. More wounded. He was looking at the carnage. His plan. His work. His conscience. They had tried to kill Dawn. In the West, you had one chance to kill someone. Fail, and this would be the result. Those were the rules. The only rules.

"Those who did not run farther than I care to chase are dead," Red Bear told Crayne when he and Dawn returned from chasing Anderson. He looked a long time at Crayne. "It is not your people who were killed so that others could carve them apart and hang their hair on a wall as a trophy. I do not take pride in killing, Crayne. I have done what had to be done not with joy in my heart, and not even with hate, but because all who wish to dishonor the People need to know there is a price to pay."

Dawn was standing beside him. Her face told the story.

"Don't be angry, Crayne," said Dawn, putting a hand on his arm. "Jack wanted him dead. He's dead."

"I must see him," said Crayne. "There is something I have to do."

They led him to the place where the man lay.

Crayne looked at the body impassively and reached into his saddlebag. He tossed the ripped playing card on the colonel's body. The colonel wanted a war to the death. He got it. Crayne knew he could not have killed the man except in self defense, but neither could he feel his death was anything more than what Jack wanted all along—justice.

"Now, they will be afraid of a man who does not die," he said. "I hope you like what you see, Jack. Dawn and I—we kept faith."

They rode in silence back to where the Indians had gathered.

"How many escaped?" he asked Red Bear.

"A handful. Three horses. Perhaps four."

"They will reach Cheyenne in a few hours; we will have company this night or perhaps early tomorrow," Crayne said. Dawn agreed.

"You need to leave," Crayne told Red Bear. "You know what happens when they chase 'marauding Indians.' The army will be coming soon, too. Lietenant Phillips said he would, and I think he wants this to end."

"You and Dawn can ride with us."

"Can't," she said. "I made a promise, and that promise ain't kept yet. Gonna keep it, aren't we, Crayne?"

"The job is half done," said Crayne. "Anderson said one true thing: as long as someone in the East is paying money, there will be men like him to earn it. We're going back to the ranch to see what we can find. There have to be records, names, something. A friend is helping me find out what was sent where, but there has to be something at the ranch we can use."

"We shall go, but we shall not go far," said Red Bear. "The wind is our master, and it shall blow us through your tomorrows again. This is not over. We shall be near until this ends, Crayne." He explained how to make a signal only he and his men would understand.

He gave Crayne a long glance, then turned to Dawn. "You have my blessing." He grinned at the look of embarrassment across her face.

With that, he shouted instructions to his men. In moments, they were screened from Crayne by a cloud of dust. In time, even the dust was an insubstantial dot on the endless expanse of the prairie.

"Where's Sherman?" growled Southern as he stepped off the train at the Cheyenne station. Sullivan went to gather baggage.

"Sherman?" answered Newsom.

"Sherman. Telegram from him. Sent from Laramie City. Meet him here."

"He's supposed to be in Dakota, they say," Newsom replied. "Maybe Kansas. I don't rightly recall, but I know he is not in Wyoming."

Southern felt a vague unease. He shook it off. "Where's Marshall?"

"Coming from Laramie. He holed up there. Said he had threats in Cheyenne. Felt safer. There was a telegram from there saying so. Man hired bodyguards. Drunk more like. I will send men to fetch him."

Southern snorted. Marshall was scared of his own shadow.

"As long as he shows up for the lecture," said Southern. "We have two days. Tell him I have arrived, and I want him here tomorrow. This Fat Creek place, can we ride there in a day?"

"Colquitt Springs," corrected Newsom. "There is a place we can stay. It is not grand, but it is clean."

"See to it," Southern commanded Sullivan. "Have Marshall meet us at Colquitt Springs. Make the arrangements. Telegraph New York. Messages to this place. Go, Sullivan, go!"

Newsom and Sullivan exchanged glances. When the Old Man raved like this, whatever they needed to say would have to wait until he was not present.

Bryce Smith had always hoped one day to keep company with Martha Taylor. Now, she was laughing with him in a conspiratorial fashion as he showed her his copy of the latest telegram that had been received from New York City. He agreed to continue the subterfuge they had begun, having no idea what it was about but willing to do whatever Martha Taylor wanted. Sending telegrams to New York City about things he knew nothing about might get him fired, but, if the price of it was time with Martha Taylor, it was a price he would happily pay.

She was also very pleased to play a role in a game she was told would make the world better for girls like Amelia. And, she admitted, Bryce Smith was not quite the dry old stick he appeared while sitting in his Western Union office.

She was not quite sure what Crayne and his partner were doing, but, even for a woman who owned a saloon and a business, life could become humdrum at times. Whatever adventure, or misadventure, she was now a part of, it was something diverting from drunks and gunfights. Crayne had been right. Information was so easy to find if you asked the right people. They would have shot him on sight. But she had what was needed and had sent it by a trusted courier to Colquitt Springs. Why on earth it mattered what box went where she could not imagine, but if it was important to Crayne and that mixed-blood woman who was far too intense, it was important to her.

It was a game, and it was interesting, even exciting. After all, she thought as she and Bryce giggled by the telegraph set, you can never be too sure with these wires and machines to whom you are communicating.

Matthew Sullivan was more than a little irritated that Newsom and Southern left him to make all the arrangements for baggage after they arrived in Colquitt Springs. Once settled, he decided to go exploring after asking directions.

"Franz!"

The printer smiled widely. He was glad he had never underestimated Crayne.

"Matthew, how did you appear? Magic? It is such a surprise to see you."

"Marshall has a lecture tour starting on his Jack of Justice series, the one that was Crayne's," said Sullivan. "Southern wanted him to practice in front of a small audience. Have you seen him? Crayne, that is."

"There are rumors he was killed the night he left; there are rumors that he hid out in the mountains," said Franz. "I can tell you no one has seen him. How long will you be in Colquitt Springs?"

"Do you think he really is alive?"

"The last thing he told me when I went to see him was that he had to finish the Jack of Justice series, Matthew, and you know what he is like when something like that dominates his mind. I don't know how badly he was shot when he escaped. He could have died out there. He would not be the first to simply disappear and never be heard from again."

"I'll be here a few days. Where do you think Crayne has gone?"

Franz professed ignorance. They talked printing and writing for a while. Matthew met Clara and was charming, then he left with the admonition to have Crayne find him as soon as possible if Crayne returned in the next few days, or to write him in New York if Crayne returned after he went back East.

Franz watched him leave, the smile that had been plastered to his face during the visit swiftly falling as he stroked his mustache in concern.

At the colonel's ranch, Crayne and Dawn stood in mute disbelief at the sight before them. During the fight, the fire from the shed had spread to the main house. A few hands had tried fighting it, but the flames won. By the time Dawn and Crayne reached the ranch, the walls were flimsy black sticks, and the roof had collapsed. If there were papers inside, they were gone.

"Now what, Crayne?" asked Dawn.

"We have one name left," he said. "I wanted proof before I confronted him, but I suppose the law wouldn't be on our side anyhow." Then he thought about proof. Writers made up facts all the time. Proof was like facts. If he could make up one, he could fabricate the other.

"We could join Red Bear and tell him we changed our minds," she said. "We don't have to go back, Crayne. Even Jack knew he could not stop all of it. You can't kill them all; you can't stop them all. We can't do anything dead, Crayne."

Crayne looked out silently at the plains, then back at the smoldering ranch house. He reached under Dawn's hat to touch the thin scar that still remained on her cheek.

"This isn't business, Dawn. This isn't even for Jack. Not anymore. This is personal. They will not walk away. Let's go."

The Palace was the largest of the saloons in Colquitt Springs. When traveling actors and shows came that did not bring their own tents, or were of the more genteel variety that included lecturers and writers who read from their books, its small stage where the Golden-Throated Elise sang nightly was converted for the occasion.

Southern surveyed the scene. So raw. So dirty. He wished Sherman had not gone off, if the general was ever there. No one had seen him. He wished Marshall would arrive. There were only about twelve hours until the lecture was to begin. The man should have arrived by now.

"Mr. Southern! Mr. Southern!" The town was small but it was knee deep in urchins who ran errands for small change.

"Here!"

Another telegram. From Laramie City.

"Hiram Marshall missing. Unable to locate."

Southern growled and stomped his foot. Now what?

Fairweather, who now walked with a thick oak stick as he patrolled the town, had heard the story of the raid on Colonel Anderson's place. A posse was sent and would be back later that day. The colonel had been a hard man who made his own laws. Someone who had been pushed too hard pushed back even harder. The law of the wilderness. Fairweather was glad he had no obligations beyond Colquitt Springs. His mind was so much on the raid that he did not see the figure in the shadows by the doorway until it was too late.

"Hello, Marshal. Hope you are feeling better. I hear the wife recovered."

"Crayne." If Fairweather was surprised to see him, his face did not let it show. "She did. You have been busy."

"Big lecture tonight. Man who brought down the Jack of Justice."

"Yup. Talk though that he's alive."

"Ought to attend the show tonight, Marshal. Should be interesting. Should settle all questions for all time."

"Am I gonna know what all this was really about?"

"You might, Ben. You just-indeedy might."

"Crayne?"

"Marshal?"

"They tell me I would have been dead without you. But that ain't the reason I didn't hunt you down. Know that."

"Never doubted it. Eight o'clock. Sit up front. Don't come looking for me. You'll find me then."

The pressure of the gun left Fairweather's back. Pinkerton man pretending to be a writer. He shook his head. Used to be a good town. Too many newcomers. Indians were wild, but they came at you face to face. Well, Crayne promised a show. He'd see.

Chapter Fifteen

The Palace was full. Tables had been pushed aside and stacked one atop the other. Every chair in the place, and a few borrowed from other saloons, was as close as it could be to its neighbor. Four officers from the army post at Rawhide Butte had arrived, explaining that they were ordered to attend. Ernesto the Basque had come, explaining that a messenger reached his ranch and told him he should attend.

Southern, Newsom, and Sullivan had spent the day putting together material for the lecture. Southern and Sullivan would speak. Newsom prepared notes for them. Southern had vowed to visit various heinous crimes upon Marshall if the scribbler ever surfaced. The pulpit at the church had been laboriously dragged to the saloon so that Southern could have a place for his notes.

A small storeroom near the saloon's bar had been converted for the night into a room for the speakers to wait. They did so, pacing like caged animals as the noise of conversation grew, shadows lengthened, and the moment for their presentation began. Newsom had arranged material on a table by the stage, in case Southern or Sullivan forgot something. Southern looked at his watch. It was eight o'clock. Showtime!

Southern strode to the center of the stage.

Sullivan, who would also speak, sat in a chair behind him, sweating as he made his first-ever public appearance. He kept scanning the audience.

Southern, who had spoken to many crowds in his day, put his hands to his lapels and began, explaining that Marshall was on the hunt for another story—a lie that no one would disprove. He then started to talk about the outlaw whom Marshall, with help from the army, had found and who was no longer prowling Wyoming.

"Newsom!" Southern exclaimed as the fool came stumbling out onto the stage from his right, almost falling flat on his face. "What are you doing?"

"Sorry, everybody," explained Crayne as he moved out onto the stage, having pushed Newsom there ahead of him. "The show is going in a different direction."

Southern exploded in rage. He took one step toward Crayne.

"No," replied Crayne calmly, pointing a pistol at Southern.

The older man's eyes went wide, his mouth gaped open, and he held his arms high as he recoiled. The cowboys in the crowd chuckled. This show was better than the usual entertainment.

"Dawn?"

She emerged from the far side of the stage with a rifle ready and a handgun strapped around her waist. She covered Sullivan, Southern, and Newsom. "Can't we simply kill them now and figure we did the world a favor by gettin' rid of this lecture? You white folks talk everything to death."

Crayne turned to Newsom and Southern.

"You see, gentlemen, she means it. I would suggest all of you stay where you are until the entertainment for the evening is concluded."

He turned toward the audience.

"Friends, we have a tale to tell. It is a story about murder. It is a story about greed. It is a story about those who think they are powerful preying upon those who are not. Settle back." He found Fairweather in the front row. "All questions will be answered, Marshal. Promise.

"As you all know, the Jack of Justice emerged to kill a number of people before allegedly disappearing. I daresay the burning ruins of Colonel Anderson's ranch, where Jack's calling card has been found, will challenge the assumption that he has been killed. Jack is working his way through a list—a list of men who murdered Indians—Indians who were too old, weak, or drunk to fight back. These Sioux and Cheyenne were not killed in battle, they were out-and-out murdered so that they could be scalped, cold-bloodedly—and their scalps sent East, where men like Mr. Southern here put them on their wall to impress the guests at dinner parties with authentic relics of the Great Sioux War."

A buzz went through the crowd. Everyone knew scalps were taken on all sides in the heat of battle. To sell them? To hang them on a wall? The soldiers seemed stunned and angry. Stirring up resentment among the Indians meant their lives were at risk. The Basque was nodding as Crayne added, "And attacking anyone else whose hair could serve to make as much as they could before they had to shut down."

"Mr. Newsom here was in charge of collecting them and sending them East. The colonel identified him as the leader of the operation out here that—"

"You can't go in . . . No!"

The scuffle by the door turned everyone's heads. A dozen Indians walked in silently until they stood by the small stage. Red Bear looked at Crayne and nodded fractionally. Sweat stood out on Newsom's forehead.

"Where was I? Yes. Mr. Newsom here paid everyone off—including some soldiers at the fort who made sure no one listened when the Indians complained—and made himself rich in the process."

"Crayne, this is all a lie!"

"No," replied Crayne, pulling a small notebook from his

jacket pocket. "I have here the list of every payment to the colonel, every single one . . ."

"No, no," Newsom muttered.

"Oh yes! I found this at his ranch, a little singed but legible. While you were helping write the script for tonight, I helped myself to your office. The dates and numbers match perfectly. I hope you don't mind. Perhaps you might want to have some time with Red Bear and his men, to explain it all to them, Elezial?"

"No, Crayne. You can't do that. You can't do that. It's not human." As Newsom begged, Fairweather rubbed his chin. The marshal interrupted Crayne.

"Good story, but it ain't against the law much unless you can prove he told people to murder Injuns for their hair," said Fairweather. "Not long ago the territory talked about a bounty for scalps."

Red Bear took a step forward. Fairweather checked him. "You know I am only telling the truth, fella," the marshal said.

"That truth was evil," Red Bear replied. Crayne motioned for the Cheyenne to stop.

"Jack—the Jack of Justice—was on that trail, Marshal," Crayne then said. "The notebooks show money paid to men who tried to kill Jack. They tried to kill me. Newsom, what was supposed to happen to me in jail here?"

"I have no idea."

Dawn's rifle barked once, loudly. The bullet buried itself in the floor next to Newsom.

"Shall we ask again?"

"No! You were supposed to be killed. It was supposed to end there. It was becoming too hot. There were too many questions."

"And when I was going to be hanged?"

"That's what they wanted," Newsom said. "It was not my

idea. It was theirs."

"Who wanted me killed, Elezial?"

Newsom was trapped. His eyes darted from Crayne to Red Bear in fear. He reached into his jacket.

The explosion of the pistol was loud. Smoke curled from the small weapon in Southern's right hand. Newsom fell, landing on his side at Sullivan's feet. The small, redheaded man felt the injured man's chest and turned Newsom over. Red had stained the shirt beneath Newsom's vest.

"Wretch," called out Southern. "Traitor. Fiend. I saw him put a derringer in that pocket, Crayne. He was a weasel, Crayne. Useful, but a weasel."

"Got them covered, Dawn?" She and all of Red Bear's men raised their rifles.

Crayne patted Newsom, who was bleeding profusely but not quite dead. Yet. No one seemed to care as the drama went on without him.

"No gun, Southern. I do wonder what he was going to say next? Whose name he was going to mention?"

"He had one."

"I never saw one, Crayne," said Sullivan blandly. "Perhaps someone did not want him to talk?"

Southern started to bluster but was cut off with a gesture by Crayne's gun hand. Crayne gave Sullivan a long, lingering look, then turned to the men packing the saloon who had come for a lecture and seen a tragedy unfold.

"Fortunately, the story does not end here. Newsom ended up on the floor here mostly dead from the looks of him, which is what he deserved, because he approved of murders and arranged them for the man he worked for. I know who that is. You see, when the booty left here, it went East. What is shipped out must be shipped somewhere. I know where. It went to New York City, where a man kept all of his treasures until he could sell them. A man who believed he could buy and sell anything and anyone."

"Crayne, I demand . . ." Southern began.

The old Basque lifted the pistol he had under his jacket and pointed it at Southern. Southern sputtered.

"Cavendish Street was where you once lived, Matthew," said Crayne, turning his back on the crowd to confront Sullivan. "All those warehouses. Including one at 114 Cavendish, which—according to the shipping manifests that the railroad makes up—was the address of the boxes sent from here. A small warehouse filled with the scalps of old men, old women, and others murdered so you could sell trophies to men who never earned them."

"Is this true?" thundered Southern. He reached out and grabbed Sullivan by the scruff of his jacket collar. "That scalp you told me was from Sherman who said it was a trophy from the Little Bighorn was something you took from a drunk or a child who you murdered? You dishonored me that way?"

"Do not be so moral with me, Jacob," said Sullivan, pushing Southern away. He straightened his collar, adjusted his cuffs, and spoke coolly to his employer. "You and all of your friends you sent to me, so they could hang an actual scalp on their walls, never cared about the price that was paid for those trinkets so that you could have a share of the glory that went with fighting the Indians."

He turned to Crayne.

"Why, Crayne? What is any of this, any of them, to you? I handed you a story—a chance at fame. All you had to do was write about that man. Write about his actions. Write about his death, which would have been a prize-winning final chapter if it could have been accomplished as planned. Look what you did with it. Do you think these men"—he gestured to the crowd—"care about Indians who were scalped? The same savages would slit their throats on a whim. I could make one hundred dollars off of each one, even after my expenses. It was so easy."

"Men kill men all the time, Matthew. Not trying to change the world. Preying on people the way you have done is monstrous and wrong. The Matthew Sullivan I knew would never have done this. What changed you?"

Sullivan jutted his jaw at Southern.

"Him and his kind. They swill down money like it was water. I was tired of never having the best . . . always hearing from my wife that we never had the best. I went to an affair at one of his pompous friends, and he had one on his wall. The rest were jealous. Newsom knew he could help. He was useful, Crayne. He could obtain anything and contact anyone. He was well paid for his pains. Then this fool Jack started sniffing the people who supplied him. We had to stop him. All you had to do was find him, and the rest would have been so simple. You are a fool, Crayne!"

Sullivan tried to make Crayne understand.

"This was simple business, Crayne. Nothing more. When you sent that telegram that you wanted to change the assignment, I knew it was all up. Everything else worked as planned. You found the man, didn't you? And he died, didn't he? He is dead? Tell me! I know all this is pretense. I know you."

Crayne said nothing.

"You were supposed to lead us to him, but you would not do it. Then after you made things worse, it grew out of control. Sherman was so easy to manipulate. Newsom simply told his army friends to alert Sherman that the killings were creating another war. There was no question what he would do next. The army came in; this renegade was gone. And now, what of any of it, Crayne? Sheriff or marshal or whatever you call yourself out here, you with the badge there, have I committed a crime? My army friends? What do you have to arrest me on? A man who lived out here sold me a product. I sold it in New York City. Do you plan to arrest me because some of you"—he sneered at the Indians—"are offended? In this world of business, I may have run afoul of a few rules, and some of you may be squeamish over the process or the product, but there is nothing I have done where any court would convict me of any crime. If Newsom, who I did not shoot—if you would be so kind as to notice—was a criminal, he has paid the price. I am not, and I shall not!"

Fairweather had to admit there was nothing he could do.

"Sorry, Crayne. Look at it that way, there's nothing the law can do. It ain't right, but it ain't against the law. Not out here, it ain't."

Crayne looked sad. "I am sorry, Matthew." He moved his hand towards his gun. Sullivan had Newsom's derringer in his hand aimed at Crayne's midsection before Crayne could touch the weapon.

"I believe that I will leave now," Sullivan said. He smirked at Southern. "You are a fool, old man. You are all fools. Newsom was useful, but he had served his purpose. You did me a favor in shooting him. Now, I have his gun, and I only need one more thing so that I can leave here in safety."

"You," he called to Dawn. "Come over here. You can be my hostage. Drop the gun."

Dawn obeyed, keeping her eyes on Crayne. She licked her lips nervously and took hurried, shallow breaths, eyes locked on Crayne the whole time.

"All of you," Sullivan said to Red Bear and his men. "Guns down. Now!"

They complied.

Sullivan now spoke to the crowd. "You men who have fought the Indians are armed. If they make a move to kill me, shoot them. You know what Indians and Indian lovers deserve."

There were some rumbles of agreement. A few men reached for their guns.

"And what do I deserve?" yelled back Dawn. "I'm all of you here—Sioux and Cheyenne; Irish and Welsh. My hair deserve to be on your wall? Every mother's son of you that ain't some purebred deserve to be killed and scalped? Those Basque girls deserve that?"

"Knew she was Irish," said one cowboy, looking at her admiringly. Another hooted.

"I think it is sick," said one cowboy rising to his feet. "I'll fight anyone anywhere tries to take my land or hurt my family, but killin' people to sell their hair goes too far, mister. You Eastern people like hair on your walls, scalp yourselves and leave us alone. If I was that Cheyenne fella there, I'd kill you and not care what your law says, there, Marshal. Might be of a mind to help."

More cowboys roared agreement. Others shouted back against them. Sullivan pushed the derringer harder into Dawn's back and hissed for her to be silent. He turned to Fairweather.

"Marshal, I am an innocent citizen, and I expect protection if I am assaulted," said Sullivan. "I demand protection."

Fairweather squirmed unhappily but rose, leaning on the walking stick.

"Don't like it, Crayne, but he didn't break no law here." He spoke to the crowd. "On my authority, he is allowed to leave here. Understood? Everybody put their guns away. Not having no shootout here. Too many people would be hurt."

"Understood, Ben." Fairweather searched Crayne's expressionless face for a clue. There was none. He could see the man focused on the woman. Fairweather knew he could stop it. He could let it happen. He waited. Crayne had started this dance. He had to know it might not go the way he planned it. A wave of pain erupted from his side. The marshal sat.

"It is time to go, half-breed," Sullivan told Dawn. He spoke to the room at large. "I am going to the train depot. When the eastbound comes in a few hours and I leave this place, you can see her again, because killing her would be a crime, and I am not a criminal. She will live as long as no one bothers me."

"Sullivan . . ." Southern started to approach.

"Oh, shut your mouth, you sanctimonious, bullying hypocrite," Sullivan told Southern. "You were so proud to be so manly. You can take your job. I've been feathering a new nest away from the tiresome routine of your society and all of its silly pretensions. I will have a new name, a new home, and a new life. You and your magazine can go to the devil!"

He pushed the derringer once again into Dawn's back. "You always were a fool, Crayne. Always."

Crayne seemed to blink in the dim light. "Good-bye, Matthew." His lips kept moving. Dawn watched them closely.

Something in the tone seemed to catch Sullivan's ears by surprise. For a moment he focused intently on his former friend.

Dawn used that moment to kick Sullivan, hard, and fall to the floor. Sullivan pointed the tiny gun at her but never pulled the trigger as the room exploded from the sound of Crayne's gun.

Sullivan danced jerkily from the impact of three knives flung by Red Bear and his men as well as a second bullet from Crayne's gun. The third shot ended his staggering dance.

Crayne walked over. A playing card drifted down next to his former friend. It was over.

"A little close, Crayne," said Dawn. "Made a squaw wonder if her man was going to protect her or not. What made you guess I could read lips?"

"Nagging again," he replied, their eyes sending a different, private message. "Like the man said. Those Irish. You could understand Jack when not a breath was coming out of the man.

Watched you watch his lips. Knew then. You did it again when you were shot."

A few men laughed nervously.

Fairweather had hit the floor with the rest to avoid any stray shots. Now, he rose painfully, grasping a chair to do so. The chair slid on the floor. He slammed it down angrily, stood, then strode over to Sullivan's cooling body, stick thunking on the floor as he did. He looked around as he took the temper of the room.

"Everybody! Way I see it, this man who's about as dead as dead gets went for a gun and found out what happens when a man does that and ain't fast enough." He turned to Crayne. "Was the rest of it true?"

"It was."

"Never cared much for people that shoot at me, Crayne, and I don't like them Cheyenne much after the scrapes we had back in '74 and the Sioux even less over what they done to Custer, but it ain't right what that man did."

"Nope."

"So, I guess it's over and done, and can you tell me that this Jack of Justice is not going to come into my town tomorrow and kill someone? I can assure you, Crayne, that the law and the army and the territory are all going to have a real problem with you and him if this does not end right here and right now. You talk to him?"

Crayne caught sight of Franz, trying desperately to write down everything that was going on. He smiled grimly. Jack would reap what he wanted, and then some, as the story made the rounds.

"I can make that promise. The Jack of Justice will not trouble you, Marshal. He has accomplished what he wanted."

"Then the two of you and you from that New York City place might all want to leave here now while the leaving is good.

Them, too," he added, pointing at Red Bear and his men. "Too many hard feelings here for everybody to stay friends much longer than the next five minutes."

Red Bear and his men were already filtering toward the door.

One of the cowboys said Newsom was still alive.

"Fetch McHenry, the barber," called out Fairweather. "Patch the hole so we can charge him with something. If he lives. Them little guns never kill a man proper."

Fairweather caught sight of Ernesto moving toward the stage.

"No, friend, no!" he called, hobbling toward the man, who was heading for the prone Newsom. "If I was you, I'd want to kill him, too, but if you kill a man, even one that deserves it, even one that's half dead, it's murder. If he lives—and he don't look real good to me—he'll pay. Don't know how, friend, right now, but we'll find a way. Let the law settle it."

"Army justice punishes men who incite Indians," said one of the officers. "We promise."

Ernesto nodded, lowered the gun, and moved toward the door.

A chair scraped, and boots moved quickly.

"Anybody thinking about anything, don't," Fairweather said as he watched the last Indian leave. "Don't know that what happened here tonight is the law, but we'll call it justice. Now can we set up the bar and have some drinks? Night like this makes a man thirsty."

It was dark as Crayne, Dawn, and Red Bear—followed by his men—walked out into the street and the cool night air.

"Brother, that was foolish," said Dawn. "Those men could have turned on you."

"Your friend said ten bold men can face down one hundred. He was right. Jack's spirit said I needed to be there," he replied. "His spirit is yours. Now, we will go." He called to his men, gave Crayne a nod, and they were gone into the night.

Southern emerged, having already had some whiskey. "Crayne!"

Crayne kept walking. Southern reached out and pulled at his arm.

"Crayne, I am sorry. I apologize. Come back to New York. Take Sullivan's job. Take any job you want. I . . . I never knew. I know how much you wanted to be the editor. I can make all of that happen. Five times any salary you can name. Ten times."

Crayne looked at the man, wondering how he could ever think a job would make up for what he had allowed to take place under his nose. Crayne had come to realize the price of peddling lies was higher than he wanted to pay.

Dawn shoved Crayne roughly aside and barked into Southern's face like an angry, vengeful terrier.

"You knew enough to stop this. You put Indian hair on your wall like it was something to be proud of. Maybe the law won't tell you that you did wrong, but when you cross the river, Old Man, there will be a spirit waiting to take yours." She started to walk away, then turned back. "And it will be the Jack of Justice." She stalked away.

Southern fumbled for words. He looked at Crayne for understanding. There was none.

"You have one more job, Jacob," said Crayne. "In the morning, you will pick up a paper from Franz Schultz's print shop. What is written on the piece of paper will be the front page of the next edition of the *Global Reporter.* That and nothing else. Nothing. Not one other thing. I hope you take its message to heart, because, if you don't, be very clear, Jacob Southern, that you and I will see each other again. There is a playing card left. Understand? Someplace else. Anyplace else. I promise."

He followed Dawn into the night.

Clara said she had come like a whirlwind, grabbed a bag of

clothing, and left.

Franz tried to slow him down with entreaties to write about what had happened.

"Why were the Indians there? With all those cowboys?"

"They had the right," said Crayne. "I left them a signal. They've been watching. They needed to see justice happen to ever believe in it."

"Crayne, can you please slow down and write this for me?"

"Tell it plain, Franz. Tell it plain," Crayne said. "No tricks. No fine talk. Tell it honest. All anyone can ask."

"How did you know?" Franz asked.

"Newsom did their dirty work. I knew that. That meant either Southern or Sullivan. Southern would never have tried to hide his tracks," Crayne said. "Sullivan wanted to be respectable. He wanted them to think he was a gentleman. I had to manipulate Southern to drag Sullivan out here, or Sullivan never would have come. He was a coward. He was everything Jack wanted to stop. We stopped him. Southern only is allowed to live because he has one more thing to do. The envelope on your desk, the one I left there this afternoon, make sure he takes it and does what it says."

Crayne ran out the door, leaving the old man writing as fast as he could to print his newspaper the next morning

He found her in the stable, saddling her horse. He called her name.

"You did it, Crayne." She did not stop. She did not turn to look at him. "Good luck in New York."

"*We* did it." She shrugged. Nothing brought Jack back. She should feel something. She was tired and felt dirty, and her wounds hurt.

"You in some all-fired hurry to meet a train heading to some important place?" he asked, grabbing her arm hard and turning her to face him.

"Going back to your world?" she asked, bitterly. "Your writing? White man offered you a job writing for the rich people who hang hair on a wall and think they are fine Christian people. Go take it! What's a half-breed girl compared to that? I should have known. Why did I ever think you were any different?"

Her anger stunned him. He held her by her shoulders and moved her against the wall of the stall where her horse was kept.

"Let me make one thing perfectly clear. There is no future for me in New York City, Dawn. Not now, not ever. Whoever the man was who came out here to write a story is long gone, woman. Long gone. Maybe it is just as well he did what a woman told him to do—stop writing about life and live it." He shook his head. "I have written my last words. I do not know what I can do for a living, and right now I do not care. You have had my back the way you had Jack's. I could never in this life betray you by going back to those people. Never. I do not care what I do, or where I go, or any of the things that mattered not that long ago. Do you really think I am nothing more than another one of them? After all this, Dawn?"

He waited for an answer. None came. It was time to go. Time to leave all of it behind. All of it. All of them. All. He looked at her eyes, bright and glittering.

"Are you coming?" he asked her, so lost in thoughts he forgot he was still holding her against the wood of the stall.

"Crayne, you want to make some sense, here? Plain old for the sake of something different? Coming where? That hole of a place that man came from? Not me, not now, not never. And if you think I ought to be going someplace else that you ain't bothered to tell me about yet, maybe you should let me go, since I'm about ready to remind you how well I can kick unless you can give me a good reason why not."

He blushed, mumbled, and released her. For a moment her anger glared forth, then she shifted her eyes from his face.

"Shadowlands," he replied. "You and me. Alone. Some place out there nobody can find us, nobody can decide where we belong and where we don't. And if the rest of them all decide to go and kill each other, we can be so far away we never hear about it, have to mop up the mess, or spend more of our lives trying to stop people from hating each other."

"Probably not a place that far away."

"Worth looking. We can hole up in Top Hat. Don't care. Don't care who anybody's parents were. Don't care if you are not the proper Whitechapel girl I wanted when I was young who drinks gin and has black teeth going to rot from the stuff. Willing to overlook that. Mostly."

He had her full attention. Now he would find out if she was listening. He could hear the pulse in his ears as he waited for a verdict on his life from a jury of one. The smile took a long time emerging from behind the impassive facade.

"Then saddle up, Crayne. Ain't got all day to wait around on scribblers that talk and talk and talk when there's work to be done. Move! Can't be making a poor defenseless woman do all your work—and if you say that word, I *will* kick you."

He opened his arms, and she came inside them. In time she leaned back in his arms and looked up at him.

"Not a whole lot of time for talk where I come from, Crayne. Sometimes, when my Sioux family was on the run, and folks wanted to be sure they would be reunited on the other side if things ended bad, and they wanted to tell one another they would be looking for them when they were all dead and all just spirits, there was only time for one word."

"Which one, Dawn?"

She looked him full in the face and said it.

"Always."

He echoed her back. "Always."

"Then let's be done with them all, Crayne. All this death . . . all this hate . . . this ain't life. Let's ride."

Epilogue

A beaten man who had grown older these past hours, Southern walked through Colquitt Springs in the early hours of the morning to the print shop he had been instructed to find. His hair and clothing were askew after a sleepless night of misery. The disgusted officers leaving for Rawhide Butte made it clear that, even if Southern had not been involved, he should have known what was happening. Their reports would ruin him and destroy the magazine he had taken a lifetime to build. He could picture his idol, Sherman, reading what would be sent. Word would soon filter everywhere in the world of publishing. He almost envied Sullivan the rest of the dead instead of the lot of the disgraced.

Franz Schultz, who was eagerly printing his version of the events that had transpired—a news sheet that would be shared thousands of times across dozens of territories—gave him the envelope Crayne had sealed the day before. Inside was a short, hand-written message.

Southern, looking drained, wrinkled, and battered, moved over by the light where he could see as Franz and Clara chattered and worked.

"You agree?" asked Franz after the older man had been silent too long. "You agree that this and this only will be the cover of the next edition of the *Global Reporter*? No illustrations? Nothing else. If you do not agree, I am to send a message."

"I will print it; I will print it," Southern said, holding up his hands as if warding off blows. It was a manifesto, short and to the point. It would be read across the country. He thought of how it could be typeset for maximum effect. For a moment he tried to calculate the profit he might make, only to realize in the next thought that once the full tale was told, the best he could hope for was to sell the magazine and not lose everything.

"Read it out loud," Schultz said. Crayne had been clear. Southern should not be given any room to wiggle out of doing what must be done.

"All right," replied Southern in a shaky voice that sounded ten years older than the booming one he used when he entered town days ago. He cleared his throat and read.

"I am the Jack of Justice. My work in Wyoming Territory is done. The guilty who preyed on the lost and the lonely are punished. The innocent are avenged. The dead of all peoples sleep peacefully now. I will live in peace with all men.

"I send this message to those who may think to once again prey on any of my brothers or sisters, Sioux, Cheyenne, or white: I will know, and I will return to once again deal out justice.

"From the high places I will be watching. Beware."

ABOUT THE AUTHOR

Sam Hill is the pseudonym of a Spur Award–nominated writer. Over the years, Sam developed a fascination with the ways of frontier-era newspapers and magazines. The book grew out of his admiration for the creativity of both writers and publishers to chronicle the spirit, if not the facts, of the Wild West and lay the tale before readers whose endless fascination with the West and their willingness to suspend disbelief and enjoy the tales are a hallmark of a colorful and bygone era of journalism. He can be reached by emailing him at Samhillwriter99@gmail.com.

ABOUT THE AUTHOR

The employees of Five Star Publishing hope you have enjoyed this book.

Our Five Star novels explore little-known chapters from America's history, stories told from unique perspectives that will entertain a broad range of readers.

Other Five Star books are available at your local library, bookstore, all major book distributors, and directly from Five Star/Gale.

Connect with Five Star Publishing

Visit us on Facebook:
https://www.facebook.com/FiveStarCengage

Email:
FiveStar@cengage.com

For information about titles and placing orders:
(800) 223-1244
gale.orders@cengage.com

To share your comments, write to us:
Five Star Publishing
Attn: Publisher
10 Water St., Suite 310
Waterville, ME 04901